"Haven't you ever been swept away?"

Samantha asked Rick the question as they walked through the mall. She referred to something the massage therapist had said, but then realized too late how provocative it sounded.

"Not on a massage table," he said in a tone that made her heart pound.

"I know what you mean," she said, though she really didn't. She'd never been that lost in a physical moment. She wanted to be. With Rick. Forgetting everything but him and what he was doing to her.

She sighed as they stopped outside a lingerie shop, its display windows holding naked mannequins. For a moment they stood staring at the naked women with their plaster hips thrust provocatively forward, fingers extended, inviting, teasing. In her mind she saw Rick staring at her instead of them, sliding his hot, green gaze over every inch of *her* naked body.

"I'd ask what you're thinking, but I bet I'm better off not knowing," he said, his voice low.

She turned to him. *I'm thinking, You...me... naked...now.*

Blaze™

Dear Reader,

Lord knows I'm a hazard with a camera, having snapped more than one shot of my own thumb, and a disaster as a subject—I've ruined countless wedding and graduation photos with a loopy grin or eyes tightly shut.

That said, I *love* photography. The power of a perfectly captured image sets me back on my heels. I can stare at a photo for hours, reading between the pixels, interpreting emotion, guessing at character. Can a photograph capture your soul…your true self? Can you ever hide who you are from a camera or the world? The questions give me the chills and keep me writing.

I hope this book gives you insights into how you see yourself, or at least makes you want to rush out and take some snapshots—striving for that double image of inner truth that my heroine, Samantha, captures so well. Me, I suspect I'll still be photographing my thumb.

I'd love to hear what you think. Drop me a line at dawn@dawnatkins.com. And visit my Web site at www.DawnAtkins.com.

All my best,

Dawn Atkins

DON'T TEMPT ME...
Dawn Atkins

TORONTO • NEW YORK • LONDON
AMSTERDAM • PARIS • SYDNEY • HAMBURG
STOCKHOLM • ATHENS • TOKYO • MILAN • MADRID
PRAGUE • WARSAW • BUDAPEST • AUCKLAND

ISBN 0-373-79257-3

DON'T TEMPT ME…

Copyright © 2006 by Daphne Atkeson.

ABOUT THE AUTHOR

Dawn Atkins wanted to be a novelist since she put fat pencil to brown paper in the second grade. She's won the 2005 Golden Quill for Best Sexy Romance and was a finalist for the 2005 *Romantic Times BOOKclub* Reviewer's Choice Award for Best Flipside. She's written for several Harlequin lines, and this is her fifteenth published book. She lives with her husband and son and a cat named Lenin in Arizona, where she takes many so-so photographs.

Books by Dawn Atkins

To Renata,
for generously sharing your gifted eye

1

"LEATHER SHOUTS, lace whispers," Samantha Sawyer said to her new client, who'd flung off a red silk cloak to reveal her outfit for the portrait Samantha was about to snap of her.

The black leather bustier, red fishnets and glitter-flecked stilettos did not flatter the softly feminine woman before her. In that god-awful platinum flip, Misty looked like a plus-size dominatrix from a 1950s sci-fi movie.

"From what you told me earlier, I believe you want to lure Tony to bed, not chain him to the headboard and whip him into submission," Samantha said gently.

"But Tony loves leather. Leather clothes, leather furniture, leather everything." Misty swirled diamond-heavy fingers through the air.

"Tony loves *you,* Misty. And your body screams for lace."

"It screams for air, that's for sure. I can't breathe." Misty unhooked the top two grommets and exhaled in deep relief.

It saddened Samantha that instead of showing off her zaftig curves, Misty had crammed them into torturous fashions. Too many of Samantha's clients did the same—wore too-small clothes, stripped their hair of natural color and turned their faces into exhausted masks with chemical peels and BOTOX shots.

"What did Bianca wear?" Misty asked. "However you fixed her, fix me. My Tony is…wandering." Her summer-gray eyes went murky with worry.

"Let's see what set feels right," Samantha suggested, determined to cheer the woman. "And we'll choose an outfit that suits you."

"Okay." Misty loosened a third grommet with a whooshing exhalation. "Bianca told me you're a miracle worker. She says Darien's a new man."

Bianca Sylvestri, who'd sent Misty here, believed the boudoir photo Samantha had taken of her had saved her marriage and since then had referred a dozen family members, friends and associates for photos. In fact, her grateful husband Darien had offered Samantha a killer lease on the ground floor of his empty building and now she had Bedroom Eyes, plus shops for three friends— a massage studio, a hair salon and a lingerie boutique.

Samantha led the way to the velvet love seat in the corner of the anteroom, and Misty sat beside her, corset creaking like a saddle. Samantha put *The Book of Fantasy* in Misty's lap. Her portfolio featured tasteful erotic shots in a range of settings from exotic harem to medieval castle to country meadow.

Samantha believed the shots had special appeal to her clients because they came from her own sexual fantasies. Fantasies she planned to bring to life once she found the time. And the man.

Six months ago, she'd made the decision to break out with her photography and her personal life. At the ripe age of twenty-seven, it had dawned on her that her strict upbringing had cramped her style more than she'd realized.

Enough already. She'd launched Bedroom Eyes and soon enough she'd go for some heart-stopping, take-me-now sex.

Her first step to a bolder Samantha had been giving herself permission to have sexual fantasies: elaborate ones with exciting lovers—pirates and princes and high-waymen and cowboys and cops—in imagined settings similar to the ones Misty was slowly flipping through, pondering each with a smile, a sigh or a closer look.

Misty studied the woman on the tiger chaise in a re-vealing dress of liquid velvet. This came from Samantha's fantasy of willing ravishment—being gently tied and invited to surrender to passion by a lover who knew her white-hot core as well as his own. Her personal favorite.

Next, Misty came to the shadowed nude—Samantha's friend Mona, owner of the massage studio, with her head thrown back, a faint smile on her face, light falling provocatively on her lush curves. Despite its simplicity, the shot required the precise use of fill and re-flector to create a sensual, but modest, effect that suited Mona perfectly. Samantha matched pose, set and costume to personality, which gave her photos their special magic.

Misty flipped past that one fast. She didn't have the confidence for nudity. Not yet, anyway. Samantha's mission was to help her clients honor their natural beauty, but she never pushed them beyond their comfort level.

Two pages later, Misty gasped and put her fingers to her mouth in delight. Light zinged from her diamonds, as if from a magic wand. "This is it. What I want."

"Ah. Sleeping Beauty. I love this one." In this fantasy, Samantha was awakened by the kiss of a prince who'd searched the world over, risked his life to possess her with his hot mouth, tender fingers and thrusting—

Stop it.

Soon, Samantha would live these scenes instead of imagining them. Once she'd hired her assistant—which she'd just decided to do—she'd have more free time for her manhunt. She had to take action soon, before the ache between her thighs became a permanent charley horse.

"I know the perfect costume for you," she said to Misty, closing the portfolio and pushing to her feet. "Come on."

Samantha led Misty to the dressing room, with its two changing stalls, elevated try-on area with mirrors, lit makeup table and racks of fantasy clothes for men and women. Exotic shoes—spike heels, marabou slides, elaborate platforms and boots—were stored on racks along one wall. Hats, tiaras and headdresses rested on foam heads lining the top cupboards.

The overall impression was that of backstage at a theater—in fact, she'd scored most of her costumes, props and furniture from a defunct theater company. The lingerie, stockings and garters were on consignment from Valerie's lingerie shop.

For Misty, Samantha flipped past the red teddy, black silk kimono and white peignoir and grabbed the pink satin camisole with an organdy robe that would flatter her curves. Clear acrylic kitten heels and a satin cone hat with a sheer train completed the princess effect.

Samantha swept the robe around the teddy, held it under Misty's chin, then turned her toward the mirror. "Gorgeous, huh?"

"Very nice," she said with barely a glance.

"You're nervous you won't look how you imagine?"

Misty nodded.

"That's normal, but don't worry. The lights I use, the

angle, the costume and, mostly, who you are, Misty, will shine right through."

"Really?" Misty's don't-dare-hope smile filled Samantha with renewed fire. Her very best work shored up an uncertain woman's sense of her own sexual power.

"Absolutely." Samantha grasped the locket she always wore, the talisman reminding her of her mission. "You'll have fun, I promise." She thrust the clothes at Misty. "Change and meet me in the first studio on your left."

Misty headed for the dressing stall and Samantha took off for the fairy-tale studio to bring Misty's fantasy to life.

One day soon, she'd do something about her own. She had a whole mental checklist of sexual adventures besides her fantasies—drizzling chocolate on naked bodies…sex in a hot tub…sex under the sky…beneath the stars…in an elevator…in a rainstorm. Tons of ideas. For when she had time.

Her focus so far had been on launching Bedroom Eyes. She had a five-year plan with firm benchmarks and steep targets. Specialty photography required a huge client pool to survive and her corporate accounts and catalogs could only sustain her so long. If she did well, she would consider expanding, perhaps adding a second photographer when the time was right.

The unexpected bounty of having Darien offer her the entire floor had complicated things. Managing the space had proved time consuming. For one thing, construction seemed continual. Darien was a nut about storage. The lingerie shop could hold Valerie's inventory twice over and extra cupboards were being hammered into place in the hair salon right now.

Because she'd talked her friends into opening their shops here, she felt responsible for handling the tenant snafus. She'd dealt with the phone-line crash in Val's lingerie shop, but she still had to look into the plumbing problem in Blythe's salon and the AC glitch in Mona's massage studio.

She planned to hand off the property management duties to her assistant, too. Just yesterday she'd slipped a help-wanted sign in her window and ordered a classified ad for next week's paper.

Now she checked the digital Canon for image space—plenty. She used the digital for test shots to show the clients, but made prints from the richer film images. Ensuring the Hasselblad on the tripod held a full roll, she pulled down the castle backdrop, dragged the bed into position and was draping a garland of white silk roses over its canopy when the front door buzzed.

Damn. She had no time for a walk-in now. Maybe it was just Valerie wanting to pin down the details for the afternoon—Samantha had promised to help her arrange her stock and dress the mannequins in her windows. Her artist eye and all.

But it wasn't Valerie at her counter. It was a man. Handsome and tall, wearing a chambray shirt and 501s, with crisply cut black hair and a stance as square as his jaw, he was so masculine he made the studio look as froufrou as a dollhouse. And he seemed so familiar....

She knew immediately why. He was the spitting image of the weather-beaten cowboy in her fantasy—the sexy loner who smelled of wood smoke and leather and tenderly ran his rough palms over her delicate skin.

He set a scuffed leather portfolio on the counter and gave her a wicked smile. Maybe he was more like the highwayman risking arrest to enter her bedchamber by moonlight and possess her utterly.

"May I help you?" she asked, managing to sound normal.

"Rick West." He held out a hand so big it swallowed hers up. No calluses, so forget the cowboy. And his expression was strong and no-nonsense. More like the hard-bitten cop catching her speeding, then patting her down and losing all restraint.

"Samantha Sawyer," she managed to say, fighting her urge to add, *Have I done something wrong, Officer?*

He was clearly not here for a photo. Men's men only came in when they were dragged by the women who'd conquered their hearts. Rick West was alone. And without a ring.

Stop it.

"I'm here about the job," he said, giving her a blast of remarkable green eyes that made her want to say *yes, yes, oh yes.* He unzipped his portfolio, biceps tightening. "I'm a photographer."

"A photographer?" Not the cowboy, highwayman or cop. He was the artist, slowly peeling away her clothes so he could capture her on canvas or film or in clay. "But I'm only looking for an assistant."

"No problem. I can assist. Hold reflectors, deliver negs, answer the phones." He snatched her gaze up tight. "Whatever you need me to do."

Would you wear leather chaps? How about handcuffs? His eyes were a rare green. Not as bright as emerald or as subdued as jade. Nature's green—a Scottish hillside, a particular moss she'd seen on Oak Creek's red rocks.

"It would be a lot of errands, some marketing calls, low-skill stuff," she said, but he'd flipped open the portfolio to get his résumé, and she went close enough to peek at his pictures, bumping the counter, which wobbled. She had to ask Darien's crew to attach it properly to the floor.

"Wow," she said. The first photo was a startling shot of a big-winged bird that seemed to dance over a hillock of gold-and-yellow desert poppies. "Is that a falcon?"

"No. Turkey vulture."

"But it's so elegant." She glanced up at him.

"Yeah." He smiled mysteriously, as if the grace of the bird were his private secret. She could picture that wicked grin beneath a Zorro mask, with him all in black and her in a low-cut peasant blouse. *Tell me what you desire of me, mysterious outlaw.*

Your breasts, your thighs, your silky skin, your fiery soul.

He turned the portfolio at a better angle, so she could flip through it. Misty was waiting, but Samantha could at least glance at what he had. The second shot held racing clouds dusted by gold over an up-jutting desert promontory in an iridescent blue sky. "Gorgeous." She glanced up at him.

"Canyon de Chelly," he said, a flicker of pride in his Scottish-moss eyes. Forget the Zorro mask. She'd want those green eyes boring straight into her soul.

She was close enough to pick up his scent—lime-spice aftershave, fresh air and starch. His shirt was stiff, the sleeves fiercely creased. He'd ironed it? Masculine, but deliciously domestic. Mmm.

She flipped through breathtaking wildlife and land-scape shots—mostly Southwest, mostly desert, mostly color, though there were a few dramatic black-and-whites. Subtle emotions played over every print. His work was technically brilliant with an artistry that made even the familiar seem new.

"These are wonderful, Rick," she said, "but I take specialty portraits, as you can see." She motioned at the framed prints that surrounded them.

He thrust his résumé at her.

She looked it over. Freelance work for several magazines. He'd also been an automobile mechanic and had served in the army. His references included the photo editor at *Arizona Highways,* whom she knew.

"You can see my work's mostly landscape and wildlife," he said, "and I'd like to add some portraits to my portfolio. Glamour sells." He shrugged, as if that were an obvious motivation.

"But there wouldn't be much photography if any. I'm just growing my business. I'm only paying minimum wage." She extended the résumé, but he didn't take it, just held her gaze, something flaring in his eyes. Attraction spun hot between them and made the air seem to crackle.

"I'm flexible," he said, a sexy edge to his words.

"Oh, I'm sure you are," she blurted, surprising herself. He stood arrow straight, but there was an animal grace to him that made her want to see him in motion. She felt light-headed and a little weak. "But still…"

She just didn't see him doing this job.

Now, doing *her…that* she could definitely see. He'd slipped into her fantasies as easy as a night swim in August. What about making them real? She tugged on her locket, sliding it back and forth on its chain, pondering the idea.

Ask him out. You want him. He wants you. Simple.

Mona claimed Samantha used Bedroom Eyes as an excuse to back-burner her love life. Mona thought she was chicken.

Brrock, brrock.

So prove her wrong. This is the man. This is the place.

Still watching her, Rick braced a hip on the counter. When it shifted under him, he turned to jiggle it. "I could fix this. Someone could get hurt." He winked. *Hire me. You know you want to.*

"I can't offer you the job, Rick," she breathed, "but how about dinner?"

"Dinner?"

"Or maybe just dessert." She'd blurted the words before she'd absorbed the utter surprise on his face. He evidently hadn't been flirting so much. Oh, God. She'd gotten so caught up in her imagination, she'd assumed they were doing that sexy subtext repartee she loved in the movies…and her fantasies.

"Just kidding. Heh-heh." She laughed a fake laugh, madly grinding her locket along its chain, embarrassed as hell.

"Uh, that sounds…tempting…." He nodded a little, awkward, opened and closed his mouth, as if not sure what to say next.

The door buzzed and they both turned to watch Bianca Sylvestri rush in, her timing either perfect or rotten, Samantha wasn't quite sure which.

Bianca, a chubby dynamo, wore a knitted dress of multicolored nubby yarn with a matching pillbox hat. Her own creation, no doubt, since her ankle boots were trimmed in the same wool. Bianca loved to knit and was about to open her own yarn shop.

"You *have* to help me, Sammi," she said with breathy drama. "My niece Angela and her new husband Joey are desperate for a photo."

"I've got a client right now, Bianca. Misty's here."

And I just asked a man out for dessert. Dessert, *can you believe that?*

Even mortified to her roots, Samantha wasn't done fantasizing about Rick. Even now she could picture drizzling chocolate over his naked chest and flat belly, could see him licking her own swells and dips absolutely squeaky clean.

"Misty? Bless her heart, she does need you. But Joey's going to Chicago for three whole months and Angela needs a picture to keep her warm while he's gone. They'll be here in a blip. Joey doesn't know and we can't give him a nanosecond to think. Strip-sit-click, you know, before he starts whining."

"I'd love to help, Bianca, but Misty's waiting for me."

"Is she in the fairy-tale room?"

Samantha nodded.

"Great, because we need the exotic studio. You just go on and finish up with Misty." Bianca waved her away with diamond-heavy fingers. "I know exactly what we want and I'll set up for you." Bianca had helped with several friends' shoots, so this wasn't unusual behavior.

"I don't know..." Samantha said.

"I can help her." Rick said. "So you can finish."

"I can't ask you to do that, Rick."

"Sure you can," he said, low and steady, coaxing her.

"Perfect!" Bianca sang out. "Rick, is it? You're a life-saver."

"Anything I can do," Rick said, keeping his eyes on Samantha, still angling for the job.

He could save her time. Plus, moving props on Bianca's command would undoubtedly prove to him he didn't want the job.

Now dessert...that might still be on the table. She'd have to wait and see.

2

MAYBE JUST DESSERT? Damn. Rick followed the hot photographer deeper into her studio, figuring his next move. He'd meant to be friendly and helpful—a Boy Scout, not a horn dog—but his attraction to her obviously showed.

Now the woman didn't want to hire him; she wanted to screw his brains out. He'd been close to saying, *How about dinner* and *dessert?* As if he regularly traded sex for a W-4.

He was rusty at this.

Granted, the old Rick would have been happy to share dinner, dessert, a midnight snack and breakfast in bed with a woman like her. Not the new Rick and certainly not the Rick who was on duty.

He hated undercover work, despite the prestige. He hated wearing a different persona, keeping his lies in order, cozying up to suspects and scumbags. He liked things clean and straight and honest and simple. But his photography background made him ideal for the assignment, so here he was.

And he'd struck gold already, whether or not Sawyer hired him. He was about to question the wife of the mobster they were after. Darien Sylvestri owned this building and had set up Sawyer and her friends in business.

Exactly what kind of business the organized-crime task force hadn't yet pinned down. Money laundering, stolen goods or bookmaking, if Sylvestri stuck to his Chicago specialties. Pornography? Possible, considering Darien's in-town associates and all the strippers and hookers prancing through the Mirror, Mirror Beauty Center, the complex that housed the studio, salon, lingerie shop and massage place.

Something was definitely happening in Bedroom Eyes, they knew. Just before Sawyer had opened shop, the task force had triangulated a juicy call between Sylvestri and an associate. *The photo studio's prime,* he'd said. *We're all set with the tenant…. God bless Bianca.* The caller had said something garbled about a shop and some deliveries, then they'd lapsed into small talk. That was enough to move on the building.

Whatever was going on, Rick's job was to expose it from the inside as an employee. Which meant he had to get the damn job. Say whatever he had to say to get Sawyer to hire him.

He'd have to work the attraction angle. Just enough to get the connection going. Keep a tight rein on his reactions, of course. Go by the book, but he could be friendly, couldn't he?

She'd caught him off guard with that offer. Very direct. She almost seemed to have surprised herself.

She was hotter close up than she'd seemed from the surveillance. Smarter, too. And more intense.

Interesting.

He followed her down the hall, scanning every detail of the place in case this was his only chance to check it out.

Sawyer stuck her head into the first room. "Go ahead and pick out a CD to play, Misty, and I'll be right back."

Misty Simone, Rick knew. He and his partner Mark had watched her enter the studio earlier. Her husband Tony was small potatoes compared to Sylvestri. So was Joey Balistero, Sylvestri's son-in-law, whose shoot Rick was about to help with, but the more they knew about everyone who frequented the center, the tighter the case would be.

He wondered how deep in Sawyer was with Sylvestri, who'd relocated from Chicago a year ago, supposedly to retire, making a few quiet property purchases—a big house in Paradise Valley, a small commercial lot in Scottsdale, some horse acres outside Cave Creek and this two-story office building in a faded Phoenix strip mall.

Sawyer's help-wanted sign had been the first solid way onto the scene. Infiltrating the cleaning crew had failed—Sylvestri's people handled that—and trying for a lease or posing as shop customers was too short-term. Once he got hired, he could freely search the building, get to know the players, locate the action.

In a few minutes, he was about to see Balistero stripped to Skivvies. Not a pleasant prospect, but if it helped with the case, he'd hold the guy's, uh, belt for him.

Glancing into the first studio as he passed, Rick caught sight of a medium-format camera on a tripod pointed at a castle backdrop, a couple of lights on stands, a three-panel reflector, and Misty, who gave him a shaky smile.

Dressed in a pink nightie and a party hat, the woman was obviously not there for a porn shot. Probably didn't even know her husband was dirty. The wives were always the last to know.

Farther down the hall, Rick noted another studio to

the right, followed by a service door to the parking lot, then a tiny office, which he was staring into when Sawyer stopped short.

He bumped into her full on, enjoying her firm backside, and got a blast of flowers. Her thick red-brown hair snagged in his chin stubble.

She turned and looked up at him, her burned-in blue eyes wide with surprise. "Well, hello there," she breathed, trying to act cool, but flustered. Very flustered.

"Sorry," he said.

"Oh, don't be." Her eyes gave him a once-over, her pink tongue peeking out. "It was nice." She dragged a medallion on a chain, which drew his gaze to her spectacular set of nature's own.

He lifted his eyes to meet hers. "Yeah. Very nice."

For just a second, case or no case, he wished he'd met her before he'd decided to settle down, start a family, back when he was content with an occasional night with a warm and willing female.

"Here's Bianca," she said, waving him into the next studio, where Sylvestri's wife was rummaging around in the fake fur, pillows and vases on shelves. The room looked like backstage at a strip club, with elaborate furniture in animal prints and a black metal arch, along with photo equipment and three rolled backdrops.

"You sure you're up for this?" Samantha asked him, her eyes twinkling. "It's nothing like snapping a sunlit vista, you know."

"I'm up for anything," he said, letting the sexual undertow tug at the sand beneath their feet. He would have to tactfully backpedal if she went for what he was hinting at, but for now he had to keep her interested.

"Okay," she breathed. "Set up two reflectors and the

tungsten. I'll bring in the Hasselblad when I'm finished with Misty."

"You got it, boss."

She held his gaze for a second, turned away, then glanced back at him, biting her lip, as if she was in over her head. Pretty charming and he found himself smiling at her back as she walked away.

Maybe that was what had happened with Sylvestri. She just got in too deep. Wanted a studio and closed her eyes to the crimes that made it possible. It was a shame when bright people turned their talents to bad ends. Genetics, upbringing or something big went south in their lives. It wasn't his job to feel sorry for the perps, though. It was his job to stop them.

"Grab that chaise, Rick, will you?" Bianca said, calling him back to the task at hand. Right now, he'd learn what he could from Sylvestri's wife. He moved the chaise to where she wanted it, then two plaster columns, which were so heavy he felt like Samson in that old movie tearing down the pillars he was chained to.

Bianca tossed two velvet pillows at him. "Fluff those up and arrange them, please. See if you can wrap that red silk around the arch like a curtain, hanging down, but swept back."

Good Lord. If Mark and his squad could see him now— fluffing pillows and draping curtains. He wanted to laugh.

When he'd finished, Bianca surveyed the results. "Not bad." Then her gaze landed on him and stuck. "So, Rick, you're a friend of Samantha's?" She looked him up and down, like she was checking out a daughter's prom date.

"Actually, I applied to be her assistant. This is kind of an audition, I guess."

"So you need me to put in a good word." She tapped

her lip. "I'm glad she's so busy she needs an employee. I've sent in all my friends and family to get their pictures taken."

So the mobster's wives and mistresses trotting in for photos over the last few weeks had been referrals from Bianca. The task force had assumed they were doing business for Darien out of the studio. Maybe not. Hmm.

"Samantha took a photo of me that saved my marriage."

"A photo can do that?"

"When Sammi takes it, you bet. That woman knows how to yank out your beating heart and wave it under your nose." She smiled. "That sounded positively Aztec, I know, but what she does is a pure miracle." She sighed, adjusting a pillow.

"I can imagine," he said, thinking she had to be exaggerating. It was just film, angle and light, after all.

"We still need something," Bianca said, eyeing the set. "I know. Put the fat candles around that table, which should go there." She pointed at each item in turn and Rick moved things as indicated.

As they worked, Rick asked questions and Bianca was happy to explain that she and Darien had come from Chicago to retire and that the "dear, darling man" was setting her up in the knit shop she'd always wanted.

Before long, Rick knew about the horse property they'd purchased and the electronics store Darien wanted to open on the second floor of this building. He memorized everything as best he could, wishing he'd requisitioned a mini recorder. First chance he got, he'd slip away to take some notes.

Mark ribbed him about how scrupulous he was about notes and reports, but being thorough and organized kept his head straight when he was undercover, helped him remember who he was, kept the lies in order.

Again, Bianca stepped back and examined the set, then beamed at him. "Nice work, Rick. I'll definitely tell Samantha how helpful you were. And so easy to talk to. I've blabbed on and on…." She pondered him, speculating. Wondering why he asked so many questions? He braced himself to deflect her suspicion.

"Would you do me a favor, Rick?"

"Sure. Anything."

"Convince our Sammi not to work so hard. She needs to get out more. My Darien has a nephew who would be perfect for her—handsome and successful…he's in vending machines and concessions, I believe. There was a tiny misunderstanding with the authorities, but that's been straightened out."

"Sounds interesting." And criminal, actually. The mob was all over the vending world. He wondered if Bianca even knew she was surrounded by wise guys. She seemed completely guileless. People were always harder to read close up, when you saw things from their side, heard their rationalizations, their hopes and dreams and plans to change, to go straight….

"So, with you taking over some of the work, maybe Sammi can go out with him. I'm not thinking marriage necessarily, but…you understand."

"You bet. But first I have to get the job. If you could help her see I'm the guy she needs…" That hadn't come out quite right.

"We'll see about that, won't we?" she said, another speculative look on her face, as if she'd read a little too much into what he'd said. "For now, we need to light the candles."

He patted his pockets. Pointless, since smoking was a habit he'd quit along with so many others when his brother Brian had died.

The door buzzer sounded.

"That'll be the happy couple," Bianca said. "You get matches from Samantha and I'll get them in here. Hurry back. I might need you to convince Joey to co-operate."

God, would he have to hold the guy down and strip him? Samantha was right. This was nothing like snapping sunlit vistas. Wildlife didn't primp and preen and prance around in costumes. Getting a load of Joey in his undies sounded like a bad breakfast.

He headed for the studio where Samantha was photographing Misty Simone. The woman's breathy gasp made Rick wonder if they were shooting porn after all, but once he stepped inside, he saw that she was watching a slide show on a computer monitor.

Each image appeared, then faded, accompanied by music. In the shots, Misty lay on her side on satin sheets, her robe slightly open, looking remarkably hot. Not shy or silly or even overweight, and the goofy hat looked like it belonged on her head.

"How did you do that?" Misty asked Samantha, her voice faint with amazement. "I look sweet and sexy… not even fat."

"Lights and angle and you. That's all there is to it."

"Tony won't believe it's me."

"Sure he will. He'll see you clearly again. He'll remember why he fell in love with you."

Sawyer was so damned earnest, Rick was ready to believe that Tony Simone, as sensitive as the long-shoreman he'd been in Jersey, would drop to his knees at his wife's feet and beg her forgiveness for being a neglectful prick.

The last photo faded, the music stopped and the screen went black.

"Bianca was right," Misty said. "You do make miracles."

"I just capture what's there." Samantha caught sight of him. "Yes, Rick?"

"Uh…oh, I—" He realized he was standing there like a dick-dragging idiot. Why had he come again? "Matches. We need some."

"There's a lighter on that shelf." Sawyer nodded at the spot. "Everything ready in there?"

"Lights and set anyway. Bianca went after Angela and Joey."

"They won't know what hit them."

"No kidding. She's something else." They shared a smile that felt comfortable, so he pushed a little. "She thinks you should hire me to give you more free time."

"She does, does she?" She tilted her head at him.

"I think she's right."

"You do?"

"I'll make your life easier, I swear."

"I don't know about that," she said, searching him out, prying, asking him about the heat simmering between them. He knew what she meant, but he had a job to do. He had to keep her guessing for a while, at least.

"Hire me," he said with a wink. "You know we both want it."

He watched a tremor pass through her and felt an answering quiver in his own limbs. *Get a grip.* He felt so rusty at this flirting thing. He'd been kind of isolated lately. His wife hunt had been going way, way slow.

Or maybe it was something about Samantha.

Probably being undercover. He hated undercover.

Samantha watched Rick go back to Bianca, admiring his muscular behind in well-worn jeans. He'd flirted with her. At least that. But he also wanted the job. How about the job *and* dessert?

She could hardly date an employee. Assistant by day, fantasy man by night? Too weird, even for Samantha the Bold. Rick was either her assistant or her date, not both, and the next two hours would tell her which.

She said goodbye to Misty and sent her off to change, warmed by her parting words: *This means more than you know, Samantha. Even if Tony doesn't change, I'll never see myself the same again.* Mission accomplished. Samantha was thrilled.

In studio two, however, things weren't going so well. The newlyweds, sitting on opposite ends of the chaise, looked miserable. Joey slumped, fully clothed, hanging his head like he awaited a prostate check. Angela sulked in a red lace teddy, arms folded, legs crossed, foot wagging angrily.

Bianca flung up her arms. "I give up, Sammi!"

"Joey's ruining everything," Angela cried.

"I'm not taking off my pants," Joey said. "I am no fag."

"Don't say *fag,*" Angela said. "Being gay is perfectly okay. Have some respect."

"*You* have some respect and don't make me into a fool."

Angela bickered back, but Rick cut through her words in a take-charge voice. "Just do it, man."

Everyone stared.

"Look, if your lady wants a shot of you in a bird suit with feathers sticking out your ass, put on the damned suit. Hell, if it makes her happy, cluck a little."

There was a pause, then Bianca spoke into the stunned silence. "Well said, Rick. Wasn't that well said, Sammi?"

"I've seen her work," Rick continued. "You'll look good."

She could almost read Joey's mind. *If this guy thinks it's not gay…* "Okay…but just the shirt."

"But I like those boxers," Angela whined.

"The shirt's enough," Samantha said, deciding to go with a simple clinch and just two positions, not her usual six. She'd use the digital, which hung from her neck, and move the camera, not the couple, to maintain Joey's tentative goodwill. "Angela and Joey, find a comfortable position lying down. Bianca, you've done all you can. How about you wait in the lobby for us?"

"Whatever you say, hon," Bianca said. "Smile nice, you two."

While Joey uneasily unbuttoned his shirt, Samantha hit the CD player's remote, filling the room with soft music. "Grab that stepladder," she said to Rick, winking at him as a thank-you for getting Joey's cooperation.

"Whatever you need," he said, winking back. There was that snap of heat between them again, that tug of man-woman connection and her embarrassment from earlier was completely erased.

Rick braced the ladder while she climbed. She felt his eyes on her body, was aware of the strength and warmth of his arms almost touching her thighs. It was a good thing he held the ladder or she'd have wobbled right off the rung.

To steady herself, she focused in on her subjects, lying hopelessly tense on the chaise beneath her.

"Look into Angela's eyes, Joey, and forget we're

here," she said in the low, even register that worked best with self-conscious clients. "Let Angela be all you see."

"This is so lame," Joey said.

Angela grabbed the back of his hair.

"Ouch. Okay, okay."

"Won't you miss me?" Angela asked in a little girl's voice.

"Sure I'll miss you, baby," he said slowly.

"Like the moon?" she coaxed. "And all the stars?"

Sweetness softened Joey's hard features. "Every friggin' twinkle," he said, sinking into the rhythm of what must be a lover's ritual they shared. He leaned down and kissed her.

Samantha sighed. She loved when couples got tender with each other.

"This is all you'll have of me while you're gone," Angela murmured, holding Joey's gaze.

"Yeah," he said, getting into it now. "So it has to be good. It has to last."

Samantha took a shot. Perfect. When she shifted, she accidentally bumped Rick's forearm, remembering he was there, which was strangely reassuring, even as it put her on sexual alert. After a few more snaps, she needed to get down the ladder to try for some shots from beside the couple.

She turned toward Rick, signaling her descent, and he moved slightly. Her butt brushed his chest as she lowered herself, and, once on the ground, she turned, hesitating in the cave of his arms.

He struggled, too, for a moment, and almost seemed to force himself to step away from her. Whatever was percolating here was definitely mutual. She took a shuddering breath and went to crouch beside the couple.

She looked up at them, framing their faces between their forearms. Nice shot.

Rick moved to the Hasselblad and in a few seconds, he snapped a picture, setting off the strobe. She smiled her approval. She'd have two camera perspectives after all. Twice the photos in the five minutes they had before Joey lost interest.

"Imagine you're saying goodbye," she said to pull a little more emotion from the couple.

Angela pulled Joey in for a kiss.

"Baby," Joey murmured.

Click. Perfect. Samantha looked over at Rick, who'd fired off more frames, and they smiled at each other. They'd made the most of a delicate moment, working as a team, in wordless sync. Which was surprising considering they were virtual strangers. Rick had potential as an assistant.

But what about as a dinner partner?

She watched her couple, moved by the way Joey cupped Angela's cheeks with his entire palms, as if he couldn't touch enough of her, and how Angela pointed her toes between Joey's feet, utterly thrilled to be in his arms.

Samantha wanted this intimacy, too. Eventually. After she'd been wild and free and wanton for a while. She would know when she was ready. In a couple of years. Maybe three. She had a lot of fantasies to live out.

She caught Rick looking at her. He seemed puzzled, as if she'd somehow surprised him. What was that about?

"Maybe we should go for a different position," Joey said. "Move around, try some poses, mix it up?"

In the end, Samantha had to stop him before he asked for a wind machine and baby oil to make his muscles gleam.

She loaded the digitals on the computer, invoked the slide show and stepped back so the couple could admire themselves in peace. Rick stood beside her, looking on, too. She glanced at his profile, with its straight, masculine lines. He was deliciously male.

She could picture him with her on the big bed in the fairy-tale studio. She would pretend to be asleep. He would wake her with a kiss. Or maybe they'd be on the tiger chaise in this studio…her hands tied with a red silk sash…no, the black velvet one. *Please…don't… stop…. More…more…*

"And bigger. More and bigger, right?"

Samantha jerked back to the moment. "Bigger? Huh?"

"And matte, not glossy," Angela said. She meant print size, quantity and finish, Samantha realized. Whew.

All three people were staring at her. Hell, she'd lapsed into a fantasy in the middle of a shoot. It was Rick's fault. He was the living embodiment of her fantasy man standing right here beside her, so broad and tall and handsome.

And he wanted her to hire him.

This could be a problem. Or a gift. He could help her in the studio *and* the bedroom.

"Many clients prefer matte," she said, but she had to clear her throat to get out the words. "Less glare, but it's up to you." She babbled on about the proof book and the order, but she was thinking about Rick.

Could he want more than the job? He seemed mysterious to her. Which was partly why he was so hot. He could be anyone she wanted him to be.

Bedroom Eyes was the most important thing to her, right, and he could be a good assistant. She hadn't counted on photography experience in her employee, but it could only help. Maybe she should give him the job and forget dessert altogether.

She and Rick walked the couple out to Bianca. Joey and Angela strolled arm in arm, looking at each other every few seconds as if they couldn't believe their luck. Like a bride and groom faltering in the middle of their vows, awed by the power of their symbolic act, appreciating each other anew.

Samantha was so glad she'd given them this reminder of their love. Maybe couple shots were the best of all.

The clients gone, Samantha turned to Rick. "So what do you think?" she asked, knowing his words would tell her what to do.

"I'm impressed. You got those two from divorce court to a Hallmark card in two minutes flat. The digitals were great."

"The prints will be better. I combine flash with tungsten so the golden highlights are warm, not cloying."

"It's more than the lights, Samantha. You have a gift."

He wasn't about to let her hide behind her gear. She liked that.

"There's a lot you can teach me." He stood a little closer, drawing her out, stretching the tension between them like a fine, tight wire.

There was a lot he could teach her, she'd bet. *Naked.* "You did a good job of getting Joey to cooperate."

"Probably would help you to have a man around for that," he coaxed.

"We did have a nice rhythm going."

"Yeah. A nice rhythm." And heat. They had heat going. His irises flickered with gold—candles shining out of all that green moss—telling her he wanted her.

Her knees turned to flan.

"It's mostly clerical, Rick. Really. You might have to clean out drains and change AC filters for my tenants."

"I don't mind. Like I said, anything you—"

"Need. Right. You said that." She held his gaze, her knees of flan jiggling beneath her.

"And I meant it."

Did he really? Could he possibly? Could they work together *and* sleep together? Insane idea or time-saver?

"Okay. We try it for a week," she said, trying to be firmer than her custard knees. "But if it doesn't work out—"

"It'll work out." His eyes burned through her. He looked dark and dangerous, with stubble just emerging from his firm jaw, and he was so big. He'd have to bend down to kiss her, even if she went on tiptoe, and when he wrapped her in his arms, she'd be overpowered, overwhelmed, swept away.

"How can you be so sure?" she breathed.

"I am. Trust me."

"We give it a week," she said firmly, showing him who was boss. But there was a flicker of something in his green eyes that made her think that maybe she wasn't quite as in charge as she should be.

3

SCORE. HE WAS IN. He had the job.

Of course, he'd practically sworn to be Sawyer's love slave with the looks and dripping hints he'd delivered. The worst part was that it had come out so easily. Like butter, like cream, like sliding into bed with a hot, hungry woman.

Something about her dug at him—the yes-no vibe she gave off. Flirting, then backing away, as if she'd stepped too far out on a tightrope on a dare.

He wanted to reassure her. *Yeah, you're hot. Yeah, I'd jump you if I could.*

He liked her. She had this bizarre business, but she seemed sincere. *Forget liking her.* He had to keep personal reactions under control. Constant awareness, attention to detail and neutral detachment were the secrets to successful undercover work. The less personal he got, the better.

Except she wouldn't trust him if he didn't connect with her, so he had to engage in some repartee. Within reason. *Work it for the case.* He'd given her mixed messages, too, which wasn't fair and hadn't helped.

God he hated being undercover.

It made him feel out of control. He hated checking the rearview, doubling back over every story for consistency and cracks. Hated pretending to be someone he wasn't, hated living with his lies. For now, he contented himself with his success.

Telling Sawyer he needed a bite, he headed out to his Jeep to phone his partner, grab a burger, then return so she could go over his duties.

He crossed the lot, liking when the mild October breeze kicked up, promising change, just like the case. Adrenaline rushed his pulse and he felt primed for action. Easier to ignore that lust-pumped charge he'd gotten over the fact he'd be hanging around Sawyer for a while.

Lot of good that did him when he had to avoid *dessert* at all cost.

He climbed into his Jeep and took off for Jade's, the squad's favorite bar and grill just down the street.

"Got the job," he said when Mark picked up his call. "Tell the lieutenant."

"You lucky dog."

"What are you talking about, Trudeau? You'd hate this assignment. Gloria'd hassle you about the overtime and you'd miss your kids."

"But Sawyer's hot," Trudeau said.

"So?"

"I'm just saying, if the case calls for you to get sweaty with her…"

"Are you nuts?" The idea sounded so damned good he had to sit down. He could picture those muscular legs wrapped around his ass, that curly hair falling over his face, that snapdragon mouth against his, that pink tongue doing things…

"I'm trying to live through you," Mark said. "Except you don't do jack shit worth hearing about, letting alone tracking with binoculars."

"What are you talking about? You've got a great life. And a wife you don't deserve." Mark was deeply devoted to Gloria, despite the studly bullshit he trotted out for the squad. No one bought it, but it made Trudeau feel invincible, when, in fact, he could be felled by a mere blink of his wife's lashes.

"I'm saying, make an effort, West. Quit hanging with us so much. Or at least bring over a woman when you do."

"I will, don't worry." He'd dated two women since he'd decided to look for a wife. Laura, then Theresa. Both nice enough, but the minute he'd dropped them off after a date, he'd felt the relief of a duty done, and they'd slid from his mind like minnows down a creek.

Lately, he'd spent his free time throwing back brews with squad mates at Jade's or over at Mark's. Gloria made the best rib sauce and a terrific pecan pie. Their place was homey and Rick loved their kids. He should get back to the wife search, though. He'd do that. Sure. One of these days soon.

"Alex wanted me to tell you he beat the top boss on *Dragon of Doom 3.*"

"He didn't download the cheats, did he?"

"Nope. Worked it out on his own. Couldn't disappoint Uncle Rick with his rules for every flippin' thing, including video games."

"Good for him. I'll check it out when I'm over next. This weekend, maybe?"

"What are you, thirty? You act like an old married drone. When I was your age, it was a different woman every weekend. If Gloria hadn't gotten pregnant, I'd have—"

"You'd have begged her to marry you. She's the best thing that ever happened to your sorry ass."

Maybe that was what was missing in Rick's search for a wife—a woman who made him feel the way Trudeau felt. The man nearly glowed when Gloria came into a room, even if it was just to rip him a new one, which she had to do from time to time. The man was in sore need of female guidance.

Truth was that Rick wanted what Trudeau had—a settled place in the world, a wife and kids to work for, someone to help him sort out what mattered from what didn't. Something Brian had never had the chance to have.

"So now that I'm in," he said, getting back to work, "I'll be checking out all the shops, verifying IDs, seeing who's connected. Looks like some of the photography customers came from the wife, not Darien, and are straight photo shoots, nothing crime related."

"Interesting. It's good you're inside. We can figure this out a hell of a lot faster."

"That's the idea."

"And on that other thing, you'll be surrounded by naked women, West, so drool a little. Pretend you got a pair."

"The equipment's intact, not to worry," he said. His reaction to Sawyer was proof. He grimaced, especially because he got a rush when he thought about getting back to her now.

He hung up with Mark and headed into Jade's, determined to keep his mind on the job and forget how hot Sawyer was, no matter how many ways she reminded him with her twisty hip-walk and her teasing smile and flirty remarks and her tight backside, and that great set of—

Stop it.

Maybe he'd learn something from her, like he'd said, though he hated how personal portraits got. Samantha Sawyer sure knew what she was doing in the studio.

She'd turned the shoot with that lowlife Balistero into a tender moment. And Rick couldn't see her shooting porn, not from what he'd seen so far.

On the other hand, sociopaths were skilled liars, so he'd stay on guard. Remain clearheaded, neutral and completely controlled. Evaluate all evidence, examine all options, ask and answer all questions.

And stay way clear of dessert.

"IS THE BOOKKEEPER spelled *T-A-B-O-R or E-R?*"

"*O-R*," Samantha said on a sigh. "I promise I won't quiz you later." Since Rick had returned from his lunch break, he'd asked a million questions about the center, dragging the twenty-minute orientation into a ninety-minute ordeal. It was as if he thought he'd have to run the place without her. Just now he'd honed in on the fact that Darien loaned Samantha his bookkeeper.

"Let's get going, Rick," she said, "so I can introduce you to the other shop owners." The day was nearly over and she'd promised to help Valerie after work.

On the way out the door, Rick paused to rattle the loose counter. "I'll bolt this first thing tomorrow."

"The construction crew should handle it, but thanks." He was obviously trying to reassure her of his usefulness. His tone had changed over lunch. When he'd left, there had been flirtation in the air, but he'd returned all facts and figures.

Which was best, she realized as the time passed. Rick's role as her assistant—and a photographer at that—was far more important than any sex they might share. Samantha would find her fantasy lover elsewhere.

She led the way to Healing Touch, Mona's massage studio, where there was an AC problem. The delicate bell over the door tickled Samantha's ear as always, pouring calm through her. She associated the sound with her once-a-month gift to herself of a Mona massage.

Mona's was the smallest shop, consisting of a tiny reception area, two small massage rooms, a restroom and overlarge closets—Darien and his storage space.

Mona emerged from the first massage room. "Hello," she said, smiling at them. Short and curvy with open brown eyes, she moved in an eddy of palpable warmth that Samantha loved. Her massages melted worries and fears, along with knots and kinks, and it was worth every word of her usual lectures about Samantha accepting herself as she was to experience Mona's tension-melting skill.

"This is my new assistant, Rick West. Rick, Mona Munro. We're here to deal with your air problem."

"An assistant already? How wonderful." Mona shook Rick's hand, then slanted Samantha a look. She hadn't believed Samantha would actually hire anyone. She thought Samantha was clinging to the excuse of being too busy. *If you're going to break out, sweetie, break out.*

"I act fast when the time's right," Samantha said, returning her look. Now she had an assistant. Soon, she'd find a man. Hit a brunch at the Phoenician or cruise a singles watering hole and reel one in. No problem.

"It's this way." Mona led them to the second massage room.

Samantha breathed in the lemon–ylang-ylang of the candle burning on the counter beside the CD player in the cozy, golden-hued room that featured a massage table covered in saffron sheets.

"The air just sinks. No movement," Mona said to Rick, waving her arms through the air above the table.

Rick looked up, studying the register, arms akimbo. "I'll see what I can do." He scooped off his shoes and climbed onto the table, reaching up to twist something on the vent, which made his forearm muscles tighten and glide.

And look at that backside, so tight and round. *Why, Handyman Rick, I think my wiring needs tightening, my pipes need, well, what pipes need. Fix me quick with your special tool.* Samantha sighed.

Rick banged the vent slats with the heel of his hand.

"So, an assistant *and* a handyman," Mona murmured.

Samantha looked at her friend, Rick's body rising between them. "He'd do whatever I need him to do," she said.

"Oh, well. That's wonderful." Mona grinned.

Samantha blushed and changed the subject. "So how's Mr. Regular?"

It was Mona's turn to blush. "Still regular." Chuck Yardley, aka Mr. Regular, came for a massage five days a week, feigning rugby strains, but really to get to know Mona, who refused to budge on her no-dating-clients rule.

Samantha understood her reluctance. Sleazy massage parlors gave legitimate therapists a bad name. Samantha had a similar problem with callers who asked for vulgar photos, using words she preferred not to think, let alone hear.

But Mona could easily send Chuck to another therapist and go out with the guy. She claimed her people instincts went amok once chemistry kicked in and she had a rat of an ex-husband to prove it. So poor Chuck forked over hundreds a week in unnecessary rubdowns in a vain effort to coax his reluctant sweetheart that he was safe to date.

Rick tested the outflow, then looked down at them. "That should do it."

Mona tilted up her face. "Mmm, feels better already."

While Rick climbed down, his back to them, Mona mimed licking her finger and touching it to Rick's behind, then yanking the digit away as if burned.

Samantha fought a laugh.

Rick reached the floor and turned. "What's funny?"

"Nothing," Mona said, her eyes twinkling. "I just mentioned how nice it is that you're so handy. I mean besides being an assistant."

"Whatever Samantha needs," he said, winking at her, teasing, turning her nerves to hot wires.

"Yes, she mentioned that." Another look from Mona.

Samantha had to clear her throat to speak. "Rick's also a photographer. He helped me with a shoot earlier."

"Even better. Photographer, assistant and handyman. Ideal in every way." Then Mona quit teasing and honed in on Rick's back, studying it with a clinical eye.

"I hope to learn a lot," Rick said, glancing from Mona to Samantha, clearly puzzled by Mona's change of focus, but when she grabbed one of his shoulders and ran a knuckle down his spine, his eyes went wide. "What are you doing?"

"I'd guess mostly Swedish with a little shiatsu," Mona pronounced, prodding him with a bent knuckle. "Maybe some trigger-point work. You've got a slight curvature…. That sore?"

"A little, yeah. I was in a car wreck in high school."

"That explains it. Makes the intercostals go into spasm." Mona grabbed both of his arms, bent at the elbow and pulled them to first one side, then the other. "Get a lot of kinks?"

"Some."

She manipulated his shoulder and he said, "Ohh… yeah," his body sagging with relief. Watching Rick's ramrod-straight frame dissolve into relaxed pleasure made Samantha want to melt.

"Better?" Mona released him.

He turned from side to side, testing his range of motion. "Yeah. Better."

"I'll get my book." Mona glided out of the room.

"She's getting her book?" Rick asked.

"To schedule you a massage. That felt good, didn't it?"

"Yeah, but…"

He seemed so flummoxed by the idea she had to smile. "Then imagine a whole, entire hour."

Mona returned with her dog-eared planner. "How about four tomorrow?"

"We'll be too busy, I'm sure," he said, looking at Samantha for a way out.

"There's always time for a massage, Rick. Consider it an employee benefit, since I don't offer insurance."

"Thanks, but I'll be fine," Rick said, twisting at the waist to prove it.

"Mona won't settle for *fine.* By the time she's done, you won't know your own name or even where you are."

When he blanched, she almost laughed, but she hid her reaction and turned to Mona. "Also, Rick will be following up on the wedding-planner mailing. Do you want me to include a coupon?"

"Sure. I'll put something together." She turned to Rick. "I'm glad you're on our team."

"Yeah. Me, too. And if you have any other problems, let me know. I'll drop in regularly, see what else needs doing."

"Sounds great," Mona said.

Samantha thought it was nice how he was taking charge, accepting responsibility for extra duties already. Maybe a little too conscientious, but, so far, a good hire.

"You didn't need to do that," Rick said as soon as they were outside the shop. "I can pay for the massage."

"Mona gives me a discount. And you'll need it. I'll be working you hard." She put her hand to her mouth and stood stock-still.

Rick chuckled. "I'm going to let that one alone."

She smiled her gratitude, liking the wicked look on his face all the same.

"I don't know that I like the idea of Mona making me forget my name or where I am," he mused.

"Why not? Haven't you ever been swept away?" she asked.

"Not on a massage table," he said in a tone that made her heart pound.

"I know what you mean," she said, though she really didn't. She'd never been that lost in a physical moment. She wanted to be. With Rick. Forgetting everything but him and what he was doing to her. *Rick, Rick, oh, Rick.*

She sighed, then realized they were standing outside Valerie's display windows, which held the naked mannequins she'd agreed to dress.

"Venus in a C-cup, huh?" Rick said, reading the shop name from above the nude figures. "This whole place is something else." He shook his head, as if mystified by it all. Again she had to wonder why he'd wanted this job.

The atmosphere was so *not* Rick.

For a moment they stood side by side staring at the naked women with their plaster hips thrust provocatively forward, fingers extended, inviting, teasing. In her mind, she saw Rick staring at her instead of them, sliding his hot, green gaze over every trembling inch of her naked and needy body.

"I'd ask what you're thinking, but I bet I'm better off not knowing," he said, his low tone vibrating through her.

She turned to him. *I'm thinking, you…me…naked… now.*

But she was spared that bold response or a clever retort when Val burst out the door of the shop. "Thank *God* you're here! My inventory finally arrived." She stopped short at Rick.

"Meet my new assistant, Rick West. Rick, Valerie Sumner. He'll be helping you with any tenant issues. We're heading over to the salon right now to—"

"Terrific. You can both help. The shipment *barely* got here and I cannot *under any circumstances* miss Lindsay's twirling tournament. Plus, you have the windows to do, Sammi." She nodded at the displays.

Samantha looked from her frantic friend to Rick to her watch. It was already four. "You don't need to stay, Rick. Blythe's plumbing can wait for tomorrow."

"I'm happy to help," he said.

"That's excellent," Valerie said. "Come on."

They followed her through the shop to the back room where men were adding a pallet of goods to the towers of boxes and crates that jammed the space.

Val named the items in each column and then indicated where in the store they belonged. "Lingerie sets there. Garters and stockings on hooks on the walls. Single thongs and panties in rows on that counter, folded. Expensive vibrators in the display case. Edible underwear, oils and genital jewels on the counter."

Genital jewels? She and Rick exchanged startled looks.

"I'll finish checking the order, bring out the boxes and handle the inside table displays," Val finished. "Holler if you have questions." She was already heading for the back room.

"Do you have questions?" Samantha asked Rick, opening a box and lifting out a red nylon bra with the nipple area cut out. She held it by its straps.

"Just one. How do you stand these things?" He held the matching thong by its thinnest strap.

"You get used to it," she said, going for breezy, feeling hot and excited and very nervous. She'd only begun wearing thongs in the last few months.

"Looks like a match," he said, dangling the panties below the bra, which she realized she held in front of her own breasts. "Very nice," he added softly.

"Cut it out," she said, fighting the warmth of his words. Heavens to horny, she had to get a grip. She thrust a two-part hanger at his chest and gave him the sexy bra. "Clip them together and hang them here." She brushed a hanger on the circular chrome rack, setting them all to clanging.

"You're the boss." He grinned.

They set to work and she decided chitchat would keep her from lapsing into any more fantasies. "So, you were in the army? Did you like it?" she asked him.

"Huh? The army? Yeah, sure."

Sounded like mixed feelings to her. "I imagine the discipline would be difficult."

"It was good for me. Made up for my misspent youth." He smiled.

"You were wild in high school?"

"No more than most, I guess. How about you?"

"I was your standard Goody Two-shoes. I lived in a little town with little ideas and parents who fit right in."

"Small towns can be nice."

"Not to me. I couldn't wait for college."

"To go wild?"

"Exactly." But she laughed. "Only it didn't work that way. I met a guy and before long you'd never know I'd left Copper Corners. All we did was study and watch TV." Spending time with Barry had been no more exciting than League Night at the Copper Corners Bowl-A-Rama, but she'd let herself get sucked into living life his way for too long.

"No more, though," she said. "I'm not letting life trickle through my fingers. I intend to splash around, make big, messy waves that practically drown me."

She realized Rick was watching her closely. Almost as if he were taking mental notes on her. Unnerving. And flattering, too. "What kind of waves are you interested in making?" he asked.

Sexy waves that peaked and crashed and climaxed, of course, but she couldn't say that. "With my work, for one thing. And my personal life, too."

"If your personal life's anything like your work… wow." His moss-green eyes heated to a sparkling emerald. He was hinting, but she couldn't quite read his intentions.

How should she respond? *Yeah, baby, I wear out my men like paper plates. Wanna be next?* But that was way over the falls.

"Yeah. Well…these things take time. I only started taking boudoir shots six months ago."

"Sure." He paused, taking in her answer. "So how'd you get into that?"

She was relieved he was going with chitchat. "Boudoir work? Or photography? I always loved taking pictures. Begged for a thirty-five-millimeter for Christmas when I was seven and after that spent all my allowance on film and developing. Puzzled the hell out of my parents."

"Oh, yeah?"

"They thought getting in people's faces was too pushy. When I won awards in high school, they were impressed, but bewildered." It had broken her heart that they were so lukewarm about her passion. "How about you? How'd you get started?"

"I was young, too. When my pop would go hunting, I'd tag along to shoot pictures. He thought it was peculiar, but he liked the company when my older brother was too busy." He was quiet for a minute and crushed the boxes he'd emptied, sending his wintry scent to her on a puff of air.

"So when did you go professional?" she asked, hanging up a black satin underwear set.

"I fell into it. Needed money, saw an ad in a magazine. Put myself out there and assignments came my way. How about you?"

"It was a hobby until late in college." She put a white satin ensemble on the rack. "I thought I'd be a psychologist or social worker, until I took this portrait-photography class on a lark and it was like lightning and thunder striking at the same time. It was a way to combine my curiosity about people with my interest in art. I was absolutely electrified by the idea. I never looked back."

"I can see that." *I see you.* He had an unnerving way of pulling her in tight. Nice, really, and it made her feel like they'd known each other longer than the couple of hours that had passed since he'd shown up at her counter. "Photography can take hold of you for sure," he added.

"You love it, too, huh?"

"Half the time when I was freelancing, I'd forget to bill the magazine." He smiled wistfully.

"It shows. Your work is remarkable. That vulture shot…"

"Yeah. I waited all day for that one."

"All day? That would kill me."

"That's how it is with wildlife. You have to be patient. You have to know the animal's habits and you have to be willing to wait."

"That's positively brutal. And unpredictable. I like to plan out a shot, get everything just so, full control."

"But what about the surprise factor? You know the shot at Canyon de Chelly?"

"With the surreal blue sky and gold light?"

"Yeah. For that my batteries were almost drained and I had one frame, but the scene stopped me dead. That one ran in *Arizona Highways*."

"I'm not surprised."

He gave her an unguarded grin of pride. "I was lucky."

"No. When you're good, you make your luck."

They looked at each other, connected by the shared love of taking pictures. She'd never dated a photographer before. Interesting….

You can't date him. You hired him.

"So, how did you get into sex shots?" This question came out a little hard and startled her.

"*Boudoir* shots," she corrected. "Or *intimate* photos. If you're going to work with me you need to use the right vocabulary."

"Sure. Do people ever ask for something more?"

"You mean like Joey? He was ready to strip, huh?" She started to laugh, but he interrupted her.

"I mean more graphic." His eyes dug in, diamond-sharp with focus, and she felt stung.

"You mean, do I shoot porn?" Angry, she slid her locket back and forth hard on its chain. It was bad enough she got those awful calls, now her new employee was asking her the question. "Absolutely not. I believe the human body is beautiful. Sex, too. And I won't exploit either one. I would think that you would already get that. And let me add that if that's what you're looking for, then—"

"Sorry. No. That's not what I want. And I get it. I'm sorry I asked."

He wore the strangest expression, as if she'd just passed some test she didn't know she'd been given. He looked *relieved*.

So strange. He'd insulted her and he was relieved she'd snapped at him.

Worse, she was glad. She wanted him to like her. Part of her wanted to slip into a comfortable intimacy with this man. Part of her held back, sensing there was something he wasn't telling her that she needed to know.

And the rest of her just plain wanted him.

4

RICK'S GUT CLENCHED at Samantha's reaction to his question. Her cheeks were splotched with red, as if he'd slapped them with his words. He'd *had* to ask. It was his job. Now she was dragging that pendant along its chain so hard it seemed about to cut her pretty neck.

"You're going to snap the links," he said, catching her hand over the medallion. "I'm sorry, Samantha. I didn't mean to offend you." He released her hand, still feeling her warm fingers against his palm.

"It's all right," she said, releasing a breath, clearly trying to settle herself. "I just hate being misjudged. And if you're going to work with me, you have to understand what I'm trying to do."

"I do." More or less. And her answer had relieved him. He wanted her to be exactly what she seemed to be. Which was no way for a cop to feel about a suspect, but what the hell.

"I want my clients to see past society's rules about beauty and recognize what's uniquely attractive about them."

Like Misty in her party hat, he guessed. Bizarre, but Samantha's eyes burned with conviction and he respected that. "You did that with Misty, right?"

"Exactly. When it all works, I get this...impression...

almost a double image. Something extra shines at me through the lens. And I try to capture that on film." She shot him a look of shy pride, then blushed. "You probably think that makes me crazy. I mentioned it to a girl in my portrait class over margaritas and she looked at me like I should check myself in somewhere."

She blushed again, embarrassed by her confession.

"I'm glad you told me. I'm honored." That sounded hokey as hell, but it was almost true. More double-life confusion.

He felt split in half—intrigued by this woman and also suspicious of her, sorting through every word for inconsistencies or clues to the case even as he flat out wanted her.

"Luckily, you're my loyal assistant or I'd have to kill you. I mean, now that you know my secret." She waggled her eyebrows, trying to act cool when she clearly felt exposed.

Which made him want to look out for her all the more.

Something about her got to him. Maybe the banked fire in her eyes, that wild desire that peeked out, a kid behind a curtain, daring herself to be brave.

Which wasn't good. He had to keep personal reactions to a minimum, even as he built the illusion that they shared a bond, that she could trust him, tell him anything.

God, he hated undercover work.

"Bianca said the photograph you took of her saved her marriage," he said, folding another damnable panty.

"She believes that, yeah."

"Seems like if people love each other they don't need tungsten lighting or lacy underwear." He held up a package of garters. They looked plain painful.

"My photos can't fix a dead love," she said. "But

sometimes people forget what they mean to each other. The picture reminded Darien."

"If you say so." He shook his head, unable to hide his skepticism completely.

"The most important thing was that Bianca saw herself in a new way," she said, dragging that necklace back and forth again. It was a locket and he wondered what it held. "And whenever she doubts herself, she has the picture to remind her."

"Makes sense, I guess." He turned to the novelty items stacked behind him, picking up a plastic-lined box holding what looked like a hair curler. "What the hell is this?"

Samantha went redder than the nylon lingerie she was clipping to a rack. "It's a vibrator, of course," she said.

"It looks like it could clear out a clog."

"Or grind coffee?" she added with a nervous laugh.

He studied the thing. Clear latex, with a gold plastic base and gold ball-bearings set for rotation. A segment shaped like a bunny's head with two ears probably worked the hot spot. "Modern engineering." He tilted the box, examining it.

He could tell Samantha wished he'd stop staring at it like he wanted to try it out, but she said, "Some men feel threatened by vibrators," challenging him.

"Why would they?"

"Because they make a man superfluous."

"Superfluous, huh?" He examined it again. "Hell, if it works, go for it." He handed her the box.

"I don't want it." Her eyes went wide. "I mean I have one…but not like this. Mine is…simpler."

"What the hell. You can always use it to whip up dessert."

He watched his words register in her face.

"Couples use vibrators, too," she said softly. "To enhance the pleasure."

"Seems to me a man should find out what his lady likes and give it to her. Batteries not required." What the hell was coming out of his mouth? Of course, sitting in a sea of lingerie holding a sex toy had to take its toll on his sense.

"I like how you think," Samantha breathed. Heat spiked between them and Rick's belt felt way too tight.

"You want that, keep it," Val said, breezing by, nodding at the mix-master he held. "I owe you two dinner for the help. Anything else you'd like, just grab." She waved her arm to indicate the room full of girlie clothes.

Samantha smiled. "Anything here interest you?" she asked. "Maybe those?" She pointed at the men's rack, where some black bikini jobs had a hole for the cock to stick out.

"I don't think so," he said, aware it was his turn to go red.

"You probably need a custom fit," she teased. "Something in an extra-large?" Her eyes gleamed in triumph that she'd managed to embarrass him. She was something else. A live wire. A handful. A prize. If only…

"Look at the time!" Valerie's voice made him jump. "Lindsay will kill me. Can you two manage the windows without me, Sammi?"

Before either of them could reply, Valerie thrust a shoe box at Rick, then piled on some red filmy items followed by a black leather corset covered with zippers and grommets. "For the small window," she said. "Think Donna Dominatrix."

"Donna what?" he said.

But Val had turned to Samantha and had plopped a

load of pale silk stuff and a long strip of feathers into her arms. "Velma Virgin and the Pastel Posse in the big display." Val looked from one to the other. "I owe you two big. Make a list of what you want. I'm serious. Or charge me more for the catalog, Sammi. I'll do the finishing touches in the morning. You're angels. Kisses."

And she was gone, leaving them blinking at each other in the empty underwear store. "I hope you know what goes where," he said, looking down at his armload of lace, leather, zippers and boots.

"You mean you've never outfitted a dominatrix before?"

"This will be my first. Be gentle with me." The joke came out so easily. Samantha made him feel the way he had before his brother had died, as if life were a blast and a good laugh was worth everything.

"We'll just have to learn together," she said. She tucked her items under an arm and picked up the dangerous-looking corset on top of his pile.

"That's gotta hurt to wear," he said.

"I know." Samantha traced her finger along the curve of the thing, giving him a different kind of pain—sweet and hungry. "Women cut off their circulation, choke off their breathing, pinch their toes and make their arches ache just to please men." She lifted her gaze to him. "Does it work? Do these clothes turn you on?"

He didn't need a thing past her for that. "I think women are sexy enough just as they are," he managed to say.

Her mouth stretched into a slow smile. "But don't clothes add to the effect?" She dropped the torture vest back in his arms and shifted the pile of soft things from under her arms to the front. She fingered the feather strip. "I don't like being cramped or pinched, but I like soft things. Silk and velvet and feathers." She ran the feathers between her fingers until he wanted to rip the thing away with his teeth.

He could see her in just that, all right, feathers brushing her nipples, reaching down to her soft thatch—dark red like her hair?—leading him where he wanted to touch, kiss and stroke her…. Her gaze locked on his—she'd read him—and heat snapped so sharply between them he felt scorched.

"After this maybe we should have…dinner?" she asked, the last word as flirty as hell.

Screw dinner. Let's go straight for dessert. But he knew better. He had to control this right now for the case, so he said the only thing he could. "Looks like we'll be working through it, huh?" He lifted his armload of S and M gear as proof and started toward the windows, but not before he'd seen disappointment flood her features. He hated undercover work.

SAMANTHA BLINKED, startled and stung. Rick had said no. His hot emerald eyes had swirled to cool jade like mood rings dropped into a freezer.

Get over it, she told herself, following him to the front windows with her armload of lingerie. He wanted the job and wasn't interested in overtime. Okay. Made sense.

She'd overreacted to the situation. And no wonder. She'd just spent two hours fondling lingerie, sex screaming from every hanger, rack and shelf, with an extremely hot man who gave mixed signals. Of course she'd end up pulsing with lust.

Bummer, though, that she'd finally decided to go for it with a guy and wound up hiring him out of the running. Something in her felt relief at the turndown, she had to admit. She'd been going too fast, as if she'd hiked some dangerous hill, then looked down and realized how high she was, how precarious her footing, how easy it would be to fall.

She set her items in the larger window and let Rick help her up into the smaller one with two naked mannequins. Rick was so big, the window seemed as cramped as a jet's lavatory when she stood beside him, still feeling the chemistry between them.

Her knees jiggled and her heart banged her ribs and where had all the oxygen gone? But she took the leather bustier from him and, cool as could be, held it against the naked mannequin, who stood with her legs spread, hips thrust forward, black wig pulled severely back. "For Donna?" she asked.

Rick's eyes skimmed the clothing, the mannequin, then her face. "Looks right."

"If you're into that, huh?" She had her tie-up fantasy, after all. But it was all pretend, she realized. She'd never have the nerve to say to Rick, *I want you. You want me. Let's go for it.*

In her soul, she knew she wasn't equipped to just pick up a guy. Her mother's words were a red-hot memory, as fresh as yesterday. *Don't be a slut, Samantha Kay.*

She unzipped the bustier and loosened the laces so she could put it on the mannequin and made a joke. "This looks ridiculous. By the time the guy gets the thing pried open, you've given up and gone to asleep."

Rick laughed, then bent to the shoe box at the mannequin's feet, leaving Samantha to her painful memory. She'd been sixteen at the time. Tutoring the cool clique at Copper Corners High in trig had gotten her in their good graces and they'd helped her spend her hoarded allowance on a trendy black dress, then donated their cast-off cosmetics to her—dark shadow, goopy mascara, pale foundation and red gloss so wet it nearly dripped.

She was to meet them at the Bowl-A-Rama, so she'd dressed, put on the makeup, sprayed her hair wild and bounded into the living room to show her mother. *Ta-daa.*

The stunned gasp stopped her mid-spin. *You look like a slut.* The dress wasn't short or tight. Maybe she'd gone a little overboard on the eye stuff, but everyone was wearing it heavy—pop stars had set the pace.

I thought we raised you right. Her mother's eyes filled with tears and she sank into the chair. Thank God her father had been away on business—his reaction would have been worse.

Maybe if her mother had yelled at her, demanded Samantha wash her face, change out of that hooker outfit, Samantha might have slammed out of the house, made fun of her mother the way the cool girls did of theirs, smoked cigarettes and shoplifted lipstick from Dina's Shop 'N Go just like they did. Instead, her mother had seemed devastated, heartbroken, bereft.

Don't be a slut, Samantha Kay. It was a plaintive cry.

Samantha had rushed to the bathroom, expecting to see the cute, sexy girl who'd just left there, but what looked back at her was a cheap, trashy fool. Try as she might, she couldn't get back that glow, the sparkle she'd seen as clear as day.

"Can I help?"

Rick startled her back to the moment and she realized the mannequin was rattling on its posts as she struggled to adjust the bustier in place.

Now he was so close that arousal replaced sadness,

tingling through her like a tuning fork continually struck. She finished the ties and they both moved back.

"You okay?" he asked gently, his gaze on her, not the mannequin.

"I'm fine." She glanced at him. "I was just thinking that my folks would be shocked if they saw me now." Her parents only knew she had a portrait studio, not that she took intimate photos. Eventually, she'd have to tell them, but not until she was confident of her success.

"They might surprise you."

"I don't think so. Small towns are small in lots of ways."

"At least you know where you stand."

"Or where everyone wants to lock you and throw away the key. I didn't have the courage to rebel like you did."

"It wasn't courage, trust me. I just did what I pleased. My brother Brian had the grades and the ambition. That meant I was free to hang loose." Rick shrugged, but she could see he had regrets. And he didn't really strike her as a hang-loose kind of guy. He seemed serious and conscientious to her.

"I didn't have any brothers or sisters to distract my parents. I was the center of their universe—total focus of their hopes and dreams." And probably a disappointment, though they never said anything during formal family visits, polite smiles covering the tension of questions unasked, answers withheld.

"They don't understand why I'm not living in Copper Corners, leading the church choir, growing tomatoes, married with two kids. I mean, I'm already twenty-seven. What's the holdup?" She sighed and tried to smile.

"But you want more than that."

"Lots more."

"To splash around and almost drown?" He smiled.

"Exactly. I have to have something to settle down *from.*"

"Makes sense, I guess."

It was strange. They'd known each other such a short time, but she felt as though she'd shared a lot with Rick. He watched her so carefully, listened so closely, asked good questions. He seemed to really want to understand her.

Rick crouched to lift the boots out of the shoe box. They were vinyl platforms with stiletto heels and tons of laces. "Now these?" he asked, holding one up.

"Perfect for Donna D.," she said, turning one plaster leg so Rick could tug up the boot, his tan a delicious contrast to the pale limb. He yanked the laces tight and she could picture him doing the same thing to a velvet tie around her wrists. *Oh, my, make it tight.*

"Got it," he said softly, telling her she could let go.

"Sure, sure," she said, moving to the other leg, determined to focus on the work at hand, not the hungry fantasies that danced at the edge of her awareness.

With Donna dressed in leather and vinyl, they moved to her submissive partner, for whom Val had selected the red see-through open-nipple bra and matching thong Samantha and Rick had first opened. Rick knelt below her and pulled the thong into place while she attached the bra above him.

This was such a suggestive activity it felt like pure torture to Samantha, made worse because as he worked, Rick brushed against her calf below her capris. His gaze kept touching hers, then jerking away, and the mannequin rattled on its moorings from their shakiness. He seemed as unsettled as she was by the task.

When they finished, Samantha moved Ms. Nipples so that her arms overlapped Donna's, creating a unified picture, then backed up to survey the effect, Rick at her side.

Very hot. The open bra seemed to serve up the pale plaster nipples, carved to look very natural. The black bustier and boots made Donna seem darkly erotic.

"I think that does the trick, don't you?"

"Oh, yeah," he said, then shook his head, hands on hips.

"What?"

"I can't believe I'm doing this, that's all." He waved at the mannequins. "Dressing dolls in underwear."

"Does it threaten your masculinity?" She quickly added, "Because it shouldn't."

"Oh, yeah?"

"Let's just say a man's big hand on a shred of red lace has a certain… je ne sais quoi."

"Je ne sais what?"

"It's hot, okay? Let's go with *hot*."

"I'll take it." He held her gaze for a long moment, his mood-ring eyes swirling, all right, but murky, as if he planned to hold back at all costs. "Shall we start on the next?"

He stepped down, helped her to the floor and up into the bigger display window, which held two standing mannequins, a blonde and a brunette, with a third, honey-skinned, in a black Afro, lying on her side between them.

Samantha handed Rick a mint-green camisole with delicate straps for the standing blonde and she dressed the lounging woman in a butter-cream satin teddy. Finished, she reached for the third outfit and stopped short. "Oh."

"What's wrong?" Rick said, looking down at her.

She stood, holding the teddy. "I have this same one."

"Yeah?" He moved closer.

"I wore it for my first bedroom shot." She fingered the shimmery fabric with both hands.

"Your first shot? And it was of you?"

She nodded. "It was for my boyfriend Barry. We were taking each other for granted, so I thought…why not?"

She'd thought all they'd needed was to relight the spark, so Val had helped her gather an outfit and she'd intended to march into the bedroom wearing it. In the end, taking a photo to show him had made her feel less vulnerable. Which should have been a clue to the outcome, but she hadn't been ready for the truth.

"How did it turn out?" Rick asked softly.

The story was embarrassing, but it had been a turning point in her life. Something about Rick's gaze—as if nothing in the world mattered more than what she had to say—made her want to tell him.

"The photo turned out great." In it, she lay on her side, one leg bent, lace garters and white fishnets showing, her auburn curls cupping her cheeks, a white feather boa teasing her jaw and her breasts swelling out of the gleaming teddy. She'd been so excited by how she looked, couldn't wait to show Barry, to read the pleasure in his face.

"I can imagine." Rick's words sent a wild thrill through her. He was picturing her in the teddy she was holding by its straps. His Adam's apple dipped in a slow, painful-looking swallow. "Did your boyfriend like it?" he asked hoarsely.

"He thought it was a joke." The old hurt filled her heart. "He said, 'It's not you, Sam.' But it was. At least the me I wanted to be." Still wanted to be.

"The man was an idiot," Rick said, shifting his

body closer, as if he thought he could shield her from the memory.

"I was the idiot. I settled for Barry for too long." Right after that incident, she'd broken up with him and decided to go for what she wanted from then on.

The emerald heat was back in Rick's eyes and his breathing was rough and tight and he stood so close. That control she'd seen before had been burned away. He wanted her. She wanted him.

Go for it, girl.

They were alone in the window, surrounded by women in lingerie, who seemed to invite her to take action. Beyond them, the security lights in the Mirror, Mirror lobby glowed golden. *Do it. Do it now.*

So what if Rick worked for her? They could deal with that. The minute she'd seen him she'd known he was her fantasy lover. Everything in her was telling her to go, go, go.

She wasn't going to wait for what she wanted any longer, dammit. Taking a shaky breath, she dropped the teddy between them, rose on tiptoe and pressed her lips to Rick's.

He froze, shaking with intensity, then grabbed her upper arms and kissed her hard, angling his mouth to get closer. Their tongues met and stilled, as if surprised at how easy it had been to get what they wanted. Rick tasted of mint and man, and he used the exact right pressure—hinting at hot urgency, but not overwhelming her—as he deepened the kiss.

This is it. What I want.

Heat rose, energy crackled and her body went liquid so that it was only Rick's firm grip on her forearms that kept her from sinking to the floor.

At the same time she wanted to rub herself against him like a wild animal in heat. She wanted clothes to disappear, Rick's fingers to stroke and slide and coax and enter, his strong lips and hot tongue to seek her hot center and nuzzle and lick her to climax. She wanted the kiss to go on and on and on.

She wanted—

Rick ripped his mouth from hers and lifted her away from him, as if she presented some terrible temptation.

"What…?" Samantha wobbled, fighting for balance, and bumped into the lounging mannequin. Rick caught her before she tumbled out of the display and, in the process, knocked an arm off the blond mannequin. Flailing for balance, Samantha knocked down the other doll.

Rick steadied her, holding her at arm's length, as if he feared she might spring at him. "I'm sorry I did that."

"Don't be sorry. And I was the one who started it. I know we work together, but we're adults. We can handle this."

"But I can't." The words were hard and sharp.

A throbbing silence hung between them until the truth struck her like a slap. "There's someone else," she said softly. "Isn't there?"

Guilt and relief flickered in Rick's face. "Yeah. There is."

Damn, damn, damn. She'd geared up the courage to go after a man and he turned out to be taken. "I see. Now I'm sorry."

"You had no way to know." He bent to pick up the doll she'd knocked over.

So that explained his mixed signals. She'd been too lust-crazed to pick up the clues. She was mortified.

The doll's leg thumped to the floor. She bent and picked it up, fighting to shift gears. "Look at the mess we made."

"Yeah." He grabbed the puddled teddy that had started it all and yanked it over the naked doll's head.

Samantha busied herself fixing the lounging doll she'd practically tripped over, but in her nervousness, she turned the head so hard it came off in her hands.

Rick crouched beside her. "Allow me." He took the head from her and gently twisted it back onto its bolt. Then he caught her gaze and covered her hand at the same time. "It's okay, Samantha. And, trust me, if I were available, nothing would have stopped me."

Lord, did he feel sorry for her? That was absolutely unacceptable. "That's how it goes." She shrugged like it was no big deal. "The problem is that I've been so busy with Bedroom Eyes that I haven't had a chance to get out and…" *Get laid?* She couldn't say that.

"Splash around, make big, messy waves?" he supplied, obviously trying to lighten the moment.

"Exactly." She had to get away from those eyes of his, so she rose to slide panties onto the mannequin. Rick braced the doll that was shaking under her nervous fingers.

"Now that I have an assistant, of course, I'll have much more time, so I can get out and get…busy." Get busy? Even worse. The panties snagged and she jerked them up, making the mannequin rock back and forth. Rick steadied it.

"I don't know what's wrong with me."

"The same thing that's wrong with me." He gave her a wry smile, which made her feel better, even if he was exaggerating in sympathy.

"Anyway, looks like we're about done." She grabbed up the pale boa and draped it around the doll's shoulder.

She wanted to be finished, to get out of the window and away from Rick. "There. All done." She jumped down and Rick joined her. "Thanks for the extra help. I'm sorry I can't pay overtime, but—"

"It's fine. I'm glad to do it. When do you want me, Samantha?"

"Huh?" *Every minute of every hour.* She couldn't help it, standing so close to him, her lips still hot from his kiss. "Nine," she managed to say. "We open at nine."

"See you then. And thanks for the job."

She couldn't even remind him they were trying it for a week because she could hardly let him go now. He might think it was because he'd rejected her. "Sure, no problem," she said.

No problem? Who was she kidding? She'd attacked an employee in the lingerie window. Holy horny Hannah, she would never stop cringing.

5

RICK GOT TO HIS DESK at the station before six the next morning to key in his notes for the update with his lieutenant. He'd scribbled down as much as he could remember about the various shop owners, the layout of the building, what he'd picked up about Darien Sylvestri from his wife and Samantha, especially the details of Lester Tabor's loaned services. He hadn't learned anything significant about the case from the Joey Balistero shoot, except that scumbag mobsters needed love, too.

Insomnia had left him foggy. Going undercover was always an adjustment, but Sawyer had seriously thrown off his rhythm.

That kiss had shocked him. But he'd gotten into it fast, yanking her tight against him and kissing her deeply, his heart banging so hard against his ribs he'd feared he'd bust one out right there.

Hell, he'd wanted to throw her down among those plaster dolls and find out exactly what she had on under her clothes. One of those open bras and skimpy panties they'd been fiddling with for torturous hours maybe? Or maybe sweet cotton panties with flowers on 'em?

He'd been weak. And way too human.

There's someone else. Yeah, right. So lame. He should have cooked up some excuse, but he'd figured that since he had the job, the whole dinner-dessert idea was out for good.

But that story about how her lame-ass boyfriend had hurt her had gotten to him and then she'd kissed him and he didn't need Mona's massage to make him forget his name and where he was.

He liked how she forced herself to be bold—joking about the vibrator that clearly embarrassed her to death. He liked the sweetness she seemed to see as a weakness. She smelled good, too. Like talcum powder and flowers and apple pie and…home.

"So how'd it go with the porn queen?"

He jerked up, realizing he'd been daydreaming. "Huh?"

"Lots of sex shots?" Trudeau asked.

"That's *boudoir* shots, pal. She gets testy if you even hint about anything lewd. Straight photography so far."

"How about video? Sylvestri's got associates distributing bootleg porn."

"No video equipment that I've seen. What Samantha does is, uh, tasteful." Trudeau would laugh him out of the station if he tried explaining what she'd said about forgetting society's rules and finding that special double image and true beauty. "No crotch shots or throbbing members."

"Damn."

"She seems clueless about Sylvestri. She thinks he loaned her his bookkeeper because he's *generous.* My take on her is she's just naive."

"After half an afternoon? What the hell did you do with the woman?"

Fondled dildos, dressed store dummies and came this close to ripping off her clothes.

He remembered her bracing that black corset against the mannequin and asking him, *What do you think?*

He'd never been into kink, but if she wanted it, he'd bring the cuffs.

If he weren't working the case, of course.

If he weren't a changed man.

"We talked. Setup...inventory. I studied her... books." Yeah, right. "I'd bet my badge Sawyer's not involved in whatever's going on. But I'll poke around some more."

"You bet. You *poke* around." It was a standard Trudeau remark, nothing more, he knew. Mark would never believe Rick had done what he'd done. His gut clenched as he gathered up his notes. "Gotta meet with the lieutenant before I head out."

He left, thinking about the implication of Mark's remark. Had he been too easy on Samantha? Getting personal with suspects blurred your instincts. That's why there were regulations against it. There were reasons for most rules, he'd learned over the years. You broke the rules and the rules broke you. Sooner or later.

He hadn't always felt that way. He'd done what he wanted pretty much until Brian had died. As a kid, school had bored him, so he spent his time screwing around with friends and girls and engines.

Pushing an engine to its limit in the desert late at night made him feel fully alive, with every breath shooting down his lungs, sending fresh blood to the tips of his toes and out the top of his head.

There'd been plenty of tickets, the accident that had messed up his back. Minor troubles, really, but life had been full. And he'd kept on living it—wide open—until his brother's death had hauled him up short.

Rick had been twenty-five, working in an auto shop, living cheaply to sock away money for a muscle car, doing freelance magazine photos. He'd been in the sack with a nameless girl when his cell phone wouldn't stop ringing.

It was a buddy with the Phoenix P.D., who'd called to tell him his brother, a defense attorney, had been shot dead in the apartment of one of his clients, a drug dealer, who'd been killed, too.

The cops had kept the negative stuff out of the report—one time he'd been glad someone bent the rules. Brian's death had been tough enough on his parents without the rest.

Like the flip of a switch, a finger snap, Brian was gone and Rick had realized he'd been tossing away his own life as though it didn't matter. But it did. It mattered a hell of a lot.

He had to do something to make up for his brother. Something straight and strong and right. School took forever, so he applied to the academy and he'd been on the job four years.

He liked the work. Loved it, really. His parents seemed pleased, maybe proud.

From time to time he'd had to defend his brother's reputation—sometimes with his fists—from older cops or attorneys who made cracks about him.

His brother had done some good. He'd just been limited. And, dammit, he was Rick's brother, for better or worse.

And now he was gone, before he'd had a chance to figure it out, settle down, have a family of his own. So Rick would do it for him. For himself, too.

But lately he'd been isolated. The dates had fizzled; he'd been bored. Maybe that was why Samantha had hit him like a Mack truck. She would be something else in the sack, for sure, with all that sweetness coupled with her fire to *get busy*. That was funny. But out of the question. Even without the case to consider, he wasn't looking just to get laid. He wanted a wife, two-become-one, all that jazz.

He could see making an exception for her. If only he weren't working for her. If only he weren't a cop and she a suspect. If only everything were different.

SAMANTHA PULLED INTO the Mirror, Mirror parking lot at 8:30 a.m. Hers was the only car, so she'd beaten the other shop owners and the construction crew, which had an unpredictable schedule. There was no black Jeep, so no Rick, either. But it was still early.

She couldn't help hoping he wouldn't come at all, just quit and be done with it. But she knew Rick was a man of his word and he'd be here when she'd said she *wanted* him.

She had to stop that—wanting him. She'd already shown him how desperate she was. If he gave her another you-poor-horny-thing smile she'd die a thousand deaths.

On the other hand, Rick was the first man she'd *attacked,* so she had to expect a learning curve.

She climbed out of her Jetta, determined to act normal, no matter what. She pushed her hair, which she'd fussed with, out of her face and straightened her skirt—the short one that hugged her curves. She was primping and preening for a guy who had a girlfriend, for God's sake.

Luckily, they'd be too busy to talk much today. Several clients were due to look at proofs and she'd scheduled three shoots. She'd have to send Rick to Shear Ecstasy on his own to check out the plumbing troubles Blythe was having.

She unlocked the back entrance and blinked bleary eyes against the early morning dimness inside Mirror, Mirror's lobby. She'd hardly slept a wink. She'd tried to work up a fantasy to relax herself, going for the tiger-striped chaise ravishment, but Rick's face had appeared instead of the usual blurred features of her dream lover, and when she'd gotten close to climax, he'd said, *I can't*, and the mood had wisped away like smoke on a breeze.

She paused at the Venus in a C Cup windows to make sure the displays looked okay. The dominatrix–sex-kitten window looked fine, but the mannequins in the kiss-and-crash window looked like they'd had a drunken party. One doll's wig was crooked, her leg twisted wrong and the hand on the lounging doll looked as if she were reaching for her own breast.

Samantha went inside to fix it before Val saw it.

The instant she stepped into the window, Rick's scent mainlined to her memory center and she could almost taste the mint-and-man flavor of his lips. He'd gripped her forearms so tightly, too, holding himself back, fighting his desire.

He's taken, she reminded herself and set about fixing the mannequins, adjusting the crooked leg, turning the twisted hand, straightening the sliding wig.

Smoothing the lace over the doll in her butter-cream teddy, she imagined Rick's fingers on her body and couldn't help closing her eyes….

"I want to touch you where you're swollen and soft."

"Please," she begs, desperate for exactly that. She writhes against his body, wanting his hands on her, his fingers probing secret places, giving her pleasure and taking his own.

His hands slide down her belly and find her damp

glory—her desire made liquid. He brushes her slick, wet flesh over and over, slowly at first, then more firmly, knowing exactly the effect of his torture, and pushing, always pushing her higher and higher.

"I want to give you pleasure until you scream. Right here, in the window, so that passersby know how this feels, so that they long for what they're missing—"

Something—a sound, a flicker of light—made Samantha open her eyes. She looked out at Rick standing there staring at her. He seemed frozen by the sight, his hands fisted, then opened, his lips parted, his chest expanded and shrank in quick, uneven breaths timed with her own, a few feet away through the glass.

I want you, his eyes said. *More than ever.*

She wanted him, too, and a hot chill coursed through her.

Could he tell what she'd been doing standing here with her eyes closed? Her palm still cupped one of the mannequin's breasts, so she jerked it down to the waist and pulled the teddy straight, smoothing it flat over the doll's torso.

Be cool, be easy. You're working here, she told herself and smiled at him, wiggling her fingers in greeting.

He waved back, fingers moving slowly, his Adam's apple doing a slow glide. She turned her attention to the wig, trying to act natural, though her heart pounded, and when she glanced up again, he was gone.

"Can I help?" His voice behind her made her jump. He'd moved with silent swiftness and appeared as if she'd conjured him from a fantasy. He extended a hand, which she took, aware that her skirt rode high on her thigh and gapped open.

He averted his eyes and held on to her until she was

solidly on the floor. Rick was a gentleman. Protective, too, in a way she responded to at a primal level.

"So, you came back?" she said, forcing herself to speak lightly. "After last night I wasn't so sure. I mean all that ladies' underwear and sex toys." And that kiss. Don't forget that kiss. She never would.

"You said nine."

"You're early."

"That I am." He smiled. Whether with regret, continued interest or self-mocking humor, she couldn't quite tell. What was going on behind those lush green eyes? And why did she want to know so damn much?

"So here's what I have in mind for you," she said, and began babbling out his chores—help her with client meetings, follow up on her marketing, check the hair salon's plumbing—

"I'll stay busy, Samantha," he said, interrupting her cascading list of tasks. "You won't be sorry you hired me."

"Or that I kissed you?" The words burst out.

"Or that." His eyes held her—all of her—as though he wouldn't change a thing. "I kissed you back, remember?"

"Yeah. I remember."

"So how about if we stay out of windows in empty underwear shops from now on?"

"Sounds like a plan," she said, acting cheerful and reasonable when she secretly was wondering how he felt about empty studios with satin-covered beds. Oh, dear.

SO FAR, SO GOOD, Rick thought, heading for the beauty salon around noon. He was supposedly checking on the clogged drains, though he intended to comb every inch of the center today, with special attention to the storage the *generous* Darien had insisted on, according to

Samantha. Cupboards could hide drugs, guns, stolen goods, anything. Sylvestri showed up often with instructions for the crew, Rick had learned, so he'd be alert for any appearance the man might make.

Rick patted his shirt pocket for the tiny camera, his jeans for the mini tape player he'd grabbed before he'd left the station, eager to get going. He liked the investigative part of undercover work. It was just the subterfuge that bugged him.

Such as the fact that Samantha already trusted him, after only a few hours of work. If she knew what he was up to, she'd be shocked, hurt and mad as hell. Couldn't be helped. Nature of the work. He shouldn't care.

But he did. She was so honest—even in little things. He'd sat in on two order sessions where she'd refused to soak the eager customers for maximum prints and poses, keeping them within the budget they'd tossed out the window the instant they'd seen the shots. Samantha was good, no question, and she had integrity and a clear-eyed approach that made sense in a kooky way.

He'd found no evidence that she knew about any criminal activity occurring—or planned—in the building. He'd pored over her books, but found no double billings, erasures, odd checks or unusual cash flow. If Lester Tabor was laundering money through Bedroom Eyes, he did it with a second ledger Rick would have to locate. He planned to grill the guy when he came in to do the month's accounts in a few days.

Rick headed for the beauty salon. *Shear Ecstasy.* What a name. Everything in the center dripped with sex. It got on his nerves. He paused at the lingerie shop. He'd stood here this morning, staring at Samantha, while she'd stroked that doll's breast, her eyes closed. Had she been thinking anything like what he'd been thinking?

He prided himself on total control on the job, but he'd limped over to her, so erect it had hurt to move.

Somehow, she threw him, made him forget he was a cop, turned him into a slathering wildebeest. Or some other creature easily led by its horn.

He entered the salon and got a nose-stinging blast of hair junk and perfume. Three stacked women flipped through magazines in the waiting area, their supersized racks barely reined in by a tube top, a tank top and a low-necked leotard. Long, tanned legs extended from a mini-skirt and two pairs of shorts short enough to be underwear. Strippers, maybe? The task force had ID'd several who'd had photos done at Bedroom Eyes. A few had rap sheets for turning tricks after hours. Not that unusual for exotic dancers.

Maybe this trio just liked to make men pant. He didn't get why women had to be brazen about their assets. He preferred the pleasure of slow discovery, the secret beauty a woman shared only with her man.

He suspected that was Samantha's preference, too, despite what she said about clothes and their effect. On the other hand, the mental picture of her in that yellow silk thing shot lust through him like a high-voltage current.

Back to business. All three women smiled up at him. He smiled back, then turned to the unstaffed counter, which held a rack of lime-green flyers advertising a strip revue with three dancers in elaborate costumes. One looked familiar....

He turned back to the women reading magazines.

"Yep. That's me," said the one in the silver tube top.

"Nevada Neru. Choreographer. The other two are back there, if you want a signed flyer." She pointed at the back of the shop where two hairdressers were at work on women and a manicurist was doing someone's nails.

"Thanks," he said, grabbing a flyer. The club's name—*Moons*—rang a bell. Had there been a drug bust there? Arrests? The photo looked like Samantha's work. He'd already noticed the salon walls held framed pictures labeled Photo by Bedroom Eyes, Hair by Shear Ecstasy. Good advertising, he guessed. Samantha had a good concept. Too bad she'd established it in a mobster's lair.

"Bring a friend," the choreographer added, winking. "Your mother, even. It's a very tasteful show."

"Great." He nodded, folded the paper and tucked it behind the camera in his pocket. Though Sylvestri had declared Bedroom Eyes *prime,* the salon seemed to have its share of racy clientele. He'd keep his eyes and ears open. Where there was smoke, there was fire.

"Can I help you?" the first hairdresser called to him. Tall, thirtyish, she held up a square of foil. Metal stuck out all over the head of her customer, a redhead, who looked wired for sound.

"If you're Blythe, yes," he said, pushing deeper into the fog of hair spray. "I'm Samantha's assistant, Rick West." He extended his hand.

"Welcome to Shear Ecstasy, Rick." Blythe met his gaze as firmly as she shook his hand.

"Thank you. So, how's your plumbing?"

"Whoa…pretty bold." The words came from a dark-haired beauty in the next chair who seemed to be getting a strip of hair glued onto her head. The hairdresser banged her on the head with a comb. "Ouch."

"He really means *plumbing*," the hairdresser with the comb said. "I'm Heidi." Her smile was as no-nonsense as Blythe's. "Forgive Jasmine. She can't resist a double entendre."

"I had to pour Liquid-Plumr down the shampoo sinks first thing this morning, but since then no prob," Blythe said.

"How about if I check it out?"

"If you have the right tool," Jasmine said. "And I just bet you do. Ouch." Heidi had popped her again. "Jeez, I'm just having fun. You don't mind if I have a little fun, do you, Rick?"

"Not at all," he said. Assuming it was legal.

"The builders left some toolboxes in the back, I think," Blythe said. "Those guys are forever here and gone."

"I'll see what I can find," he said, grateful for an excuse to snoop around. He found a pipe wrench in a toolbox among painting supplies in a utility room, then checked out the bathroom, the tiny kitchen and the supply room. The only thing he found of note were a bunch of newly installed cupboards.

Out in the salon, he made a big show of running water in all four sinks, then moved a chair out of the way so he could crawl underneath and pretend to work while he eavesdropped.

"I told Jackson no way on the extra show," a woman yelled from under the dryer. The redhead, he thought, had been shifted over there. Extra *show?* Sex party maybe? "Duke's birthday's coming up and all."

Duke? Dunmore maybe? Yeah. There *had* been a drug bust at Dunmore's club. A few months back. Rick would ask Mark to track down the details. He banged on the U-joint to sound busy, listening hard.

"You'd think the *incident* was a promotion, not a…you know…*incident.*" This from Heidi. Whispered.

"Jackson's had to beat the guys off with sticks ever since," hair-dryer woman said.

"Beat them off? I didn't think Jackson swung that way." Jasmine again. "Ouch." Heidi had whacked her, no doubt.

"We know Jackson doesn't have much energy these days," Jasmine said in a teasing tone. "You've worn our boy right out. He's too tired to even boss us around. I had to make my own dental appointment last week."

Could Jackson be their pimp?

Heidi giggled, sounding like any woman in love. In the ordinary world, these ladies would be talking about dates, boyfriends and cocktail parties. Maybe to them that's all it was. Strip clubs were just entertainment, prostitution a victimless crime.

But hooking wasn't a simple exchange of sex for money. Girls didn't aspire to be call girls on junior-high career day. Hookers had no legal protection, no assurance of physical safety. With every trick, they risked their health, their dignity, their lives. High-end call girls who were smart could get out, but there were tremendous traps in that life. Drugs and exploitation and raw ugliness.

He had no interest in arresting these girls. He wanted the creeps farther up the food chain. He hoped the pros could get a fresh start—rehab, college or solid jobs. He gave money to United Way for programs that offered just that.

"And what's with the *internship,* Heidi?" This from the redhead. "Wink-wink, right? That's not really what your brother the mayor needs me for, is it?"

"Sure it is."

"Then he's paying me up front."

"It's a job. I'm doing you a favor."

"And, considering my other skills, you're doing your brother a favor, too?"

"I told him nothing. What you two do in the privacy of town hall is completely up to you."

Interesting…Heidi was helping a town official with sex? Hmm.

"You about done down there?" Blythe's voice startled him and he jerked up and bumped his forehead. "Yeah. Finishing up." He twisted the joint, then scooted out. "Everything's tight. No leaks."

"Good, because I need to wash Autumn out."

He pushed to his feet and returned the wrench to the toolbox. He looked around a little more, counted the cupboards, estimating square footage, then headed out.

In the archway, he stopped dead to watch Jasmine doing a backbend, both palms on the floor, one leg straight in the air. "How do they look?" If she meant her breasts, they looked amazing.

"Very natural," Heidi said. "As if it's part of you, as I promised. The better extensions are worth it."

He still wasn't sure they weren't talking about her breasts.

"What's up?" Samantha's voice from behind made him jump. She'd come from the service entrance.

"I was just…checking things out," he said.

Jasmine did a complex flip and rose with an erotic shimmy.

"Oh, I bet." Samantha winked at him.

"I was. Really. The plumbing."

"Like I said, I bet." She pushed his arm. "I'm teasing, Rick. She's gorgeous and you're human. I hear their cabaret show is incredible. You should take your girl-friend maybe." She patted the flyer sticking up from his pocket. "The girls will sign that for you, if you want."

"I don't think so."

"Your girlfriend would disapprove?"

Shit. She thought he was cheating on his girl, ogling strippers like a chump. He hated that. "I wasn't... That wasn't..."

"Yes?"

"Oh, never mind." Better leave it alone. He joined in the applause for Jasmine, who now bowed.

"So, Blythe, you met Rick?" Samantha said. "He tells me he's been checking things out."

"Evidently," Blythe said, winking at him. Damn. They all thought he was a dog. Then Blythe narrowed her eyes and came at him, shoving her fingers into his hair. "You have nice texture, you know," she said. "And it's thick, but you wear it too short for your face."

"He was in the army," Samantha explained.

Heidi tilted her head to the side. "Spikes would help."

"Exactly what I was thinking." Blythe squirted a blob of foam in her hands, then rubbed it into his hair.

He tried to signal *help me* with his eyes, but Samantha just grinned. "Blythe's a genius at matching people with the right do."

"But I don't have—"

"A do?" Blythe said. "Relax. I know. Men don't have a do, they have a *look* and yours needs something." She tugged his hair upward, then turned him by the jaw to the mirror. "How's that?"

Four heads swiveled toward him and eight female eyes joined his in the mirror, where he saw that his hair stood up as if he'd stuck a finger in a socket.

"Very hot," Samantha said.

"Very Brad Pitt," Jasmine said.

"Very electrocution," Rick said.

"He needs bleached ends," the choreographer said. "Much more dramatic."

"Oh, excellent," Blythe said. "Honey-blond, don't you think?"

"Or platinum-flax," Heidi said, tapping her lip.

Nevada turned to scrutinize him. "Does he need a part?" She shoved his hair down on one side, her eye-popping rack bobbing right under his nose.

"Detracts from the dangerous glare he has," Samantha said.

"I have a dangerous glare?" he said faintly. He was drowning in female attention—eyes digging in, fingers in his hair, boobs under his nose, and Samantha's wry smile just inches away.

"And you're ripped, too," Autumn said, running her eyes down his chest, making him damned uncomfortable. "You should wear tailored clothes." The other women nodded.

"Ever consider dancing?" Nevada said. "We're thinking about adding some male numbers."

"I don't dance," he said. And he certainly didn't strip.

"We could teach you," Jasmine said.

"Don't say no, say maybe," Samantha said. He could tell she was enjoying his discomfort. "Valerie has some great G-strings, remember."

"I'll give you a discount on the bleaching," Blythe said, "since you work for Samantha."

"I think I'll stick with what I've got." His masculinity was taking enough of a beating. Yesterday, he'd fluffed velvet pillows and dressed dolls in panties, and now he had strippers trying to turn him into a metrosexual. The nail girl was even eyeing his fingers.

"Don't you need me in the studio?" he said to Samantha, desperate to escape this hellhole of beauty.

"I'll just bet she does," Jasmine purred.

"Think about the spikes now," Blythe said.

"Sure. You bet." He barreled out of the shop, then waited for Samantha to catch up with him. "That was brutal. I thought they were going to hold me down and pierce an eyebrow."

"It's not too late," she teased. "But they were right about the bleach and the spikes."

"I don't think so." He ran his fingers through the goo, trying to make his hair lie flat. "You enjoyed watching them ganging up on me, didn't you?"

"It was fun to see you off balance a little."

"You've seen me that way before."

"I know. And I liked it."

So had he. And that was the bitch of it. He caught her smile and returned it like a fool.

6

RICK HELPED SAMANTHA with two shoots and made a few marketing calls for her, but managed to leave early for his Healing Touch appointment. He wanted to scope out the shop and examine Mona's schedule for names that might pertain to the case.

He'd already looked over the empty second floor of the building being renovated for Sylvestri's electronics business. One of those "Crazy Darien Gives Away the Store" places. Stolen stuff maybe? Rick didn't know yet. So far, all he'd found was a ton of construction debris.

The bell over the Healing Touch door tinkled when he entered. In seconds, Mona stuck her head out of one of the massage rooms.

"Sorry I'm early," he said, hoping she had more work to do on the client inside so he'd have snooping time.

"You can change into a robe in there." She pointed to the bathroom. "Then if you'll lie facedown under the sheet in the other massage room, you can relax until I get there."

"You want me to take off…to get…" *Naked?* He swallowed hard, mortified despite himself. He sure as hell wouldn't do much relaxing lying there buck—

"Leave your underwear, if that makes you more comfortable," she said, as cheerful as a nurse.

"However you usually do this," he mumbled. He had to sound open to something extra, in case she propositioned him. Plenty of therapists offered "full release" for the cash. He hoped Mona was as legit as she seemed.

"Strictly up to you." He was pretty sure she was laughing at him.

As soon as she closed the door, Rick headed for the appointment book. Right now, it seemed she was working on Alfred Costa. Hmm. He was connected and high up. Rick dashed for the dressing room to look through Costa's things. The oak locker was only latched, not padlocked, so Rick riffled through the pockets of Costa's hand-tailored suit, finding a thick money clip, a wallet with driver's license, credit cards, business cards for an import business—yeah, right—and what looked like one of Samantha's bedroom shots of a cute brunette.

Hidden in Costa's Italian loafers was a trim holster with a snub-nosed .22. He took down the serial number to see if it had been used in a crime.

That done, he had time to examine the rest of Mona's shop and take photos of all Mona's appointments. He noticed the name Chuck Yardley nearly every day. Who needed a daily rubdown? He'd get the task force to check the guy out.

A male voice rose from behind the closed door. Must mean Costa's massage was over. Rick ducked into his massage room and listened against the door, stripping fast. He'd forgotten to grab a robe from the rack in the bathroom, but what the hell.

After a bit of chatter, Rick heard the bathroom door open. Costa getting dressed, no doubt. That meant Mona would pop in here any minute.

Rick slid under the sheet, facedown, nervous as hell. Maybe he was as uptight as Mark claimed. A woman was about to run her fingers all over his body with slippery oil and he only dreaded it. He rested his forehead against the top of the doughnut-shaped pad. The hole seemed to be for his nose. Useful, he guessed, but it made him feel as helpless as something getting prepped for barbecue, or some mortifying exam.

There was a tap on the door.

He lifted his head to say, "Come in."

Mona entered. "All set?"

"I guess."

"This isn't a root canal, hon." She chuckled, then moved away. Music swelled into the room—a wispy female voice singing something foreign. "I can't promise you'll forget your name or where you are like Samantha suggested, but I'm sure you'll enjoy it." He heard the wheeze of a squeeze bottle, her hands sliding together, and he braced to stay alert.

He had to stay on his toes, remain poised to pick up any clues whatsoever—hell…

Mona's hands on his back felt like live heating pads. Lord God that felt good. Warmth rushed through him. He closed his eyes and let his mind just go.

She began to rub slowly, humming to the music, grinding out the knots and twists he hadn't realized were there. Tension rolled off him like water off oil.

What a great idea this was. An employee benefit. *Thank you, Samantha.*

"So, what do you think of our Sammi?" Mona asked.

He was feeling so good that he just answered straight out. "I like her a lot."

"She's a wonderful, warm woman, isn't she?"

"Mmm-hmm." While Mona did an amazing knuckle move down his spine, he pictured Samantha on tiptoe when she'd kissed him, remembered her hot mouth, her soft tongue, how much he'd wanted to keep kissing her…all over.

Stop it. Now.

His mind switched to the memory of her in the window this morning, eyes closed, fingers on that mannequin's chest. He imagined those fingers sliding down his back the way Mona's were, but with a different purpose and…

Damn. A hard-on.

"I worry about her because she works too much," Mona was saying. "She never takes time for herself."

"Yeah. She works hard." Don't say *hard*. He struggled to settle himself. He was on the job here.

"She thinks she has to be a different person to enjoy life more, but I tell her she's fine as she is."

"Mmm-hmm," he mumbled.

Mona moved to his calves with a twisting motion that dissolved every rational thought.

"She could use some company, you know," Mona mused.

"Company?" he repeated blankly.

"Maybe you can convince her to relax more, take some time off. Heck, maybe take her out yourself."

"Take her out…?" He shook his head, fighting for good sense. There was *someone else,* after all. He opened his mouth to decline, but the door tinkled and Samantha called out, "Mona? Are you…? Is Rick here?"

"In here!" Mona called loudly. "Come on in," she said, the lilt of mischief in her voice.

Lying there naked under a thin sheet, his body slick with oil, he felt exposed. And far too erect for a man on duty.

The door opened and he heard Samantha suck in a breath at the sight of him.

"You already started," Samantha breathed.

If she only knew.

"I didn't mean to interrupt. I was looking for Rick."

She'd found him, all right, Samantha realized, with only a thin sheet covering up his spectacular body in all its nude glory. She swallowed hard, battling for a clear thought.

"We don't mind," Mona said. "Do we, Rick?"

Rick lifted his face out of the doughnut and turned to her. "It's fine." He smiled, but he seemed tense.

God, he looked good. His oiled shoulders were a lovely tan and Mona's fingers expertly traced the dips and bulges of his many, many muscles. And here Samantha was without a camera.

"I wanted to catch you before you got…but I see you're already…" *Naked.* So very, very naked.

"What is it?" he asked, his voice coming out rough.

"Just a favor…I wanted to ask you a favor is all."

"Which is?"

"Which is what?" She blinked again rapidly, licked her lips, trying to focus. *The favor. Ask the favor.* "Oh. Right. Could you stop at the photo lab on your way in and pick up the order?"

"I can do that. No problem."

She couldn't quite get herself to leave. "It's the Milford, Steiner and Littlefield prints, some catalog stuff, and the Simone and Balistero proofs." She forced the words over her desert-dry throat.

"No problem," he said again, his eyes locking on hers. *Get naked and get up here.* She could just *swear* that's what he meant.

"That'd be great," she said. She could see herself moving her hands slowly down his strong back, over his round backside, thick thighs and tight calves, shiny with oil, the curly hair sparkling in the gold light of the warm room.

Even the bottoms of his feet looked delectable. Broad but with a graceful instep. She was drawn again to his backside. She felt like weeping with longing.

Rick's eyes closed.

Samantha's eyes closed, too, and a lovely fantasy flitted across her brain. She was naked, coated in Mona's massage oil, slithering all over Rick's back, then rolling him over so they were face-to-face and as slippery as seals who hadn't had sex in a really, really long time.

His hands were on her breasts, sliding down her stomach and down...there. Her sex, which felt like a tiny water balloon, filled and heavy, ready to burst.

"Uhhh..."

Who groaned? In horror, Samantha realized it was her. She'd moaned out loud. Damn. She backed up, caught herself on the counter, bumping the volume knob on the CD player. Enya's honey voice roared out.

"Sorry, sorry." She turned it down. "My stomach's been bothering me." She moaned again, rubbing her tummy. As if anyone could mistake that aroused sound for indigestion.

"I've got time after this if you need a massage, Sammi," Mona said, laughter in her voice.

"No. No. I should go...."

"It feels as good as it looks," Rick said, his voice a rumble of relaxed pleasure. Didn't this get to him? She felt as though they were playing pretend-this-doesn't-excite-you chicken and she'd just lost.

"So, turn over, Rubber Muscles Man," Mona said, "so I can do your front." She patted him lightly on the shoulder.

Rick frowned. "I, um, think one side's enough."

Mona paused, then something registered. "Okay. Sure." She looked straight at Samantha. Another beat and Samantha figured it out, too. Rick had an erection. Because of her? She had to hope so. Mona had told her that once in a while men got hard-ons on her table. She ignored it, sticking strictly to the "civilized" muscle groups, and it was never a big deal.

"We'll let you dress," Mona said to Rick, and motioned for Samantha to leave with her.

"Look what you did to that poor man," she said as soon as they were outside the door. "And you with your moan."

"It just slipped out."

"He likes you."

"How do you know?"

"He told me so. And, hell, I could see he had you in three Kama Sutra poses in his mind just saying hello."

She moaned again. "But it's no use. He has a girl-friend." Her disappointment swelled, filling her chest with pain.

"He told you that?"

"Yes. After I threw myself at him."

"You threw yourself at him? I'm proud of you, girl. I never thought you'd have the nerve." Mona hugged her.

"But so what? He's taken."

Mona considered the idea, tapping her lip. "I didn't get that vibe. Maybe they're about to break up."

"He was very firm."

"Oh, he was firm, all right."

Samantha slugged her on the arm, then shook her head, staring at the door behind which Rick was covering his gorgeous, oil-slick body. She sighed and changed the subject. "So, what's happening with you and Mr. Regular?"

"He's still regular," she sighed. "I have to practically pour him out of the shop every day, he's so loose. He must be doing great at rugby."

"He's not coming here because of rugby, Mona. Give the guy a chance. He's decent, he's kind. He's loyal."

"So is a beagle, but I'm not dating one."

"How can you give me advice about men when you're locked up as tight as…what? The trapezius on a gymnast! That tight."

"Ooh, muscle names. Excellent, Sammi."

"See, I listen to you. Now listen to me."

"It's not professional to date a client."

"So send him to another therapist."

"I make him feel good, so he has a crush on me. Big deal."

"He brings you lunch, he listens to your problems and he tells you his. That's a relationship, hon."

Before she could protest further, Rick emerged, dressed, but rumpled and pink in the face. "Thanks, Mona," he said. He twisted his head from side to side, testing his neck. "I haven't had this much mobility in a while." He shrugged his shoulders. "Everything's looser."

Then his eyes snagged Samantha's. *Not quite everything.* "Thanks for paying for this," he said.

"My pleasure." And her agony.

"You were right. I hardly know my own name."

It's *Rick, Rick, oh, Rick.* "I'm glad you enjoyed it," she managed to say. At least she'd gotten a new fantasy for her checklist—oiled-up, naked massage. She sighed. She'd better start looking for a man to fulfill her fantasies before she was tempted to jump Rick with the nearest quart of Mazola.

"THIS IS RICK WEST, calling for Bedroom Eyes Boudoir Photography. We recently sent you a packet?"

"Yes, I recall that," Wendy of Wendy's Weddings replied.

"That's terrific. We think that tasteful, intimate photographs would enhance your clients' wedding experience." Rick couldn't believe how easily the words *boudoir* and *intimate* rolled off his tongue today. He could practically feel the testosterone draining away. "We'd be happy to draft a proposal and meet with you."

At least Samantha believed in it, so it wasn't completely stupid. He looked over at her, bent over the scheduling computer. His gaze snagged on the gold locket resting between her breasts, then shifted to the creamy swells that rose and fell with each breath. He craved the sight of her like a cold beer on a hot day. From here he could easily inhale her perfume and hair and warm skin.

He could still hear that raw moan in Mona's room. He knew how she felt. On top of that, he'd had the royal humiliation of the women knowing he'd stacked wood right there on the table.

Some undercover cop he was.

"Huh? Uh… Oh, you're interested?" Staring at Samantha's chest, he'd missed Wendy's response. "We'd be happy to do that," he said, recovering. "Absolutely. When can we meet?" He pushed his chair over to Samantha, making the counter shift a little. He'd have to fix the damn thing one of these days.

"How interested is she?" Samantha whispered.

He shot her a thumb way up.

She silently clapped her hands, then bent to click through the scheduler while he called out dates, the locket dangling before his eyes.

When he hung up from Wendy, Samantha beamed. "If we score this account, you should get a commission."

She'd told him hooking up with wedding planners was a key component of her marketing plan, and this was the first successful callback he'd made since he'd started working for her four days ago.

"I'm just doing what you pay me for." Except his real job included eavesdropping on every phone call, snapping shots of passing perps, assessing every word she said for lies.

Screw it. Right now, the Wendy's Weddings meeting felt more important than a closed case and he didn't care what that said about how good a cop he was.

Samantha was adding a note to the appointment, keying in the address, and he sat there, watching her, unable to move away. He zeroed in on that damnable locket, hanging in the air over her chest. It was the size of a silver dollar, carved with leaves and flowers. "You wear that a lot." He braced it against his palm.

"Every day." She backed away so the locket slipped off his palm and bumped softly against her breastbone. Whatever was inside, she didn't want to talk about. "I'd better get busy on the proposal."

"Sure," he said and found himself staring at where she'd gone for long seconds after she'd disappeared.

The front door buzzed and he turned back to see Valerie standing there. "Sammi busy?" She looked excited.

"She's in her office."

She rushed past him and he waited a few seconds before following her to see what was going on.

"The stuff's here, Sammi," he heard her say. "I want you to sample it before I agree to sell it."

Sample it? He doubted it was anything illegal, but he had to be certain. He listened in the hall, waiting for the women to exit out the service door, then followed, cracking the door in time to see them step behind a white panel truck, parked beside the Dumpster—away from prying eyes or just for shade?

A woman opened the back door, which blocked all three from his view. He figured out a question to ask in case they heard him approach, then moved silently toward the truck.

"If you're going to sell this stuff, Val, don't waste any on me," Samantha was saying when he got close enough to hear.

"There's plenty more where that came from." The seller.

Paper rustled, then Samantha said, "Mmm."

His next step crunched gravel, so he knew he'd have to make his presence known. With the fleeting hope he wouldn't catch Samantha with a coke spoon up her nose, he rounded the van in time to see her wrap her lips around the head of a penis on a stick. It was Pepto-Bismol pink and she bit the tip clear off.

Ouch. He resisted the urge to protect his 'nads.

Beside her, Valerie nibbled on a cream-colored breast with a pink nipple, also on a stick. The seller was holding out a small pastry box.

"Hey, Rick," Samantha said, chewing slowly, holding up what was left of the cock. "Care for a taste?"

He raised his hands in polite refusal. "I'm good."

"You sure? Belgian chocolate. Yum."

The sight of her pink tongue curling around that shaft made him go weak in the knees.

"What do you think?" Valerie asked him, picking up a plump breast from the box and tilting it for him to examine. "For bachelorette parties and bridal showers? Would you be interested?"

"Me? No, but…" He shrugged.

"I think it's a great idea," Samantha said, snapping off two solid inches of the cock pop, making him wince.

"White, milk or dark chocolate," the seller said, pointing at the items. "The pink is cherry-flavored. We offer breasts and cocks, of course, but also pussies. Small, medium or large. And hard-candy versions of everything."

"Oh, you mean *suckers?*" Samantha said, looking right at him. "*All-day* suckers?"

"Yeah," the confectioner said, not even cracking a smile. "We rotate the stock so you never have stale product, but the hard-candy pops have a longer shelf life."

"Wouldn't want a penis to go stale, would we?" Samantha asked.

"God, no," Valerie said, getting into it. "And an out-of-date pussy…unforgivable."

Rick shook his head while the girls laughed.

The candy maker rolled her eyes. *Real mature.*

"Did you need something, Rick?" Samantha asked.

"Uh, yeah. Media cards. Extras?"

"In the top drawer in my desk," Samantha said. "Sure you don't want a boob to go?" She held one out, its pink nipple shaped like a Hershey's Kiss.

"I'm fine. You just enjoy."

He headed back, smiling, and relieved, too. If drugs were changing hands at Mirror, Mirror, they weren't doing it out of a panel truck filled with edible genitalia. He should be disappointed, of course, because the sooner he found something wrong, the sooner they'd close the case.

Mark was bringing him the report on the bust at Moons at the end of the day, so that might suggest a lead. And next week, he would talk to Sylvestri's bookkeeper Lester Tabor.

But the truth was he was relieved that Samantha appeared to be innocent of any crime. He *wanted* her to be innocent.

Way too much.

SAMANTHA AIMED HER JETTA for home, biting off the tip of the all-day cherry penis she'd been sucking for Rick's benefit as she backed out the door. Cherry flavor exploded in her mouth and she smiled, remembering the way Rick had stared, jaw hanging, as she performed a few racy tongue moves. He was deliciously shockable.

A pang of desire stung her again. Why did he have to be taken? She could so easily picture him in her chocolate-dripped-on-bodies fantasy. Butterscotch, too. Maybe an entire hot-fudge sundae. Think of the whipped cream…and what they could do with the cherry on top.

She'd been waiting for the right guy to act out her fantasies. And Rick would be perfect.

But he was taken, dammit.

Her fingers stuck to the steering wheel—cherry drips—so she felt for her purse for a tissue. It wasn't on the seat beside her. Or on the back-seat floorboards. Hell, she'd been so busy backing out the door doing her lick-fest, she'd only grabbed her keys, forgetting her handbag altogether.

Damn. She whipped into a U-turn and headed back to Bedroom Eyes, blinking against the glare from the setting sun. The traffic had thinned and the air was cool in the fall dusk. Rick should be gone by now—he'd been locking up when she'd left.

Except as she turned onto the block, she could see his Jeep was still there. A guy in a beat-up white sedan parked beside him was handing Rick a folder. She slowed, then waited for Rick to drive off. It would ruin the effect if he saw her hurrying back in for her purse.

When he was gone, she pulled into the lot and parked a few spaces away from the sedan. The driver was sitting there talking on a cell phone.

When she stepped out to leave a few minutes later, though, he was changing a tire. And not happy about it, judging from the swearing he was doing.

"Flat tire?" she asked.

"Yeah." Then he saw her and blanched, as though she'd caught him doing something terrible. "Yes. Rolled over a nail, I guess." He struggled to his feet, dropping the wrench, wiping his hands on his pants.

"It's all the construction we've got going on around here. I can let you inside to call a service station if you need to."

"No thanks. I've got it."

"I saw you talking with Rick. You're a friend?"

"A friend?" Tension flickered in his face. "Sure. Yeah."

"Rick works for me. I'm Samantha Sawyer." She extended a hand.

He started to shake it, then looked at his dusty palm. "Sorry."

"And you are?"

"Mark. Trudeau. Rick's friend, Mark Trudeau." He said it in a strange way. Nervous guy, it seemed.

"Pleased to meet you, Rick's friend, Mark Trudeau."

"Likewise. I've heard a lot about you from Rick."

"You have?" What had Rick told him?

"Sure. It's all good. Rick likes his job."

"I'm glad. I was afraid he'd be bored."

"No, no. He's having a great time."

"That's good then."

But she could tell there was more he knew or wanted to say. Had Rick mentioned the kiss? Maybe not if Mark knew Rick's girlfriend. What was she like? Samantha wondered.

Silence fell and Mark rubbed his hands on his slacks. "I'd better get back to this." He motioned at the tire. "My wife's expecting me."

"Let me at least get you something cold to drink," she said and went inside for a Dr Pepper. By the time she returned, he was putting on the new tire.

"Thanks," he said, taking a long swallow.

"So, you know Rick well?"

"Well enough." He didn't seem to want to say more, but her curiosity was strong.

"How long have you known him?"

"I guess three, four years." He paused, noticed her interest and continued. "Yeah, he's over to the house a lot. He likes my wife's cooking. And my kids. Gets into the video games with my son."

"Does his girlfriend come, too?" Might be a clue to how serious they were. Valerie hadn't picked up a "taken" vibe from him, after all. "Does she like video games?"

"His girlfriend?" As soon as the words were out of the guy's mouth, regret rushed across his face.

Mark didn't know about her. Which meant one thing. "Rick doesn't have a girlfriend, does he, Mark?"

Mark shrugged. "Could be new. Rick's a private guy."

"I don't think that's it." Not at all. Come to think of it, Samantha had been the one who'd mentioned *someone else* and there'd been a flicker of confusion before Rick had jumped on it with apparent relief. Why had he lied? What did he think she was going to do? Try to have his love child? Get her old-fashioned parents to arrange a shotgun wedding?

"Me and my big fat mouth." Mark looked physically ill.

"I won't tell him you blew his cover. Don't worry." She tried to laugh. "I don't get why he thought he had to lie."

"Rick keeps people at arm's length."

"Maybe." He'd literally done that after the kiss— held her away, both arms extended, fighting her and temptation.

"I'm no shrink, but I'm sure it's—what do they call it?—fear of intimacy? Gloria and me are always after him about getting involved with someone."

"I guess I can see that."

"Rick's a straight arrow. Lotta rules of conduct. No hooking up at work for sure."

"I bet that's it. Yeah."

"It's not personal, I know that. He likes you, like I said. Speaks highly of your work and your integrity and…you know…."

"Sure. I know."

Relieved, Mark got busy with his tire again.

She knew Rick was attracted to her, so it wasn't that.

Maybe he thought she'd make too much of the sex. She should have been more clear. Maybe if she'd said straight out, *I want sex and only sex,* she'd be in bed with him right now, instead of listening to his buddy cook up excuses for him.

Mark patted the ground beside him for a lug nut she could see was just out of reach. She plopped onto the curb, grabbed it and handed it to him.

"Thanks," he said.

The good news was that now she knew nothing stood between them except Rick's wrong impression of her. If all he wanted was sex, then she was his girl.

She handed Mark his wrench.

He swore mightily, then apologized to her.

"Swear away," she said, pondering her next move. As she handed Mark tools, then his soda, then the jack handle, a plan began to form in her mind and her hurt feelings turned to excitement.

"Got it," Mark said, sitting up, wiping sweat from his face with the back of his forearm, streaking dirt like war paint across his forehead.

"Hang on," she said and used a napkin to clean him off.

"Thanks for the help," he said to her. "You okay with the Rick thing? I mean if what I said causes a problem, I—"

"I'm fine. Better than fine. Understanding Rick better can only help us work better together."

"Rick would kill me if he knew I told you."

"Trust me, Rick will be fine." If she had her way, Rick would be thanking Mark, not killing him. She would, too. If all went well, Rick would get laid—and what man didn't want that?—and she'd get the fantasy sex she'd dreamed of.

7

WHAT THE HELL was Samantha up to? All morning, she'd been giving him *looks*. Sexy, take-me-now looks. It had been bad enough Friday when she'd left the studio. Watching her little pink tongue perform tricks on a cock lollipop as she'd trotted out the door had just about killed him.

Now on Monday, she'd escalated her behavior, playfully hip-checking him as they moved around the office together, brushing his arm with her fingers as she made a point, allowing her glance to linger. What the hell was she doing? Had she forgotten about his girlfriend, dammit? Did he have to announce his engagement or something?

To make matters worse, just now, she'd rushed out, claiming she *had* to talk to Blythe, and asked him to get started on the upcoming photo shoot on his own. She'd be there, but not for a while.

He should investigate the Blythe emergency, but Samantha had trapped him waiting for the client—Trudy Norton, who'd requested a Wild West setting for her rodeo-star fiancé.

This was her now, he guessed, tripping toward him from the parking lot in a red cowboy hat and matching boots. And a trench coat. In this heat, that could only mean she wore something racy underneath. Lord. If Samantha didn't believe in her work so much, he'd have a tough time keeping a straight face.

What was so urgent at the salon? The report Mark had brought him Friday about the drug bust at Moons had made him want to look closer at it, since Heidi, the comb-wielding hairdresser, had been a star witness against mob guys running drugs out of Moons under the nose of the owner Duke Dunmore.

Content with the drugs, prosecutors had ignored the prostitution angle, which might be playing out in the salon, judging from the conversation he'd over-heard from under the shampoo sink. For that matter, there was plenty of room for drugs in the freshly in-stalled shelves.

He kind of hoped Shear Ecstasy was the nexus of criminal activity at Mirror, Mirror. Of course, Bedroom Eyes had plenty of semi-empty closets and Samantha had photographed the hookers and strippers, too. He had yet to talk to Sylvestri's bookkeeper. Samantha could still be involved.

The thought made his heart sink. He cared far too much about her. He could not get the woman out of his head. He wanted to turn her clear blue eyes smoky with lust and drag hungry gasps from her sweet mouth.

Saturday night, he'd taken his parents to a movie and had noticed that the female lead had Samantha's pointed nose, and the sidekick her small, solid build.

He had to stop this shit. He was on the job. But Samantha's morning torture had made it a hell of a lot harder...so to speak.

The cowgirl in the trench coat pushed through the door. "Howdy," she said, tipping her hat, trying for ballsy, though he could tell she felt nervous. He understood completely. He was pretty uncomfortable with his role in this deal.

"Trudy? I'm Rick West. I've set up the studio if you'd like to come this way."

"You're taking my picture? But I booked with Samantha. Angela told me she was great." She stopped walking.

"I'll just be taking the preliminary shots. Samantha will take the final ones." And the sooner she got back, the better.

"Okay. That's great. No offense."

"None taken." He led her to studio three, which they used for outdoor settings, Trudy's boots clicking cheerily beside him, while he soaked his undershirt with sweat.

"Do you need to look at our costume options?" he asked her, waving at the dressing-room door. *Could he sound any more gay?*

"I'm wearing what I want. Under here." She blushed. "I'm not sure it'll work. I've heard that the camera makes plaid look smeary and is red a problem?" She untied her belt and held open the coat, revealing a red-checked bra with matching panties. "What do you think?"

Lord almighty. He felt himself go as red as her hat. Mark would have loved being flashed by a cowgirl, but Rick was mortified. "That should work...fine." He swallowed.

"Good. Travis, my fiancé, is such a rodeo fiend."

"I'm sure he'll be pleased." He led her into the studio he'd set up with a barn backdrop, a short stretch of raw-wood fencing and a large hay bale.

"How perfect," she breathed, shrugging out of her coat and handing it to him before she rushed to position herself on the bale, on her side, legs extended over the end. "How's this?"

She looked like she'd been dumped from a horse.

"Maybe lean a little to the left."

She did.

"Not so far…that's it…a little more…to the right now." He felt like he was directing traffic. "Not so far…whoops."

She'd slipped to the floor, but gamely climbed back up.

He approached and patted the end of the bale. "Maybe put your foot here and lean on one elbow." Now one breast seemed to smother the other, but what was he going to do about that?

"Better," he said, adjusting the reflector and the hair light. Much easier than handling her boobs.

Using the digital, he checked the shot. Nice rim effect around her shoulders and maybe the suffocated breast wasn't *so* bad. "Great," he exaggerated. "All set."

Poor Trudy froze up like a corpse.

This was why he disliked portraits. He didn't care to stare into people's hearts through a lens. He didn't want to see their fears, their doubts, the don't-dare hopes behind their shaky smiles. Animals were so much simpler. And a mountain sunrise didn't care who loved it. It just was. In all its glory.

"How about you think good thoughts," he said.

She produced a grim smile that matched her rigid body.

Where the hell was Samantha?

"Maybe just relax everything," he said. *And could you straighten your breasts?* Samantha would have the woman posed softly, her eyes glowing with love, with minimal direction. He was failing wildly and confusing Trudy while he was at it.

Trudy blew out a breath, but that made the tit problem worse. "Does my stomach pooch too much?" she asked.

He looked through the lens. "Nope. Pooches just right." Lord. He snapped a couple horrible shots, then slid one sweaty palm down the side of his pants.

Maybe Bianca would pop in. She'd come in for a couple friends' sittings and never hesitated pointing out when they looked goofy or wrong. Somehow no one got offended.

"Should I smile or just look sexy?"

Her smile looked like a grimace. "Let's try the sexy look."

She straightened her mouth and tilted her head, looking like someone had stabbed her with a pitchfork.

"Okay…" Click. He cringed at the digital image he'd captured. "Maybe the smile again?" Just as bad. Click. Click.

Emboldened by the clicks, Trudy widened her smile, leering like a bad jack-o'-lantern.

This was harder than it looked.

Come on, Samantha. Get in here.

If he uploaded these shots for Trudy, she'd burst into tears and run out the door in her tablecloth underwear.

Samantha peeked in the door to see if Rick was twisting in the wind yet. Looked that way. He wiped sweat from his forehead, took a shot, then grimaced, wiped more sweat and took another shot. Poor Trudy looked like she'd lost her prom date or had her car stolen.

It was go time with her plan. It was a good one. Not only would she and Rick have sex, but she'd have turned him into a decent boudoir photographer at the same time.

Still, her heart bumped her ribs and she had to take deep breaths to steady herself. "So, how's it going?" she said, waltzing in.

Rick shot her a grateful look. "See for yourself." He handed her the camera in play mode.

Holy moley, Trudy looked like a wax museum figure. *Fix this. Please,* Rick's eyes begged.

"We're getting there," she said to Trudy. "But how about we try a different tack?" She squatted beside Trudy, instructing her how to shift her body, coaching her into warm thoughts about Travis. In a few seconds, Samantha had a comfortable rhythm established.

Rick took over the digital and she headed for the Hasselblad, and before long, she was delighting Trudy with the best of the digitals. As soon as Trudy had tapped happily out the door in her red boots and trench coat, Samantha turned the sign to closed, locked up and faced Rick. "How about we debrief the shoot?" she said.

"What's to debrief? It was a train wreck until you got there," he said, shaking his head, a self-mocking smile on his face. "You proved your point. It's harder than it looks. I assume that was your point?"

She smiled. "Let's take a look. Shall we?" In studio three, Samantha clicked through the horrid shots Rick had taken followed by the good ones she'd snapped. It was like some extreme makeover show—before and after—horrible grimace followed by warm smile, wax figure versus sexy woman. "What do you think?" she asked him.

"That I'd better stick with sets and lighting," Rick said with a rueful grin.

"I think you just need a little practice."

"You want me to torture another poor client?"

"No. I have a better idea. Practice on me."

"On you?" He swallowed hard.

"Exactly. Just like learning CPR on a doll. I'll pretend to be a client and you take a boudoir shot of me."

"A shot of you? I don't think so. Maybe I'll just watch you more closely."

She shook her head. "We learn best by doing."

"You expect me to take a picture of you…dressed like…" He shook his head. "I don't think that's a good idea." He pulled at his collar.

"We can be professional about this, Rick."

"Like I said. Not a good idea." He folded his arms. No way.

"It's not your girlfriend, is it? She trusts you to work here, right? Surrounded by nearly naked women? I mean she knows about your job…?"

"It's not that. It's…"

She was enjoying seeing him squirm a little. After all, he had lied to her. "What? What is it?"

He swallowed again, then seemed to think it through, take on the challenge and leveled his gaze at her. "Okay. You win. If you can handle it, so can I."

"Great. Let's start with my outfit." She took a deep breath and let out the words in a slow tease. "How do you see me, Rick? In leather? Velvet? Silk? Something see-through perhaps?"

His eyes went bright and his words were low and serious. "You'd look great in all of it and I think you know that."

Warmth shot through her at his tone. He felt the tug of lust, too, thank goodness, because she needed his resistance to collapse fast. She had only so much boldness in her.

She maintained her professionalism for the moment. "Generally, Rick, you'll want to offer direct guidance to the client, but for now, let's say I've already decided what to wear. Because I have. I'm going for an exotic temptress look, so how about you set up studio two for me?"

"If you say so." He sighed. "Any particular backdrop or props?"

"Surprise me."

"Somehow, I think that's impossible." *What are you up to?* he asked her with his eyes, but she only winked and hip-swayed away, pretending a calm she didn't feel. Her heart tripped like a hummingbird's wings.

In the dressing room, she grabbed the leopard-patterned bikini top with a matching skirted bottom she'd decided on. It had a wide woven band that would de-emphasize her little tummy bulge. Trembling, she changed into the outfit. No shoes or stockings. They'd have all Rick's clothes to deal with as it was. She looked at herself in the mirror, hoping for the best.

She looked…exposed. And too obvious.

She hated how fast *sexy* turned into *slutty* in her mind. But there was no help for it. To make herself feel better, she threw on a purple silk cape, hooking the gold-braid clasp and letting the hood bunch at her neck. The cloth whispered across her arms and brushed her thighs in a luxurious way. In the cape, she looked regal and sultry. Plus, now Rick could adjust the fabric around her body.

She looked better. Well, except for her flushed face, feverish eyes and the way she was shaking. How could she draw Rick into her fantasy, when she looked downright scared?

Light flashed off her locket where it lay over the cape and she opened it, turning the photograph inside so she could take some courage from it. In the picture, she looked a little nervous, but still very sexy. Seeing the photo again made her breathe more deeply, feel more calm.

Samantha looked from the locket to the mirror and realized she looked great. She would *be* great. With a swish of her cape, she strode off to make something wonderful happen for herself.

When she entered studio two, Rick turned, holding a blue velvet pillow in one big hand, the digital camera around his neck. At the sight of her, something powerful seemed to pass through him. "You look...wow," he said, his eyes raking over her. "I picked this to match your eyes." He lifted the blue pillow.

"You noticed my eyes?"

"Sure." He shrugged as if it were only one of many things he'd cataloged about her. He gestured at the set. "Look okay?"

He'd placed the tiger-striped chaise at an angle, with the wire arch behind, twined with swaths of faux leopard fabric that happened to match her bra. There were two other pillows—one purple, one black resting against the head of the chaise.

"It looks perfect," she said.

"So do you." His voice sounded thick with hunger and that made desire pool in her abdomen.

"So how do you want me?" she said.

He stared at her. "You don't really want me to answer that."

"Sure, I do. You're the photographer, remember?" Oh, she was getting into this.

He sighed, shook his head, resigned to his fate. "Why don't you just make yourself comfortable?" He patted the chaise.

She held his gaze as she approached, then lowered herself onto the item, bracing herself on an elbow, covering herself with the robe so Rick would have to open it up.

He adjusted the blue pillow behind her back, then crouched beside her, inches away, frank appreciation in his gaze. He looked at her through the viewfinder. "Very nice," he said, letting the camera fall away.

"Don't you think I'm too covered up?" She tugged at one side of her cape. "Reveal me for the camera, Rick." She was damned pleased with her tone.

"I hope you know what you're doing." He unlatched the clasp at her throat, his fingers brushing her skin, lingering a little. She breathed in his spice and starch, felt the heat shiver in the air between them. The robe teased her skin as it escaped her body, revealing her leopard-spotted bikini top and the gold-trimmed skirt.

Rick stared at her breasts. "You match the arch." He seemed to struggle to keep his voice steady.

"Excellent choice," she breathed. "You read my mind."

"I'm afraid so." He arranged the cape around her arms with care, but his fingers brushed her bra. He hesitated.

"Move me the way you want me," she said, shifting her breasts closer to him.

"You're not making this easy."

"Oh, but I think I'm making this very easy." She shrugged so that one side of the cape slid completely off her body to the floor, exposing her to the heat of the lights. Already a sheen of sweat made her thighs slippery. She wanted to wrap them around Rick's hips and hold on. Her sex pulsed like a tiny, hot heartbeat, wanting so much more.

She guided Rick's hand to her hip. "Move me, Rick. The way you need me."

She felt him slide into her words, as silky as the robe falling away from her body, and he pulled her hip toward him, then brushed the top of her thigh with trailing fingers. "Bend your leg," he said, and pushed gently at her ankle to show her how he meant her to move.

"Like this?" she asked, bending her knee, resting her foot on the chaise. "Is that better?"

"Depends what you mean by better." Another wry smile.

"Now you need to get me in the mood," she said. Here was where she had to handle this just right. "Ask me why I want this photograph."

"Okay… Why do you want this photograph?"

"It's for a man who wants me, but not…quite… enough." She paused, settling into the role she'd decided to play.

"I see." Rick was wary, but listening closely and his green eyes gleamed with heat.

"He wants me, but he won't do anything about it." She let her finger slide down the edge of her bra, gratified when Rick's eyes followed the path her fingernail took.

"Samantha, I…"

"I don't know why he's resisting." She slipped down to her stomach and made a circle around her navel. "He even made up a girlfriend to scare me away. Can you believe that?" She met his gaze.

Rick blinked, then stilled, caught and waiting for her reaction.

"I figure he must think I have…expectations. He doesn't realize that all I want is a chance to explore our attraction, to enjoy each other physically. That's all I want."

Rick's face had gone rigid, his breathing raspy, and his body vibrated with the effort it took to hold back, but he didn't speak, didn't make a move. Why wasn't he giving in?

She would just have to keep coaxing him. "He doesn't realize that I have these...fantasies that he would be perfect for."

"Fantasies?" he said faintly.

"Yes. For example, here's one of my favorites." She rolled onto her back onto the soft pillows. The other side of her cape fell to the floor, leaving her body fully exposed on the chaise. She was going for broke here. "Here I am, dozing, and my man finds me. Because he thinks I'm asleep, he dares to touch my body."

She waited for a second, eyes closed, hoping Rick would put his hand on her. But he only released a ragged breath.

She opened her eyes and met his gaze. He was staring at her, wanting her, but fighting himself, too.

"Go ahead, Rick," she whispered. "Do what you want to do."

When he didn't move, she took his hand and guided it over her stomach, letting his fingers barely skim her flesh. "He's so afraid to wake me, he barely brushes my skin. Like this."

Rick shifted closer to her and she moved his hand in a wider circle, so his fingertips brushed the underside of her breasts through her bra, then the top of her skirt, making her stomach twitch and jump.

This was the sexiest thing she'd ever done in her life, but he had to take over soon or she'd start to feel foolish.

"Then what?" he said hoarsely, hunger in his eyes.

"Then he wants to kiss me."

"Samantha—"

"And that's what I want," she rushed to say. "I want

you to kiss me, Rick. Make love to me." She released his hand and slid her fingers into his short hair and waited and watched.

She saw the moment he gave in. His green eyes flashed like heat lightning and his hands seemed to convulse around her face. He held her cheeks between his broad palms. Then he kissed her, shaking hard, as if he were doing something terribly wrong.

Samantha kissed him back, showing him with everything in her he was doing something absolutely right.

8

SAMANTHA WAS RELIEVED when Rick deepened the kiss, easing his tongue into her mouth as if it belonged there, and she opened wide, giving him room to move and explore and take all he wanted.

Still holding her face, he broke off the kiss and looked into her eyes. "This is what you want?" he said fiercely, his entire body shaking. "Are you sure?"

"Yes." But the word came out in a gasp because he'd slid his hand between her legs. She spread her thighs, welcoming his touch, and he brushed her crotch with his fingers, while she quivered and panted.

"I can't leave you alone," he said. "I can't stop wanting you." He ran his finger deliberately across her with the exact right pressure.

"Good. That's good." She fought to hold a thought while fireworks shot off everywhere inside her. An entire Fourth of July under her skin. She gasped for air, knowing this was happening too fast. She'd been too abruptly excited. She needed to slow down a bit.

As if he'd read her mind, Rick removed his finger, easing the too-swift tightness there. He lowered his mouth to hers. "No hurry," he murmured, telling her he understood. When he kissed her, his tongue was easy, coaxing her to gradual heat with slow, sure pressure, and she felt the delicious building tension that would lead to a sure climax.

If only they were naked. If only clothes could whip away. She had condoms in her purse—cherry-flavored novelty ones from Val's shop—but her bag was across the room and she hardly had the strength to speak, let alone move.

She wanted to reach for his shirt buttons, but he undid the front clasp of her top and she couldn't do anything but enjoy the pleasure of his eyes on her bare breasts.

"Beautiful," he said, leaning down to suck one nipple deep into his mouth, sending a ribbon of desire to her sex, twisting it exquisitely tight. At the same time, he returned his fingers to the place between her thighs, setting off vibrations like guitar strings continually brushed as he stroked and stroked.

"Oh, that's so good. It's so…so…" She couldn't get out the words. She was flying away, skimming through the air as he stroked and sucked her. She dug her fingers into his hair to hold on to her sanity and moaned helplessly.

After lovely moments, Rick shifted his kisses downward to the underside of her breast.

Don't go, she wanted to say, but then he ran his tongue down the middle of her torso and kissed her stomach, his hands sliding down her body, moving down and down.

"What are you…?" *Doing,* she wanted to say, but couldn't…quite…get it…out.

"I'm tasting you," he said, tugging her gold-trimmed skirt down, too, then all the way off. She was all but naked now. Her bra hung by its straps on her arms, her breasts bared, the air teasing her nipples, wet from Rick's mouth, and now her sex was open to Rick's gaze.

And his kiss. Oh, his kiss. *Holy Hannah in July,* Rick was going down on her. That was such a personal, intense thing to do.

He softly brushed his lips along the top edge of her hair, melting her. Her stomach jumped under his mouth, tickled and thrilled by the intimate touch.

He slid his hands down to hold her bottom in place, as he teased her through her hair, close, but not quite there, warming her up, getting her ready for the experience.

He angled her sex toward his mouth, looking at that secret part of her as if he'd craved a taste all his life.

"Yeah," he said in satisfaction and lowered his mouth to barely brush her mound. His breath rushed between her folds until she seemed to liquefy like chocolate in a fist. If he kept this up, she might dissolve altogether.

Then Rick slid his tongue into her space and the sensation was a hot arrow piercing the neediest part of her. She tensed and cried out. Too loudly, but she couldn't help it. How else could she tell him how wonderful this was?

Prince Charming was waking her with a kiss. Rather, he was sending her into a spasm of luscious pleasure. She could hardly believe this was happening. Could hardly believe she'd made it happen. Rick had given her the courage, in the way he looked at her, wanted her, even as he held himself back.

For the first time, she knew clearly what her painful yearning had been all about. It was no longer just a mental picture, a longed-for fantasy. Rick made it real. She knew what she wanted—Rick. She was safe with him. That fact was as vibrant and true as the sensations coursing through her body.

He thickened his tongue, cupped it around her clit and pressed on both sides of the sensitive flesh.

Her cries lapsed into unintelligible syllables and she gasped for air while Rick moved his lips and tongue slowly, then faster, at exactly the pace she needed.

She pivoted her hips, spread her legs, baring herself to him, wanting more and more. *Do me. Keep doing me. Don't ever stop doing me.*

Then he sucked her tight and closed his teeth in a sweet pinch so abrupt and delicious that she rocketed off, exploding wildly, crying out, almost screaming.

Rick managed to stay with her, gripping her hips, fingers digging into her bottom, his warm breath on her, his tongue cupping her, while her climax went on and on, and she floated on clouds of ebbing pleasure that slowly faded away.

Rick pressed his lips to the inside of first one thigh, then the other, then kissed his way slowly up her body, while she shook and struggled for deep breaths.

"Omigod," she said, lifting her head to look into his face. "That was amazing." Better than her imagination for sure.

"Yeah," he said, kissing her mouth. "It was."

Her light musk on his lips reminded her how intimate this had been. He had pressed his tongue to her deepest need. She felt surprisingly close to him, connected, as if they'd been lovers for years, not just a few hot minutes.

She wanted to thank him. She wanted to cry. Which was silly, considering this had just been sex.

Besides, there was so much more to do. She had to touch Rick, taste him, too. "Now it's your turn," she said and reached for him through his pants.

He was thick behind his zipper under her fingers. His eyes flared with a fierce desire until he closed them, frowning, mouth taut, as if he were engaged in some intense internal battle.

She started on his belt, but he stopped her hand and opened his eyes. She saw that he'd dredged up some reserve of self-control. He lifted her hand to his mouth and kissed her knuckles. He tried to smile, but his jaw quivered with the effort. "That was great," he said tightly.

"We're not stopping now," she said. "You haven't even—" Climaxed. Or been inside her. They'd barely started.

"I know." But he reattached her bra, focusing in, as if he had to cover her up before he lost all restraint. "I shouldn't have done that." He found her skirt and slid it up her legs, watching her body as though he didn't really want to cover it. "I got carried away."

Lotta rules of conduct. That's what his friend Mark had said about him. *No hooking up at work for sure.* That was probably the problem.

"I know we work together, Rick, but this doesn't have to change anything," she said, gripping his upper arms.

"It should," he said, holding her gaze.

Maybe he thought she wanted more than she did. "I meant what I said. I really want just sex."

"But I don't." He wrapped the cape around her, as though she were a package he was afraid he'd rip wide open. "I want more than that."

"You're kidding." She sat up and looked at him.

"When I said there was someone else, it wasn't exactly a lie. I haven't met her yet, but she's out there."

"And you're waiting for her?"

He nodded, his smile self-mocking. "Hard to believe, but, yeah, I want one woman for the rest of my life."

She felt her jaw drop. Rick had rules, all right. And

one of them was that sex mattered. It was sweet, really, and old-fashioned. And the worst thing in the world for her. She'd finally snagged her fantasy man and he wanted true love.

"I'm sorry I let that happen," he said, the soft green of his eyes going muddy with guilt. "It wasn't fair to you."

"Fair? It was heaven. And it was my idea, remember?" There was something more here that bothered him. She didn't understand it, but it made her feel guilty for dragging him onto her wanton couch—like the wicked, selfish Delilah, seducing the hapless Samson into his downfall.

Rick still wanted her, she could tell by the way a muscle jumped in his cheek and how he kept tightening the cape over her body to keep himself away. She'd bet if she kissed him or touched him, his self-control would snap like a twig.

He brushed her hair away from her face. "I should go. Before I…" Raw longing flooded his features, but he turned away and pushed to his feet. She couldn't imagine living a life so bound by rules. "Shall I take the film to the lab?" he said, clearly trying to sound normal. He strode deliberately to the Hasselblad.

"Yeah. That would be great," she said, her voice still shaky.

"There's another frame here," he said and looked down into the readout, adjusting the focus. "I still have to take your picture, right?" He smiled.

"I think you got the idea," she said, confused and a little sad.

"Think back on what happened," he said, "for just a second."

She smiled, realizing how much better she felt after

those glorious moments. The camera clicked and the flash fired in the middle of her memory.

"Beautiful," he said with a sigh. "I'll get this developed and we'll see if I learned anything from your lesson." He held her gaze while he rewound the film, a sad wistfulness in his eyes.

"You regret this?" she asked him.

"Not nearly enough," he said, popping out the film, which he lifted, then turned and left.

Samantha sighed and leaned forward, flexing her bare toes against the cool tile. She felt…good. Calm. Settled into her body, and also sensitized to everything—the air in the studio, the nap of the faux fur beneath her, the silk cloth against her skin. She could still smell Rick, could almost taste him, could feel his tongue right…*there*. And she wanted more.

Just her luck that she'd finally been bold enough to go for it and she'd chosen a man with the small-town attitudes she'd been eager to escape.

No way could she be with a man who felt guilty about sex. She also wasn't interested in being a man's one and only. Not yet. Not until she'd sampled her fill.

At least she'd done it—splashed around a little, made a wave. There'd been that alarming jolt of feeling close to Rick, which made her wonder if maybe sex wasn't as simple as she wanted it to be, but she'd made progress.

Though she hadn't come close to drowning.

THE NEXT DAY, Rick skimmed over the dozen proof sheets he'd picked up on the way to the station. He wanted to check in with Mark before he headed to Bedroom Eyes for the day.

While he waited, he flipped through shot after shot

of women and couples in skimpy clothes in front of romantic, exotic or outdoor backdrops. Nice. Nice. Excellent. Gorgeous. Samantha was good. Very good.

And there it was—the picture he'd been looking for. The last frame on the last strip. Samantha. Sitting there in her jungle bra, her lips swollen from his assault, but offering up a soft smile, her blue eyes shiny with new bliss and fresh heat. She looked both innocent and carnal—a combination that had turned his self-control into ice on a frying pan.

Look at her. Her tiny photo sent lust pulsing through him and seemed to suck all the air out of the station.

She'd figured out there was no girlfriend. But that wasn't what had washed away his resistance like so much sand in the surf.

She made him forget himself. Forget all that had happened in the last four years. She turned him into just a man who wanted her with everything in him. When she'd placed his hand on her body, he'd been lost, swept away, aware only of her skin under his fingers, and after that her wet mouth, her sweet tongue and, later, the wet swollen need of her, the taste of her sex, tangy on his tongue, the way her cries declared he was the only one who could touch her this way.

He'd managed to stop short of taking her with his body—as if that were somehow more honorable. But if she'd done one more thing—kissed him, grabbed him, looked at him that way—he'd have caved for good.

He'd been on duty, for chrissake. Samantha was still a suspect, though he was reasonably certain she was oblivious to whatever crime was going on under her nose. Even if Lester Tabor was using her books for illegal purposes, Rick would bet his life Samantha knew nothing about it.

He stared at her photo, feeling the tug of desire all over again. Damn. He prided himself on being able to rationally assess any situation and take the right course, no matter how tough. He was losing it.

"So, what's cooking at ye olde sex shoppe?" Mark said behind him, looking over his shoulder.

Rick shuffled the pages so Samantha's picture was hidden.

"Are those sex shots?" Trudeau reached for the proofs. Rick let him take the top few sheets. "Damn. Were you in the room when these were taken?"

"For some." He shrugged like it was no big deal and put the rest of the pages in the lab envelope.

Mark lifted his gaze. "Hell. At least act interested."

"Oh, don't worry. I'm interested." Yesterday afternoon was terrible proof.

Mark shot him a look. "What's up? You look sick."

"It's the case, I guess. I just wish we'd get a break."

Mark seemed to figure something out. "The problem is you feel guilty, West. You're having too much fun." Mark slapped him on the back. "Forget it. There isn't a cop here who works harder and we all know it." He handed him back the photo proofs.

Rick winced and his gut tightened. Mark thought he was some kind of saint. He had that reputation, irritating his squad mates with his insistence that no stone remain unturned, no regulation not be followed, no report left incomplete. Never a shortcut to good police work.

What the hell had happened to him?

He should be in the lieutenant's office right now reporting his inappropriate actions. Except that might jeopardize the task force's work, a lose-lose for everyone.

He looked across the room at his crew, all working hard. Jessie, on the phone, and Rocky, studying a file, had volunteered to pretend to be a couple coming in for photos at Bedroom Eyes if he needed them to.

Craig and Dave, interviewing a suspect by Dave's desk, had jumped on the tedious chore of running Mona's client names through records. They'd all pitched in, even when they had other work to handle. They were a team. They trusted him. He couldn't let them down.

He had stopped things with Samantha, right? No harm done?

"Listen," Mark said. "You never called me back, but I needed to let you know I ran into Sawyer Friday after you left."

"You what?"

"She came back for something. I had a flat and we got to talking."

"You talked to Sawyer and didn't tell me?"

"I tried, man. It was nothing big. The only thing was that she figured out you didn't have a girlfriend. She mentioned her and I sort of hesitated."

"You hesitated?"

"Hell, you didn't tell me you made up a squeeze. I covered it up—told her you had intimacy issues."

"Intimacy issues?"

"Hold on. It worked. Also I said you had rules against hooking up at work. She bought that. And she said that understanding you better would help you work better together."

"Oh, yeah. It did that, all right." Now he knew how she'd figured it out, why she'd been so bold. *Thank you, partner.*

"What's up? You look like you ate something a week

old and ugly. Did she hit on you? She did. She hit on you! You dog."

"Keep it down." He looked around, but everyone else seemed busy and no one looked up.

"What do you know. You do the deed?"

"No. I stopped it. Would you forget it?" He knew he must look as guilty as hell.

"Hey…it's cool. No worries. Whatever the case calls for."

But Rick could tell that Trudeau was completely blown away. And no wonder. He couldn't believe he'd let things go that far himself. "It was a mistake, okay? It won't happen again."

"Sure." But Trudeau grinned at him as if Rick had just sold his soul to the devil and Trudeau was the welcoming committee at the door to a happy hell. "We all make sacrifices for the greater good."

"Cool it," he growled, hating that he'd sunk so low. Even now, he realized Samantha made him want to forget all about the case, screw the rules, and be with her. What was happening to him? If he wasn't who he thought he was, then what?

"I'm just glad you have more than yarn balls and a sock puppet between your legs."

"Let's stick with the case, all right? And try not to have any more heart-to-hearts with any suspects about me."

"Deal."

"The bookkeeper comes in a couple days. I'll see if he's running double books."

Mark nodded. "Craig says half a dozen of the massage clients are connected. Costa's gun? Clean."

"What about Chuck Yardley…the guy who gets a

daily rubdown?" he asked, happy to focus on the details of the case that didn't concern Samantha.

"Accountant. Not even an outstanding parking ticket. Bean counter with a jones for massage, I guess. Full-release maybe?"

"Doubt it. Mona's legit."

"And how do you know?"

"I just know."

"How? Wait. You got a massage?"

He felt himself redden.

"Shit. You should look a hell of a lot happier than you do right now, West. What a racket."

"What's up?" Rocky Marston called over to them.

"West here. Getting massages. Taking pictures of buck-naked hookers."

"How do you rate?" Marston asked him. "My last undercover was pizza deliveries on 110-degree summer nights."

"Rick deserves it," Jessie said, looking up from her file. "Unlike some cops I know who take advantage of people's good nature and drag ringers into a friendly game of ball." Jessie and Rocky played basketball with a coed league.

"I can't help it those guys went to college."

"On basketball scholarships?"

The pair settled into bickering, ceasing their harassment of Rick, thank God.

"What's happening with the upstairs space?" Mark asked him.

"Still building out. Counters and cupboards this week. I check in with the crew every day. What about the Sylvestri horse property? Anything unusual there?"

"Retired racehorses and manure. Nothing out of

place in the barns. Not even a small plane. We're keeping an eye on the store in Scottsdale, too."

"Bianca's knit shop. I can't imagine Sylvestri'd do anything there. He's pretty devoted to his wife."

"The only thing Darien Sylvestri's devoted to is lining his pockets." Mark stopped, studying him. "What are you saying?"

"Nothing. Bianca's at the studio a lot. Raves about all Darien does for her." He shrugged. Was he getting sucked into sympathy for the suspects he'd grown to like? When the shit hit the fan, what would happen to everyone at Mirror, Mirror?

He didn't want anyone to get hurt—Valerie with her G-strings and genital lollipops and Blythe who wanted to bleach his hair, plus Mona, who'd done something to his spine that made it easier to breathe. Would they be forced out of business by all this?

He shouldn't care so much. Which was exactly why cops weren't supposed to get involved with suspects. Innocence could twist into guilt in a heartbeat. He knew that to his soul.

He was suffering from the confusion of living two lives. He had to focus on the case. Get that bastard Sylvestri behind bars and leave Samantha the hell alone.

9

"Need any help?" Rick's words were weighted with meaning. He stood in the doorway of studio two looking in at Samantha, where she crouched, trying to snag a velvet pillow from beneath the chaise. She was instantly transported to the previous afternoon when he'd stripped her naked and kissed her *there* on this spot.

"Just trying to grab a pillow that fell." *The blue one you chose to match my eyes.* She ached at the sight of him. He looked as desolate and lost as she felt.

But that was only natural. Everyone longed for what they'd denied themselves, right?

He came to crouch beside her, dropping the lab envelope he carried onto the chaise between them. "The proofs," he said, running his palm across the striped surface until his fingers connected with hers. *I remember, too.*

"Thanks." She couldn't hold his gaze, couldn't stand the heat swelling between them, so much swifter after what had happened.

He'd seen her naked, heard her wild cries, kissed her breasts and her sex. She'd felt him behind his zipper, the hard length of him, proof of his desire for her.

"I can't quite reach," she said, bending again.

"Let me." He leaned down, the tendons in his neck

rippling beneath the clean line of his crisp haircut. The animal power of him made her feel faint. She was like a young girl with her first crush. *Grow up. You had your fantasy. Be content.*

Rick nabbed the pillow and when he put it in place, she could see that he'd gotten himself under control again. Rick seemed to be able to turn his lust on and off like a light switch.

She could do that, too, dammit. She grabbed the envelope and plopped onto the chaise, turning it into a seat, not a spot to make love. "Let's see how they came out."

Rick sat beside her, while she scanned the pages, mentally noting her favorites. She'd take the loupe to them under better light, but it was fun to get a preview. The Trudy Norton shots were especially great….

There it was. The picture Rick had taken of her. Sitting right here just after her shattering climax.

She looked…wonderful. Satisfied and still eager and as sexy as hell. The light was golden even without the tungsten, as if the warmth of the moment had colored the air around her.

She felt Rick waiting, so she lifted her eyes to his. "This is a great photograph."

"I thought it came out good."

"You really caught me." She realized abruptly that his shot was better than the one she'd taken of herself. She grasped her locket, toyed with the clasp and looked at Rick. The photo was her personal treasure, but Rick deserved to know how good he was.

Holding his gaze, she pried open the locket and cupped it in her palm like a butterfly for him to admire.

He looked, then lifted his eyes to hers. "This is the one you took?"

She nodded.

He studied it. "It's very good."

"Not as good as yours." She pulled the chain over her neck and held the locket next to the proof, angled so they could compare the two images. "In my shot I look nervous. In yours I look happy and hopeful." Eager, really. With a sigh, she closed the cover and put the chain over her head, adjusting the locket between her breasts.

"You wear that every day." He tapped it and she felt the vibration in her bones.

"To remind me to go for what I want, to never settle."

Rick cupped her cheek with one hand. "You deserve to get what you want, Samantha." His words made her feel like releasing a breath she'd been holding for years.

But I want you.

There was a velvet sash on the shelf a few inches away. She could hand it to him and her willing ravishment fantasy could happen right here. *Tie me up, Rick. Make me beg.*

Except that ship had sailed. They'd both agreed. There were other guys out there, just as hot, just as worthy, just as in tune with her body.

She sighed.

The door buzzer sounded, breaking the tension.

"That's probably our one o'clock. Mary Jane Sizemore," she said.

"Which studio do you want to use?"

"One. She wants a romantic shot." She glanced at the stack of proofs. "I should really organize these orders. Why don't you go ahead and handle her? I'll assist, but you run the sitting."

"I don't know if I'm ready for that."

"Sure you are. We just saw the proof." She tapped the envelope that held the shot he'd taken of her.

"That was different." His voice was low, serious and his green eyes crackled. Lord, she wanted him.

"I certainly hope so," she said, struggling to keep it light. "You can't be seducing all my clients or they'll never want to leave."

"It's only you I can't resist," Rick said with a rueful smile. At least it had meant something to him, too.

"You'll do fine. Make suggestions on positioning and talk her into the right mood."

"Easy for you to say. Just don't leave me hanging long. Who knows what awkward position I can get the woman in." He pushed to his feet, straightened his shoulders as if he faced an unsavory duty and marched off.

She started for her office, but she heard Bianca's smoke-rough cackle instead of Mary Jane's voice, so she changed direction and headed to the reception area. "Bianca," she said in welcome. "You look gorgeous."

"You like? It's my own design." Bianca did a quick twirl in her gold-threaded knit suit with a leopard-spotted collar, cuffs, belt and pillbox hat. "I call it 'Sheena, Businesswoman of the Jungle.'"

"It's perfect for you."

"Bianca has *good* news and *great* news," Rick said, winking at Samantha, clearly fighting a grin. The woman had charmed him, too, when she'd popped in for a few sittings, and Samantha could tell Bianca adored Rick.

"More business for you!" Bianca said. "One of Joey's buddies is getting married and they want you to do bedroom shots. I'm talking the entire wedding party—bridesmaids, groomsmen, ushers. Twenty-five people!"

"Wow," Samantha said. "That *is* great news, Bianca." She winked at Rick.

"No, no, no. That's only the *good* news," Bianca said. "The *great* news is that I'm taking a photography class."

"You are?"

"At Phoenix College. Darien's idea. I was telling him about helping out at Bedroom Eyes and he said, 'Why don't you take the blankety-blank pictures, baby, instead of talking about them all the blankety-blank time?' He has a potty mouth, my Darien, but, anyway, he got a catalog from the college and there was a class so I said, why not?"

"You'll do great, Bianca. You have a great eye." If she had the patience for the technical aspects of the craft, Bianca would make a respectable hobbyist.

"And you'll give me tips and show me tricks?"

"I'll help you however I can."

"I knew you'd say that. I wouldn't have the nerve to do any of this stuff—the knit shop or the class—if it weren't for you." Bianca lunged at Samantha for a bruising hug.

"I only took your picture, Bianca."

"You did more than that, hon. You unleashed me." Still hugging Samantha's shoulder, she turned to Rick. "Isn't this woman amazing?" She shook Samantha so hard her head wobbled.

"Yes," Rick said softly, his eyes warm. "She is."

"See that you remember that." Bianca wagged a finger at him. "Or you'll answer to me. And my husband knows some pretty tough customers, let me tell you."

"I'm sure he does," Rick said in an odd tone. Then he looked out the window. "Looks like our client's here."

Rick took Mary Jane down the hall and Samantha blocked off most of the following week for the wedding shoot, while Bianca leaned over the counter, making it jiggle, watching her work the mouse.

"All set," she said, standing straight.

"Now tell me what's going on with you two, Sammi. The looks flying back and forth almost melted the gold in my suit."

"He works for me, Bianca, that's it."

"And this is real leopard skin, hon." Bianca tapped her hat. "Come on."

"Real or not, the hat's gorgeous," she said to change the subject. "Are you going to sell your designs in the new shop?"

"That's the plan," she said, successfully distracted. "Though Darien's gotten so involved lately. He helped me with the yarn order, if you can believe that."

"That's nice of him." The man seemed to have too much time on his hands since he'd retired, Samantha thought. He was always popping in at Mirror, Mirror, too.

"He's full of surprises these days, my Darien. So tight with a dime, but he insists I order the exotic yarns. He doesn't care about the price. Lightweight is important, he says." She sighed. "He's even talking to the carpenter about the shelves—he wants them all deep and wide."

"Are you getting excited about the opening?"

"Oh, yes. The only tragedy is the shipment comes in next week, so I'll be so busy I don't think I can help with the wedding shoot. I'll buy the flowers, though. I want you to use them in each shot. The colors are garnet and goldenrod and I'm thinking of red-grape clumps, huh? Luscious as the blushing bride." She kissed her fingers. "So symbolic. The perfect motif."

"We'll be fine with my silk flowers, Bianca. You

have a lot on your hands, it sounds like, so don't worry about—"

"I insist. And I'll pay. But I am busy, that is so true. My class starts next week, too." Her gingersnap eyes sparkled as brightly as the diamonds on her fingers, which flashed as she talked. "Oh, I almost forgot. My niece Elisha will help with the costumes for the wedding pictures."

"I don't think we need any help, Bianca."

"Sure you do. You won't have me, so Elisha's my stand-in. This is a big job, hon."

"But I don't really—"

"Okay. Truth time. Darien promised Elisha's daddy he'd get her a job and I said I was sure you could squeeze her in. Pay her something token—say ten bucks an hour?—and up your rates to cover the cost. Kenny can afford it."

"I'm sure we'll be fine without—"

"She's very bright. She had a little attitude problem—kids, what can you do?—but she's turning that around. Will you help me out here? Please? As a personal favor?"

"We'll work it out. Sure." Bianca had done so much for her, Samantha could hardly refuse. Though she had noticed that Darien had a remarkably large family, and they all seemed to owe or be owed tons of favors.

"Terrific, then. You'd better hurry back to Rick now." Bianca patted both her hands, smiling affectionately. "I'm so glad this all worked out."

"Rick's been a big help."

"Oh, I'm sure he has." She winked. "I'll just tell my nephew never mind."

"Your nephew?"

"The single, handsome one? Duke Dunmore? Owns

a bar?" She winked again. "I'll just tell him the position's been filled."

"If you mean the assistant position, you're correct. Because that's all that Rick is. My assistant." The woman would not let go of the impossible idea.

"Don't say another word, hon. Might jinx it."

"There's nothing to jinx, Bianca."

Bianca just winked and smiled a cat-in-the-cream smile as if she knew something Samantha didn't. For just a second, there, Samantha wished Bianca was right. She said goodbye to her and headed down the hall to see how contorted Rick had Mary Jane.

THE SETUP WAS FINE, Rick realized, looking at the shot through the viewfinder. The fake-fur throw offered texture, the translucent lace backdrop gave an ethereal effect and the hair light made Mary Jane's dark hair gleam golden. The combination of tungsten and a reflected fill-flash would give a warm white glow. The setup was great.

The costume was fine, too, if a little hokey—a short red robe with a deep vee trimmed with white lace, making Mary Jane look like a Valentine heart.

But the woman needed work. She looked morose and miserable, and her position was far too tense.

This was the hard part. The part where he had to position her and talk her into the right mood.

He went to crouch beside her, cupping the camera in a palm. "How about if you lean toward me and let your, uh, chest come forward."

She shifted as he'd asked. Better.

"Now, move this thigh a few inches to the left." He tapped the stocking-covered knee of that leg and she moved it. "Great. Now tuck one arm this way." He demonstrated on his own body.

She hesitated, tried, but didn't get it right.

"May I?" he asked.

She nodded permission and he moved her arm. It felt purposeful and professional, not at all like with Samantha, where merely placing a palm on her body had set him on fire.

"Do I look okay?" Mary Jane asked.

"Getting there." He had to do something about her wooden smile. "Tell me who this photograph is for."

"My husband Bo. For our anniversary. We've been married seven years." But she looked wistful, not happy about it. Maybe Bo was bored or had the seven-year itch.

Rick hated being this close to personal pain. Sweat trickled down the sides of his face and along his ribs. "That's a long time to be married. It's good to, uh, remind yourselves why you got together."

"You think so?" She sounded so hopeful.

"Sure." Samantha would be working her romantic magic about now, so he decided to give it a try. "How about you close your eyes and think about a special time with Bo?" *Let it not be sex.* He couldn't take that.

"A special time?" Mary Jane closed her eyes, frowned, then a smile spread. "I know. Our honeymoon at the Princess. Bo made the arrangements and he had roses for me and champagne and he'd made a heart of chocolates on the sheets. No drugstore sampler, either. Gourmet truffles."

"Sounds great." And explained her choice in lingerie. She'd dressed like a box of Valentine's Day chocolates.

"It was." She opened her eyes. "We ended up with melted chocolate all over *everything*."

Click. He'd caught a great look—sweet and wicked. She blinked. "Oh."

"That was nice. Keep talking. Try to forget I'm here. Tell me more about how Bo treated you on your honeymoon." *But, please no sex.*

He glanced up to see Samantha in the doorway. She shot him a thumbs-up and his heart swelled with unexpected pride.

"He was so sweet," Mary Jane said. "He couldn't take his eyes off me the whole weekend." She gave a dreamy smile.

Click. He caught it. Not bad.

Wordlessly, Samantha moved to the tripod and began taking pictures with the Hasselblad, nodding at him after each one.

By the time they finished, Rick was worn out and dripping with sweat, but they'd snagged some nice frames. Samantha gestured for him to keep running things, so he loaded the digital images for Mary Jane to preview. He invoked the slide show and the first shot flared.

Mary Jane gasped. "That's me?" She plain beamed at him.

"That's you," he said, pleased, too. They watched the show, while Mary Jane sighed and gasped and said *wow* and *oh* at each picture. He couldn't help grinning.

When the last shot faded to black, she turned to him with tears in her eyes and hugged him hard. "You're amazing."

"Just doing my job," he muttered, as mortified as hell, but happy, too. Samantha winked at him from behind Mary Jane.

They walked her out and, after the door closed,

Samantha turned to him, leaning against the still-wobbly counter. He *had* to fix that thing.

"You did a great job, Rick. I hope you're proud of yourself. It's no small thing to turn a relationship around."

"I just took a few pictures."

"And they'll remind Bo how he felt when he made a heart out of pricey chocolates just to please his bride."

"You're a romantic," he said, liking that about her, even though he knew love wasn't that simple.

"What about you? You want one woman for the rest of your life. What's more romantic than that?"

"It just makes sense." He shrugged. "You get to a certain age and you want to settle into a life with someone."

"I guess. Any luck, if I may ask?"

"Not so far. I've dated a couple of women, but…"

"It didn't work out?" Her curiosity made him uncomfortable, but he somehow found himself wanting to explain.

"We didn't click. Couple of dates, but we ran out of things to say. I'm not much of a talker."

"You talk to me."

"Probably too much." The more she knew about him, the harder it was to keep the lies straight in his head, to keep the case clear and his goals front and center.

"I don't think so. And, frankly, if you want to get serious with someone, you'll have to do a lot better than that."

"The less I say, the fewer mistakes I can make." That was full-out true in the moment. It was a relief not to be lying into her earnest face.

"You think a woman who loves you expects you to be perfect? If she loves you, she'll forgive your flaws and mistakes."

She was a romantic, all right. "I think you earn love

and guard it with everything in you." Sure, some people were high-minded and long-suffering, but he'd seen enough, especially on the job, to know that was mostly not the case.

"You don't give people much credit. Love is sturdier than you think, Rick." She fiddled with her locket. Her showing him the secret picture seemed almost more intimate than his making love to her. She wore it to remind herself never to settle. She'd had an asshole for a boyfriend and still believed in romance.

She deserved to be appreciated for all her depth and sweetness by a man who cared for her alone.

Rick didn't want to think of her hunting around, sleeping with a bunch of guys. She thought she just wanted sex, but Samantha put her heart into everything she did. She could get hurt so easily.

He started to warn her to be careful, but he couldn't, not when she looked so earnest and so sure. So all he said was, "Maybe you're just braver than I am."

Then he heard the buzz of saws out back. Darien was due to check in with the workers and he'd been standing here like a lovesick fool. "I need to head out back. Talk to the workers about fixing this." He jiggled the counter.

"Sure," she said. "Good idea." But she was pondering his words, worrying about him. Sweet, really. As if she hoped he'd find some forgiving woman with a sturdy love. She just reached into his chest and squeezed his beating heart like Bianca had suggested that first day.

On the other hand, he knew for a fact she could never forgive him for what he was hiding from her.

The crew boss told him that he'd just missed Darien, but he managed to get the gist of the conversation. Darien wanted the workers to quit work on the second floor so they could finish the cupboards in the beauty shop before a shipment came in that night. A *shipment*. The hairs on the back of Rick's neck rose.

Furthermore, he'd instructed them to buy locks for the cupboards.

Locks. No hair product was worth a padlock. Had to be guns, drugs or money. Adrenaline pumped through him. Something big was afoot. He'd need to be on site for that delivery, which meant a few overnights at the center.

He headed off to call Mark with the news, then scout out the best place for a stakeout. Somewhere in there he realized he'd forgotten to ask about fixing Samantha's counter.

RICK BOLTED UP from the futon in Mona's shop and grabbed his gun. He never wore it at work, not wanting to alarm Samantha, but a stakeout could be dangerous.

He hadn't meant to fall asleep—he'd chosen Mona's studio for its proximity to the service door and salon *and* because there was little chance he'd fall asleep on the incredibly uncomfortable couch.

This was his second night, though, and exhaustion had overcome the thin cushion and cramped length of it. He rubbed his eyes, then glanced at his watch. Twelve-fifteen.

The rumble of a long-haul truck's engine out back came to him. The delivery. Thank God the noise had woken him up.

He moved soundlessly to the back of the shop and cracked the door. Street sounds told him the service door was open. He listened hard, his own breathing harsh in his ears, and picked up small talk from the parking lot. He twisted his neck slowly to ease the kink. He'd need another Mona massage soon.

He'd saved himself a trip home this morning by stowing travel-size toiletries in the cargo pockets of his pants and cleaning up in the center's bathroom, zipping out before Samantha had arrived, then returning in the T-shirt he'd worn under the previous day's denim shirt.

The workers said little, then he heard the hum of an electronic truck gate lowering, followed by clunks, then grunts as the men lifted and shifted cargo.

Before long, cart wheels squeaked and feet thudded down the hall. He waited until they passed, then looked out to see a handcart stacked high with factory-issued boxes. He glimpsed a flat-screen TV on top of a column of DVD players. Electronic gear for Mad Darien's store? Stolen maybe? Why else arrange a late-night delivery?

He waited for quiet so he could investigate further, except he heard new voices and footsteps, but coming from the lobby of the center. Stuff was arriving from up front of the center, too?

The Healing Touch door rattled. Shit. Someone was headed for his hideout. He lunged into the room where Mona had given him a rubdown, leaving the door cracked so he could listen, his gun at the ready.

"I think this is a bad idea." Mona, he realized, sounding tense. Surely she wasn't helping with the delivery.

"But it's a pain that won't quit," a man whined.

"What are you trying to do, Chuck? Do you really have a muscle spasm? Let me see…."

Chuck? The guy who showed up every day for a massage? Chuck Yardley, right? The bean counter.

"Maybe not a spasm, but I need your magic fingers," he said, turning the words into a lame pickup line.

"You make me sound like a vibrating bed." That was the usual teasing Mona, but she sounded uncertain.

"That's not how I think of you at all. I'm blowing this." Yardley sounded embarrassed and a little drunk.

"Okay, then," Mona sighed. "You know the drill. Take off your clothes and lie facedown on the table."

"I'd like something different tonight, Mona."

Hell, was he going to ask for something illegal? *Don't do it, Mona. Tell him where he can stick it.*

"Different how?" she asked, her voice surprisingly soft.

Rick frowned. *Come on. You're better than that.*

"You know," Chuck said. "I've been trying to ask you for weeks, and it's taken me all night—and two martinis—to get up the nerve to get you to meet me here."

"Chuck...don't. You know I don't work that way."

Good for you, Mona.

"What are you afraid of? It's what we both want."

How the hell could johns believe hookers enjoyed the act? If this creep tried to force Mona...

"I have rules, Chuck."

That's telling him.

"Rules are meant to be broken," the guy coaxed.

There was the sound of movement, the rustle of fabric.

"Rules exist for good reason," she said faintly.

"And there's an exception to every rule." He was cajoling her, his voice low, moving in.

No means no, pal. Rick had to stop this. Screw his cover. He had to save Mona from making a mistake she'd regret forever.

"Chuck...I don't... You're my best customer." Her voice cracked.

"I want more than massage from you, Mona. Much more."

A hand job? Blow job? Half and half? Rick's stomach clenched. He eased out the door, ready to bust into the other massage room and save poor Mona. She'd probably been drinking, too, so her judgment was impaired.

"Oh, God, that feels good," Mona said, sounding, well, the way Rick had when she'd rubbed his back. "You have a good touch."

Rick stopped cold, waiting for more.

"I know a knotted muscle when I see it," Chuck said, his voice tender, "after all those hours on your table."

"You should consider becoming a therapist."

The guy chuckled. "I'm too busy falling in love with one."

"What am I going to do with you?" Mona sighed.

"Send me to another masseuse…then fall in love back."

"Keep convincing me."

"As long as it takes," he murmured.

Rick backed away, glad he hadn't burst in, blowing his cover in a rescue no one seemed to need. But now he was trapped by the lovers, who sighed and kissed and rustled around in the room until he wanted to put his hands over his ears.

To his relief, in a few minutes they departed, since Mona refused to use her massage room for anything but therapy. Thank God, since Rick had no interest in being a voyeur.

As soon as he heard the front door lock, he slid out to check the status of the delivery. From the hall, he heard only silence and through the small window in the security door he saw the truck and the crew were gone.

He headed for the salon, where he unhinged the doors on the cupboards and took digital snaps of the box labels so the task force could determine if the stuff was stolen. If it was, he'd at least proved *something* was going on.

Tomorrow, he'd find out if Blythe knew anything

about what had been loaded into her storage room. He hoped to hell not. He'd been relieved Mona wasn't doing late-night hand jobs. He liked how she looked out for Samantha, worried that she was trying too hard to change herself. Mona was right. There was nothing wrong with Samantha except her naiveté about the company she kept.

He wanted Blythe to be clean, too.

Along with Samantha, always Samantha, with her romantic views and her earnest attitude. The bookkeeper was due in the morning. He had to do everything in his power to verify whether or not the guy was legit.

The studio is prime. Darien had declared it so, so there had to be something going on at Bedroom Eyes. What the hell was it?

10

"SEEMS TO ME A MAN SHOULD find out what his lady likes and give it to her. Batteries not required," Rick drawls, standing between Donna Dominatrix and Nancy Open Nipples, tugging on the satin strings of the robe Samantha is wearing. They are alone in the window in the golden glow of the security lights and beneath the robe she is naked and aching for Rick's touch.

"What I want is you," she breathes and deliberately pulls down his zipper. His pants disappear and his arousal juts, proud and promising, and he steps close enough to trace each nipple with first his fingers, then his tongue. She writhes against the velvet length of him.

"Taste me," she commands, taking on the style of the stern mannequin in black leather behind Rick. He drops to his knees, holding her gaze the entire time, then finds her with his skillful tongue, gripping her hips, keeping her in place while she squirms and squirms and cries out and...

Samantha opened her eyes from another incredibly realistic dream starring Rick. It was so real that she patted the bed just to be sure he wasn't there beside her.

Nope. Just her, all alone, sweaty and unsatisfied, in her big empty bed. For two nights since the tiger-chaise incident, Rick had been the star of her sex dreams.

He appeared in her waking fantasies, too, especially her favorite, the velvet-tie seduction, where he teased her past endurance, while she twisted against the soft restraint, begging for mercy, begging for more.

Waking and sleeping, Rick haunted her. It was pure torture and she had to stop it somehow. But how?

Gritty-eyed and exhausted, she got up and set about getting ready for work. Pulling into the Mirror, Mirror lot early, she was surprised to see Rick's Jeep already there.

"Hey," she said, when she found him inside. "You're early."

"I had a bad night."

"Me, too." Maybe for the same reason.

He looked more exhausted than she did, his eyes bloodshot, a streak of shaving soap under one ear. Now that she thought about it, he'd been rumpled yesterday, too, and she noticed that he wore the same cargo pants as the day before.

"Neighbors had a noisy party," he said.

"Oh." So it wasn't horny dreams about her. "You've got a little…" She leaned closer and wiped off the streak of cream.

"Thanks." She could tell he didn't want her to move away. His gaze took her in like sustenance, like air or food or water.

She rubbed her fingers together and smelled the shaving soap. "Mmm. Lime and spice."

"Yeah?"

"Reminds me of you."

"Oh." Then they just stood there. This happened all the time. It was as if they kept getting snagged in each other's gravity. Every brush of arm or leg, every glance or word drew them together, hovering and circling like friendly planets.

It was killing her. Night and day, he was in her mind. Why did they have to suffer? Couldn't Rick afford a little side trip on the way to a wife?

"So, Lester Tabor is due at nine?" he asked. "Does he come into your office or work at the front desk?"

"In the office, but he won't bother us. I need to put the finishing touches on my proposal for Wendy. We're meeting her at eleven."

"Then I'll keep on eye on him for you."

"On Lester? He can handle my books in his sleep."

"You have to watch people who deal with your money, Samantha."

"You are too suspicious, Rick." He didn't crack a smile. "And don't be so deadly serious all the time. Relax. You're doing a good job for me."

That didn't seem to make him any happier. In fact, he looked positively grim.

"Maybe you need a nap," she said. "You look grouchy."

"Sorry." He forced a smile and ran his fingers through his hair. "I'll try to cheer up."

"I'm heading over to get Mona's coupon for the wedding package. If I'm not back before Lester gets here, introduce yourself. Just don't grill the poor man."

He smiled, but only a little.

Samantha found Mona on the phone, so she plopped onto the futon in the waiting area and was instantly drenched in Rick's scent—the strawberry-kiwi shampoo she'd recognized in the grocery store and his lime-spice shaving cream. Odd.

Was her obsession playing tricks on her senses? She sniffed the decorative pillow under her elbow and the smell was even stronger. Rick had been here for his massage and checked on Mona once or twice since, but he certainly hadn't hung around long enough to soak into the upholstery.

She glanced down and noticed a tiny can poking out from under the futon. Travel-size shaving cream. A picture of lime on the front. What the hell? Then she noticed a pale footprint in the futon arm that could easily match Rick's boots. Omigod.

Mona hung up and said, "What's the matter? You look like you just saw a ghost."

"I might have. I think Rick slept on your couch."

"You're kidding." Mona came closer.

"I can smell him. Here." She handed up the aromatic pillow.

"Yeah, I guess, but…"

Then she extended the can. "And this was on the floor."

"Okay, that's weird."

"And look at this." She pointed at the footprint.

"Why would Rick sleep on my couch?"

"I have no idea. If he needed a place to sleep, Bedroom Eyes at least has a real bed." What was going on?

"He didn't sleep here last night," Mona said, her face pinking up like a summer sunrise. "I know that."

"How?"

"Because I was here. Late. With Chuck."

"No! You're kidding! With Chuck?"

"That's what I said." She deepened to sunset's glow. "He had a back spasm, so I met him here for an emergency massage."

"Mona, please."

"I know, I know. I guess I was kidding myself. Which is not like me. None of this is like me."

"Sit down and tell all." Samantha patted the futon, sending more of Rick's delicious scent up to her nose. "What happened?"

Mona sat, her body angled toward Samantha. "Well, once we got here, I could tell he wasn't really in spasm. He was nervous and he'd been drinking, and he told me he wanted more than a massage from me."

"Really?"

"Then, and this is the best part, he noticed my neck was knotted and rubbed it out."

"Wait. He gave you a massage?"

"He has such a wonderful touch."

"You didn't just settle for a massage, I hope."

"No. He kissed me and I melted and we went to my place…and the rest… Well, I'm not describing the rest." Mona gave the most girlish sigh Samantha had ever heard from her down-to-earth friend.

"I'm so happy for you." She hugged her, but Mona's embrace didn't have her usual relaxed lushness. "What's the matter?"

"I don't know what to think now."

"Don't think. Just feel. Be in love."

"It's not that simple. I broke my rule and now I feel like I'm falling through space. I don't know what I'm doing."

"You're falling in love. You're not supposed to know what you're doing. Just enjoy it, go wild."

"Like you, you mean?" Mona teased.

"That's just it. I did go wild. I went for it with Rick. He didn't have a girlfriend—you were right about that— but it's worse. He has principles. He wants sex to mean something."

Mona laughed. "It does, hon. That's why I'm freaked out and why your shoulders are up around your ears. It means something to you, too. Turn around and let me do some trigger-point work while you tell me what happened."

Samantha turned and Mona dug into her shoulders, while she told her sad tale of the one man on the planet who wasn't happy just to have a good time in bed.

"Ooh, he's deep," Mona mused as she pressed out knots and relieved twists.

"And mysterious. That's why he seems so perfect. I can imagine him as anyone I want him to be."

"Have you considered forgetting your fantasies and just getting involved with him? Let it mean something."

"I'm not ready for that. Relationships confuse me. I forget who I am, slip into the guy's world, see myself through his eyes."

"You mean like with Barry?"

"Yeah."

"You didn't know what you wanted then. Now you do. And maybe what you want is Rick."

"I have the hots for the guy. I hardly know him."

"So get to know him."

"He's a private person."

"At least find out why he's sleeping here." Mona patted her, signifying she was finished.

Samantha turned back to look at her. "Yes. That I'll do."

"Go for it." Mona's dark eyes twinkled knowingly.

"You, too. Mona. With Chuck. Think of all the fun you can have, all the adventures and erotic pleasures."

"I'm not into that, Sammi. I picture us in my hammock feeding each other strawberries from my garden, sun tea at our elbows, books on our chests, reading to each other."

"So your fantasies are more domestic than mine. Take a couple ice cubes out of those teas and trace each other's naked chests while you're rocking in the hammock and you're there."

She sighed. "I don't know. I'm just…well…happy."

"You look it, hon. You're glowing right now. And me without my camera."

"Maybe one day we'll come in for a couples shot. We're taking it slow for now."

"Just don't take each other for granted or get into a rut or give up who you are to be with him."

"I would never do that," Mona said.

"No. You're right. That's my stunt." Samantha sighed, happy for Mona and, somewhere deep, wishing she was ready for love, too.

"Maybe give yourself a chance with Rick," Mona said, reading her mind.

"No. He wants to settle down and I need to break out. We're not in the same place in our lives at all."

"Maybe you've already broken out, Sammi. What about that?"

"One hot moment on the tiger chaise does not a wild sex life make, Mona. Rick and I work well together and that ought to be enough. If I could just get him out of my fantasies. It's just that he seems so mysterious and sexy."

"Ah, the dangerous stranger."

"Exactly. If I could think of him as just a regular guy who pulls his pants on one incredibly muscular leg at a time, I'd be fine."

"You have a crush, you're saying? So get to know him better, find out his warts and bad habits and short-comings. Make him ordinary."

"You're right. That's exactly what I have to do. Reduce the mystery factor and the lust will fade. Thanks, Mona." She hugged her. "And I'm very happy for you."

Mona smiled her gratitude. "So, let me get the coupon. Your presentation is today?"

"Yep. And if we score this account, I think it'll start the momentum we need. Rick's great on the phone, too. He's a fabulous business partner." *Business* partner, not *sex* partner.

She had to keep that in mind from here on out.

No matter what temptations came along.

RICK HELD THE DOOR of Wendy's Weddings for their departure and watched Samantha shake the wedding planner's hand with both of her own. "Thank you so, so much." She seemed about to explode with excitement.

"You're very welcome," Wendy said. "Really."

"We'll fax over the final notes when we get back," Samantha said. "And, again, it was *such* a pleasure to meet you."

"Same here," Wendy said, smiling back, caught up in Samantha's enthusiasm.

Samantha passed out the door under his arm, bouncing on the balls of her feet, striding so fast he had to gallop to catch up. The instant they rounded the building, she surprised him by throwing her arms around his neck. "We did it!"

He twirled her, relishing the feel of her body, small and sweet in his arms. God help him, he dipped his nose into her hair and inhaled. Cinnamon, flowers and home.

She slid to the ground and pushed out of his arms, her eyes shining so bright it was hard to look straight at them. "I can't believe we did it."

"Of course we did. You had a terrific proposal."

"Your idea of including locket-sized photos was genius."

"I got it from you." He nodded at where her locket bounced against her cleavage. Whenever he looked at it, he thought of her radiant face inside the gold frame.

"The point is that it made Wendy choose the pricier option. We *must* celebrate. Lunch at Renzio's. And champagne. On the company."

"You can't afford champagne. I've seen your books, remember?"

"If you won't take a commission, then you're taking lunch. This will mean ten high-end clients a month at least. Wendy runs big ads in the glossy mags that go free to rich neighborhoods. Once it gets out what we're doing with Wendy, other planners will be easy to sign on. First benchmark—check! I am so happy!"

She hugged him again and this time she stilled, leaned back to look into his eyes, testing. *Do you feel what I do?*

God, yes. In spades, in neon, in letters across the sky. He pulled away fast and held the driver-side door for her.

Turned out Samantha couldn't drive worth shit when she was excited. He grabbed the overhead grip when she roared onto Highland without a sideways glance at oncoming traffic. Babbling about details that remained to be done, she ran a yellow light and barely slowed for a stop sign. He couldn't help slamming his feet onto the floorboards.

She glanced at him. "You want to drive, Rick?"

"Just take it easy. This is a residential zone and you just blew by a stop sign."

"So, what, now you're a cop?"

You got me. "Traffic laws are our friends."

"I'll take the ticket. I don't care. I'll take two. I can afford them now."

He chuckled. "Sammi, I think you could burn

rubber in a school yard and still talk your way out of the citation."

"You called me Sammi." She shot him a look.

"Eyes on the road." He motioned for her to look ahead.

"I like that. It means we're friends."

"Sure," he said, adding, "Sammi," like a fool. It was worth it to see the smile sweep across her face and light her eyes.

She jerked into the restaurant's driveway and zipped to the valet stand. "Life's too short to self park," she said, jumping out and producing her key for the attendant.

Rick just grinned. She was such a ball of energy. He liked soaking in her sun. He'd never thought of himself as gloomy, but compared to her, he was a Portland sky.

In minutes, they were seated in a richly upholstered booth at the back of the restaurant. The table was set with linen, two sizes of crystal glasses and an entire drawer of utensils decorated the double plates trimmed in gold. The quiet murmurs of the well-heeled crowd lent an atmosphere of discretion and class.

The wine steward, all unctuous servitude, beamed greedily when Samantha announced they *needed* a bottle of champagne.

Rick insisted on the least expensive in the wine *book*—it had too many pages to be called a *list*—and soon he and Samantha were looking into each other's eyes, while the man drizzled gold bubbles into their glasses.

The instant the steward left, Samantha lifted her flute. "Here's to us," she said and Rick didn't even fight his grin. He tapped her glass, the sound ringing out like a warning bell. *Remember the case. Remember who you are.*

Hell, he flat-out liked being in Samantha's orbit—a cool moon to her fiery sun.

"I'm so glad I hired you," she said. "Without you, I wouldn't have made that sale."

"I just backed your play," he said.

"It was more than that. I was nervous and too eager."

"You were just enthusiastic." He loved that about her. She was as bubbly and warm as the liquid warming his insides, making him want to swallow the bottle in a long gulp, take her in his arms and make love to her.

"You moderated me," she said. "Plus you have that knowing smile. Like we had so much to offer that Wendy was lucky we could squeeze her into our schedule."

"You do offer a lot, Samantha."

"You, too, Rick. As an employee…and as a person. I mean…for the woman you're looking for…that you haven't found yet." She went pink and sucked down champagne. "Anyway, thanks for all you did."

"I'm happy to help," he said. He would make sure she came out of all this unharmed, dammit. Would he bend the rules for her? His gut burned. He'd cross that bridge when he came to it.

"You fit in so easily," she continued. "You've taken on extra duties. I feel like we're…partners, you know? That you truly want me to succeed."

"I'm glad you…trust me," he said, though that made him queasy.

"I do." Except her blue eyes darted away from his. She had doubts. "Can I ask you a question?"

"Sure." He braced himself. *Who are you really?* If she asked him straight out, he'd tell her, he knew. And that would be trouble. He'd just have to deal with—

"Have you been sleeping at Mirror, Mirror?"

"Have I…?" Shit. She'd figured it out.

"Because—" she fumbled in her handbag and held out his shaving-cream can "—I found this in Mona's studio."

Must have fallen out of his pocket when he'd jumped up last night. "Yeah," he said. "I did sleep there." How much truth could he tell her and not jeopardize the case? "I've had…problems…at my place."

"What kind of problems?"

His landlord maybe? Couldn't play the girlfriend angle. Plumbing out? Eviction? He'd already tried noisy neighbors. Damn. He needed a good lie…. "I thought it would be good for security at the center. There've been robberies in the area." This happened to be true.

"Really? Robberies?"

"I heard that, yeah." From the job, though, not media accounts.

She blinked, clearly not believing him, but not angry, either, or suspicious, which is how she should feel. She looked worried about him. "I could advance you some salary. Heck, let's call it a commission. I know you don't want that, but…"

She felt *sorry* for him, for chrissake. He couldn't bear her pity, even if it got him off the spot. "I'll be fine. I've got it handled."

"Look, Rick. I'm your friend. I'm happy to help you, if—"

"I don't want your money." He hadn't intended to snap at her, but her sympathy made him feel exposed, as if he were about to take a knife in the chest from a surprise assault.

"I just want to help." She looked hurt.

Damn. "I don't mean to be harsh. I'm just—"

"A private person, I know." She spoke softly, wounded by his withdrawal, and he couldn't think of a word to say. "But if we're friends, we should know each other better. Help each other... Anyway..." She shrugged and he felt helpless to respond.

Luckily, their food arrived and they busied themselves eating for a bit, speaking only about the food, which smelled great, but now tasted like dust in his mouth.

After a while, Samantha spoke in a low voice. "At least use the bed in Bedroom Eyes, Rick. Mona's futon is hard as stone." She was looking out for him still.

"Thanks, Sammi..." Her nickname came out so easy now. "If you don't mind me staying there for a night or two. Until I work things out at my place."

The lie came out so smoothly. He hated hurting her. Maybe he could make it up to her—do something they'd both enjoy that wouldn't jeopardize the case....

"Listen," he said, capturing her hands under his, "I'd like to pay you back for all you've taught me. How about you come with me on an outdoor shoot?"

"Really?" She blinked, startled. "That sounds fun." She looked down at where he'd covered her fingers, then up at him. "When and where?"

He squeezed her hands, then decided that was a bad idea, since what he wanted to do was bring her palms to his mouth and kiss each soft surface in turn. He let go and dropped his hands to his lap. "Say Sunday at Oak Creek? I know a great spot."

He realized he wasn't just throwing her a bone. He wanted her to come. He wanted to take her to the red cliffs he loved, stand with her beside the swirling creek and beneath the trembling aspens. He wanted to show her his meadow, watch her face when she took it in, breathe in her smell mixed with pine and green and the ironstone aroma of flowing water.

Hell, they deserved a Sunday, didn't they? They both worked hard. How bad could it be? *You want her alone in your favorite place, you chump.* That made it very bad, but when she said, "I'd love to," her eyes shiny with champagne and excitement, he hardly felt guilty at all.

11

SITTING IN RENZIO'S, Rick's eyes smoldering at her, her body tingly from champagne, an outdoor shoot with Rick had sounded glorious. Especially coming on the heels of his harsh refusal of help. *Get out of my life* followed by *Come on in, the water's fine.*

But that was two days ago. Now it was three o'clock in the morning on a *Sunday*—the one day she slept in— and the idea of tromping through the woods sounded like hell on earth.

She couldn't even hope for her sex-under-an-open-sky fantasy, since she'd determined to think of Rick only as her assistant.

What she should be doing is trolling the brunch buffet at the Phoenician, where she could snag a visiting CEO. Brunches didn't kick off until eleven. She could get some *sleep*.

She stared at the digital display—she had a half-hour before she had to shower. Her finger bumped the picture Rick had taken of her. She'd framed it and put it on her bedside table as another reminder of what she wanted. In it, she looked so ready. But not for Rick. Not anymore.

Today she planned to learn so much about him he'd stop being fantasy material. However, since she had thirty minutes to kill, one more sexy little story wouldn't hurt.

She lay back, closed her eyes and let the picture form in her mind. There he stood—Rick as her highwayman, all in black—standing in her bedroom doorway. Samantha spread out under her sheet and let the fantasy unroll in her mind.

"Why have you come?" she asks the highwayman, breathless with need and relief.

"To claim you, to make you mine, to brand you with my mouth, my hands, my cock." His voice is fierce. But she knows his anger is not for her. He is furious because his passion for her is beyond his control. Why else would he come when he risks prison, torture, death? Because he must *have her. Without her, his life means nothing to him.*

"But we agreed that you must go," she says. "It is not safe for you to stay. They will arrest and hang you."

"To hell with what we agreed. To hell with what they will do to me. I will have you now." He strides to her bed. His eyes burn as if they will brand her, too. Brand her as his until he has his fill.

He straddles her needy body—in her fever, she's thrown back the coverlet, her nightgown tossed off because of the heat—and he stretches her arms overhead, clasping her wrists to keep her in place. He lowers his head and takes her mouth with his hungry lips.

She struggles against his hold on her, but not for long. She revels in his power over her, because she knows her power over him is equal, if not stronger. His kiss deepens, liquefying her. She feels his hard need against her belly and she rubs against him. She is desperate, she is wanton, she is...coming.

Samantha's eyes flew open. Someone was leaning on her doorbell. She looked at her clock—4:00 a.m. It was

Rick, right on time. She'd fallen asleep in the middle of her very last Rick fantasy.

"Hang on," she shouted, leaping out of bed. She hopped into her shorts, yanked on a tank top and ran out of her bedroom.

Scurrying for the door, she smoothed her hair with one hand and scrubbed her teeth with an index finger.

Rick buzzed again.

"Just a sec!"

Buzz.

She twisted the knob and yanked open the door. "I'm here, okay?"

"Hey, there." Rick looked completely relaxed and hotter than hell in a khaki vest over a plaid shirt with rolled sleeves and he held two to-go-cups from Starbucks. He took a lazy, appreciative survey of her body. "You'll want jeans and long sleeves for a while," he said, handing her one of the coffees. "Two creams, no sugar, right?"

"Perfect." He'd noticed how she liked her coffee. The idea warmed her as much as the cup in her palm. She backed up, letting him in. "I was up earlier, but I drifted back to sleep." *Imagining you as a dangerous highwayman.* "Do I have time to shower?" She sipped the coffee, though she hardly needed caffeine. One look at the man had adrenaline pounding through her veins.

"Not if we want the best light. I have a spot in mind for sunrise." Early morning and dusk were best for outdoor shots, she knew. Full sun offered harsh shadows.

"Let me brush my teeth and pull on pants."

She rushed through basic hygiene, slipped 501s over her shorts, a chambray shirt over her tank, and yanked on socks and hiking boots. She'd packed her camera gear the night before at least.

In the dim living room, she found Rick studying the portrait of her parents on the mantel over her small fireplace.

"You take this?" He turned to her.

"Yes. And they weren't happy about it, either."

"They look a little—"

"Stiff? Disapproving? And that's on a good day." She shook her head, then caught his questioning look. "Let's just say their opinion about the proper way to live is carved in stone."

"So they wouldn't like you splashing around, making waves?"

"Not really, no." They wouldn't like her studio and they wouldn't like her plan to sleep with more than one man, either. Or any man, for that matter, without a ring on her finger.

"You look nice, by the way," Rick said. "Should have my camera. First rule of outdoor photography—always be ready. Good subjects don't hold still."

"I'm a mess," she said, pushing back her tangled curls.

"You look great. Soft and warm and fresh from bed." His eyes held longing. "That your bag?" He nodded at her canvas satchel.

"That's it."

He leaned forward to grab it, then went to hold the door for her.

He held the Jeep door, too, and waited for her to get comfortable before he closed it. Such a gentleman. The truck was clean and orderly and smelled of him. She was still inhaling greedily when he climbed in beside her.

He smiled—had he caught her?—but didn't say anything, just put his coffee in the holder and started the car.

"Will we be using four-wheel drive?" she said, taking a sip of the rich blend, hoping there wouldn't be a lot of hiking involved.

"No. I thought about taking my other car—it's more fun to drive—but I just painted it and don't want scrapes."

"What kind of car is it?"

"A 1969 Firebird 400." He sighed with pleasure.

"*Oooh*. Muscle car. Runs on testosterone and rocket fuel, right? What color? Let me guess. Black or red."

"Red." He smiled. "Same model I rebuilt in high school."

He'd been wild in high school, she remembered. "So, you're reliving your youth?"

"No guy grows out of his first love." Rick grinned that self-mocking smile she liked so much.

"What kind of hell did you raise in high school, anyway?" she asked. Might as well launch her plan to make Rick more ordinary by getting to know him better.

"Nothing too terrible," he said. "Drinking…drag racing…minor vandalism. Borrowed a car once and got arrested, but that was a misunderstanding—my buddy's stepdad hadn't actually okayed the use of his Corvette."

"An easy mistake to make, I'm sure. What man would object to a joyride in his expensive sports car?"

"You see our problem." He nodded, his grin spreading.

"Anything else?"

"We built a bomb and set it off in the desert. That was a close one. It didn't go off right away, so I volunteered to check. Luckily it blew before I got close enough to lose anything vital."

"You're lucky you didn't get arrested for that."

"Yeah. That was before the Corvette incident. I

stayed clear of illegal stunts after that one. Couldn't stand making my mom cry."

That was sweet. She pondered what Rick must have been like as a bad boy. Sexy as hell, no doubt. He probably had girls falling all over him. She remembered what he'd said about living down his brother. "Did you resent your brother? For being perfect?"

He shot her a look. "Why would I? I loved him." She wasn't surprised. Of course he'd been jealous as a kid—who wouldn't be—but he'd pushed past it. She'd sensed a rock-solid loyalty in Rick. When he swore to love, honor and obey the woman he married, he'd mean every word of that vow.

This was no way to make him less attractive. She had to look for warts and flaws and bad habits. He probably had tons.

"I packed us lunch, too," he said. "Hope you like whole-grain bread and I got a nice merlot."

Lord. Not only had he planned lunch, he'd planned a quality lunch. "Love it. So, after you got arrested, you straightened up?"

"That was later. After my big brother died."

"Oh. I'm so sorry, Rick. What happened?"

"He got shot by a drug dealer. A client. Brian was a defense attorney."

"How terrible. And your parents must have been—"

"Wrecked. Yeah. It's been five years and they're just now coming around. I keep them busy, take them out. Anyway, we're about to take some great pictures." He rolled a shoulder, clearly wanting to change the subject.

"I'm looking forward to it," she said.

"Sedona is unique because there are three different

life zones within twenty minutes of each other—desert to woodland."

"Interesting," she said.

"Now if we were serious, we'd set up a blind and camp out so we could catch some nocturnal action." He shot her a look, checking her reaction.

"Camping's not my thing." She shuddered. There was a wart. He was a camper. "My idea of camping is when the Hyatt only has basic cable."

"Come on. You'd love it. Well, maybe not love it. But you'd find it worthwhile. Overnight outdoors really lets you fit into the setting." He told her about the time he'd spent three days in a creek-side blind just to catch a shot of ringtail cats, about the great blue heron who'd allowed him within a few feet after many cramped, mucky hours, and the prairie falcon, rare in the Arizona desert, he'd surprised from atop a saguaro.

She was surprised how chatty he was. She barely had to ask a question before a new story rushed out. Of course, these were photography stories, not personal stories, but he seemed so relaxed and comfortable with her it made her grin.

Meanwhile, her attraction hummed along, steady as the Jeep's engine propelling them toward the red Sedona hills.

As dawn lit the sky, Rick pulled off at a lookout point and they took pictures of the lacy tangle of mesquite, rim-lit saguaro sentinels and high breaks of wispy cottonwoods that decorated the Verde Valley.

Rick let her try his 500 mm lens. She was stunned to pick out a Harris's hawk soaring over the ridgeline, the image crisp enough she could detect the white underfur on the rodent in its claws.

"That was amazing," she said. She turned abruptly

toward him, surprising him, and she got the impression he'd been breathing her in. That made her smile. He liked how she smelled, too.

They climbed back into the Jeep and, after a few more miles, Rick turned onto a narrow dirt road.

"Are we close?" she asked.

"Getting there."

This wasn't so bad, even with the early hour. They'd had a nice companionable drive. Now they would walk a short distance, take some shots, eat lunch and head home. She was an indoor girl all the way—in her recreation as well as her photography.

The winding dirt road dwindled to nothing and Rick parked.

"We're there?" she asked hopefully.

"Now we hike." He lifted a backpack from behind his seat.

"How far?" She swallowed.

"Not too far." He fished sunscreen from a pocket, opened the lid and squirted some onto her palm. "Don't skimp and rub it in thoroughly."

Two hours later, sweaty and miserable, Samantha took a gulp of the water bottle Rick thrust at her. "Are we even close?" she asked. So much for the quick jaunt to a shady spot she'd envisioned. Where the hell was Rick's precious meadow?

"Soon," Rick said. Again. He put a hand to her back in support. "Where's the intrepid lady who wants to splash around in life?"

"That's figuratively splashing around, pal," she said and decided to buck up. Ignoring the blisters, the blackberry-thorn scrapes, the mosquito bites and the sting from her brush with a prickly pear, she pushed away from Rick's support and marched faster, her mud-caked boots squishing with each step. Running from a bumblebee the size of a VW, she'd slipped off the creek rocks and gotten wet to her knees.

At least they'd gotten some good shots. Rick had spotted a small flock of wild turkeys and had insisted they wait silently in the itchy grass until the birds had gotten close enough for a full-frame shot of a tom, feathers spread in pride.

The secret to wildlife shots was patience. She'd heard that before, of course, but watching Rick work, she realized how true it was and how absolutely great Rick was at waiting and waiting and waiting and waiting.

That was not her style. She preferred to manage a photograph, arrange everything to happen her way on her time line, control every aspect of the light and shadow and angle and movement.

At least she didn't need patience to get some great shots of the red cliffs rising around them or the variegated water of Oak Creek. But now she was tired and hot and hungry and Rick kept on like a buff and brawny Energizer Bunny with a backpack instead of a drum.

She shaded her eyes and watched him mount yet one more hill. God, he made it seem easy, moving with effortless grace. Her little digital felt like an anvil after all this walking. From the top, he leaned down to offer her a boost.

"Maybe you should just leave me here to die."

"Come on. It's worth it. Trust me."

"Okay." She grabbed a tree root and yanked herself up, her calves burning, her lungs screaming. Three more painful steps and she reached the top.

She looked down and caught her breath. Spread out before her was a clearing surrounded by ghostly white aspens, the ground covered with dusky grass. Red cliffs climbed straight up on either side of the creek that gurgled, blue-green with depth, to the left. The scene was so rich with color and calm and beauty, she could hardly take it all in. "It's gorgeous," she finally said.

Rick was looking at her as if this place were a gift he'd been dying to give her. "Worth muddy boots and a few scrapes?"

"Even mosquito bites and cactus rash."

He smiled, then went still, pointing at something behind her. "Check it out."

She turned and had to stare for a while until she realized there were two coyotes on the far side of the creek. This wasn't the first time Rick had spotted an animal she'd had trouble distinguishing from the busy blur of rocks and trees. He had a great outdoor eye. "Oh," she whispered.

Soundlessly, Rick lifted out the camera with the 500 mm lens and handed it to her. Through the big lens, she could see the streaks of brown and yellow in the gray fur, which was as wispy as feathers around the coyotes' muzzles and their eyes were bright with intelligence.

She held her breath, focused, altered the f-stop to blur the background, shifted her angle a little for a better composition. If she moved a few feet closer, she'd like the shot more. She started to move.

"Take it now. They're off," Rick whispered, his other camera to his eye. He fired off several shots.

Sure enough, before she'd adjusted focus, the coyotes were gone. "Damn."

"You'll get the next ones," he said. *Always be ready,* he'd instructed her. Another secret to wildlife shots. "Let's go down."

They trekked down to the meadow and she contented herself with some still-life shots—more her speed—catching a lovely glow on some season-worn blackberries.

"Hey," Rick whispered, pointing up at the cliff. A long-legged bird poised on a narrow ledge above them. "Gray heron," he whispered, catching it on the wing like he'd read the impulse to fly in its brain. She knew it wasn't coincidence that he was getting far more animal shots than she was. His skill was obvious in everything he did. He could switch cameras and lenses in seconds flat and used minimum equipment to save weight. He'd brought just two—one with the big telephoto and a monopod he'd retooled himself—and only a couple of filters. He used molding putty so they could be attached to both cameras. And no Velcro anywhere to maintain silence.

Rick motioned her to the creek bank, where he set his camera low on the monopod and got on his belly. She joined him, aching, mucky and miserable, but trying for as much cheer as she could manage. Meanwhile, Rick practically glowed.

"How come you look so good?" she said. "Your shirt-sleeves are still creased."

"It's a gift, babe. What can I say?" She loved his grin. She snapped a photo of him. He was in his element. She was lost.

She took more photos, snapping a shot of water streaming over silver-flecked granite while tiny black minnows formed an attentive semicircle below, waiting for dinner or maybe a show?

Something buzzed near her head, then banged the edge of her ear. She tried to wave it away, but it went straight into her ear, tickling and buzzing away. "Ooh, ow, ouch!"

She rose to her knees, bent her head to the side and banged her ear, trying to knock the thing out of there.

"What's wrong?"

"A bug! There's a big bug…help!"

"Let me see." Rick grabbed her head, peered into her ear, flicked something and the buzzing ceased.

"What was it? It sounded huge."

He held up his index finger. A tiny beetle took off. "Your ear amplified the sound." He was clearly trying not to grin.

"It could have laid eggs. I could have bugs eating a path to my brain in a few hours."

"Only on the sci-fi channel." He wiped her cheek free of dust or mud or algae, his fingers gentle on her skin. Then he took a step backward and aimed his camera at her.

"What? You're making a poster for survivalists?"

"You look great." He snapped a photo. "Like you belong out here." He held her gaze for a long moment.

"You're just trying to cheer me up. Look at you. You don't even have any mud on your boots."

"That's an old trick. Don't run from bees."

"They weren't chasing you." She slugged his firm shoulder.

"That's right. It's your own fault for smelling so sweet." He smiled so warmly her heart lifted. "So, are you hungry? Shall we eat?"

"Sounds great," she said.

In a shady spot, they unrolled the thin blanket Rick had carried in his pack, removed their boots and socks and Samantha peeled off her jeans and long-sleeved shirt.

She caught Rick watching her, rapt. He flushed, then turned to his backpack, where he lifted out the food.

They were soon eating sandwiches of smoked ham,

goat cheese, spicy mustard and baby spinach on multi-grain bread, munching blue-corn chips and drinking a lusty merlot.

Being outdoors made everything taste remarkable. She relished every delicious bite of moist sandwich and crisp chip and loved the rich wine.

She finished her sandwich and watched Rick ball up the discarded plastic and paper and pack everything away, glancing at her, adding to her wine. He seemed so easygoing, his usual tension completely gone, as if he had nothing to hide anymore. She liked him even more, dammit.

"You seem so different out here," she said. "More open. You laugh more." His grin was so broad it was almost childlike.

"It's not just being out here," he said, hesitating before he finished. "It's being here with you."

"Rick…" She was so touched she didn't know what to say.

"I wanted you to see all this." He waved out at the distant creek and the high red rocks. "I knew you'd like it, too."

This trip to outdoor hell was suddenly worth every miserable minute. "It's beautiful. Thank you."

"Why don't you lie down?" he said, patting her camera bag, as if it were a pillow. He snugged his own against it and lay down himself.

Happily hazy from the wine, she joined him. Ignoring the lump of the lens under her skull, the rocks digging into her back through the blanket, she noticed instead the way the sunlight came through the aspen leaves, how the breeze lifted her hair from her forehead, cooling the sweat on her face and how close Rick lay beside her. Their arms almost touched and their chests rose and fell in time. The intimacy was as cozy and warm as a hot bath.

"So what do you think of outdoor photography?" he asked, turning his face toward her on its canvas pillow.

She turned to him, too, liking his warm breath on her face. "It's different than studio work. Quieter. Messier. In some ways faster, in others slower. You could wait all day and never get a decent shot."

"Timing is everything. True."

"Or you could sleep in and miss it altogether."

"But when you get that shot it's worth it all." He gave a sleepy smile of pure pleasure. He'd shown himself to be infinitely patient when he showed her what to do. She imagined he'd put up with a lot from the woman he loved. He'd give her the benefit of the doubt, lavish all the attention she could stand. Lucky woman.

"The best part is you don't have to please anyone but yourself," he continued. "You take the shots you want the way you want them."

"Not like with portraits, huh?" she said. "Pleasing the client is the whole point of a studio."

"Outdoor work isn't so invasive. I'll never get used to staring into people's hearts like that. Seeing their sadness, their fear, their hopes." He shuddered in pretend agony.

"But that's why they come to us—so we can see them as they really are—and capture them on film. That's what I love."

"Yeah. I get that about you."

"Feeling how you feel, Rick, it seems odd that you'd want this job. I thought that from the first day."

"I'm learning…like I said. I wanted to learn from you." There was that flicker in his face again, like he was hiding something from her. His green eyes went opaque, like a light doused, and his emotions shut down like blinds dropped hard.

"Do I make you nervous? Asking questions?"

"Not really. You make me think."

But it was more than that, she could tell. Energy changed between them, shifted, like the clouds easing by overhead, the leaves shivering in the whispering breeze. She had to push. She had to have more. "So what do I make you think about?"

"About who I am, what I'm doing, I guess."

And what are you doing? What do you want to do?

She wanted to get naked. Still. Would it ever stop?

"Cumulus...with an undercoat of nimbus," he murmured, looking past her. He'd made it sound like a sex act.

She turned to see a pile of clouds as fluffy as mashed potatoes with dark streaks beneath.

"Rain's on the way. Maybe by tonight."

"So, you're a meteorologist, too?" she said.

"I have to know my palette—sunlight and cloud cover."

"You do know clouds, that's for sure. That shot of the gold-blasted ones in your portfolio made me melt."

"Don't say *melt*," he said, pushing up on his elbow to look down at her. "I've seen you do that."

Arousal surged through her. "You made me do that." For an instant, she thought he might kiss her. Instead, he pushed her hair away from her cheek.

The breeze blew across her face and she realized she smelled faintly of dirt. "No bees will chase me now. I smell like the creek."

"No you don't." He dipped his nose into her hair and breathed in. "You smell like you always do."

"Were you smelling my hair when we took those shots of Verde Valley?"

He chuckled. "You got me. I couldn't resist. I can't tell if it's your shampoo or your hair or your perfume or just your skin. You just smell…great."

"I like how you smell, too. And I love your eyes. They're the exact color of the moss up here, did you know that?"

"I didn't."

"But they change color, too. From moss to emerald to olive-green."

"Your eyes are so blue they almost hurt to look at."

"Really?"

"Oh, yeah." He studied her. "That pillow didn't come close to the color." He slid his gaze away and it seemed to snag on her arm. "Mosquito bites," he said frowning, counting down her arm with a gentle finger. "Two… three…four."

"They're all over." She held up her other arm for his count, his tickling finger, which she wanted to keep counting down her body.

"I should have thought of repellant. Mosquitoes don't usually bother with me. Hang on. I'll be right back."

She lay back, eyes closed, waiting for her man to return to her. With a healing herb? Or maybe a flower for her hair? She heard his footsteps, felt him crouch beside her, then something clammy smacked her thigh.

"Hey!" She sat up. He'd slapped mud on two of her bites. Smack. More mud. "Cut that out!"

"It's a poultice. It'll draw out toxins."

"It's mud and it'll make a mess." She grabbed some from her thigh and tossed it at his chest.

"Hey…I don't have any bites." He gripped her wrists

and wrestled her to the blanket, looking down at her as though he wanted to just take her. His moss-green eyes lit with emerald fire.

Go for it. She liked feeling captured by him, wanted his mouth on her, his thighs trapping hers.

But he backed off, released her hands and rolled onto his side, bracing his face in a palm. "Sorry I got you all bit up."

"It was worth it. To get to know you better."

"I guess that's good." But he didn't seem so sure.

"Of course it is. It's great." She would not let him withdraw again. "Tell me more. Tell me a secret, Rick, and I'll tell you one."

"A secret?" He frowned.

"Nothing big. Just a little thing I'd love to know about you." She watched him start to object. "Here's mine. Remember that photo you took of me on the chaise? I framed a print of it and put it by my bed."

"Oh, yeah?"

"Yeah. To motivate myself to keep striving."

"What's wrong with who you are now?"

She blinked, startled by his question, and a truth pushed through. "If I don't keep trying, I'm afraid I'll just settle. Be ordinary."

"You could never be ordinary, Samantha. You are amazing." The look on his face warmed her like a sudden smile after deep sorrow.

"Now it's your turn," she said, sensing a shift between them. "What's your secret, Rick?"

She placed her hand on his bare forearm, relishing the quiver of muscle there. These very muscles could wrap around her so tightly she'd have trouble drawing a breath. She wanted that so much. Her whole plan for the day had gone up in smoke. Now that she knew him better, she wanted him more, not less.

"Okay," Rick said. "Here it is. I've never wanted a woman as much as I want you right now."

His gaze seared through her, white-hot and demanding.

Then take me. The words rose in her mind, but she couldn't say them. The next move was Rick's.

She held her breath, trembling like the leaves overhead, and watched Rick decide.

12

TAKE ME. Rick read Samantha's desire in her eyes, which had gone from clear blue to as smoky as a hot spring. Her lips parted, her tongue traced the inside of her bottom lip and her body trembled beneath his.

She plain glowed, as she had in the shot he'd taken of her in the studio. She was right about that double image that appeared when you captured the person entirely.

He'd never known a woman quite like her. Sweet and shy and eager and bold all at once.

Make love to her.

He wanted to. More than anything, he wanted to bury himself in her lush body, her smart mind, her lively soul. Maybe then he'd be able to think straight enough to do his job.

It's not about the job. You plain want her.

The truth was a gut punch he had no choice but to acknowledge. He took in the sight of her, the way she trembled, and panted, and how her smell mixed with the scent of soil and green things and water in some exotic opium that soaked in deep, making him drunk with it.

And just like that his double life melted away and he was simply Rick West with a woman he was falling for. The instant he lowered his mouth to hers, all the rules, the straight lines he hung on to, went fuzzy and soft and he had to have her.

Samantha kissed back, her tongue insistent, tangling with his. She shoved her fingers into his hair and gripped his skull as if she feared he'd quit on her.

He felt like laughing because he wasn't about to stop. Not now. This felt too right out under the open skies he loved.

Was he slipping into old habits, when he selfishly went for whatever he wanted, screw the consequences, the way Brian had lived? A warning slammed through him, but he ignored it in favor of the wonder of Samantha's mouth, the give of her body, his conviction that this time he'd get inside. All the way.

Bracing himself on his elbows, he cupped her breasts. They felt good through the soft cloth, but he wanted her naked, so he pushed up on her shirt.

She sat up and took over, whipping off the tank top. Her creamy breasts peeked above a bra, which she unclipped and flung onto the blanket, looking simultaneously like she wanted to stick out her chest in pride and cross her arms over them in modesty.

"You're beautiful," he said simply and wrapped his palms around the lush flesh she offered him.

"Oh. That feels so good." She leaned her head back, pushed her breasts into his hands and closed her eyes.

He ran his thumbs over her nipples, liking how they shrank to needy buds so fast. Was she wet between the legs? He'd tasted her there and wanted to again. And he wanted inside her. To take her from above. To lie beneath her rocking body. To thrust into her from the side and behind, and every way there was to be with a woman.

For now he settled for taking a nipple deep into his mouth, the way he knew she liked it.

She gasped and her body shook so badly, he stopped and wrapped her in his arms, steadying her. He felt her heart pounding so hard and her ribs swelled and receded in a panicked hunt for oxygen.

What about protection? He hadn't thought of that. "I think I have a condom…in my wallet," he said. God, he hoped so.

"Oh, yes." She leaned back, her eyes wide. "I forgot. I'm on the pill though. If you're safe?"

"I'm good. Safe, I mean."

They didn't have to stop. Thank God.

"Good. Because I want to feel all of you," she said, her eyes a sharp blue sting of heat.

"And I want in," he said. Desire roared through him like the Firebird on a straight stretch, fast and hard, hot and furious. Forgetting grace and slow care, he went for her shorts, flipping open the clasp, yanking down the zipper.

She lifted her ass so he could get the damn things off and he tried not to scrape her skin in his rush to get her naked and in his hands.

He made short work of his own clothes, too, then moved to take her down to the blanket.

She stopped him with a hand on his arm and stared deliberately at his cock, her pupils flaring. She reached out a sweet hand and clasped him, sliding her fingers up and down.

"That's good," he said, rocking into her palm, holding himself back, needing to make sure she had full pleasure first.

He lowered her to the blanket while she stroked him with her fingers, cupping his balls with the other hand.

He looked down at her, lust pounding through him, his

restraint all but gone. *Easy. Take your time. Make it good for her.* When had he ever wanted a woman so much?

"I want to touch you," he said, taking her fingers from his cock and putting her hands around his neck, needing to slow it down so he could take care of her right. He slid his hand up her thigh and she spread her legs for him the way she had on that bench in the studio.

"Please. Touch me," she breathed and he dipped his fingers where she was swollen and so wet. "Yes, like that. I like that." Her eyes rolled back and she relaxed into what he was doing. She trusted him and that made him want to please and protect her.

She felt familiar and new at the same time. He stroked her slowly and she cried out, then whimpered, writhing under his fingers. Reading her body, he moved faster, adding pressure, sensing she was close.

"S-s-stop," she managed to say, fighting for words, stopping his hand. "I want you inside me."

"Yeah," he said, his blood surging, grateful for the invitation. He situated himself over her parted thighs, nudged at her entrance, then plunged deep into her. She felt good—a perfect fit—smooth and tight and holding on.

"Finally," she breathed. Sparks flared and subsided in her eyes like embers in a campfire.

He pulled out and pumped in deep.

"That's it… Keep doing…that."

He repeated the move, loving the length of her and the way she held on to him with her sex, squeezed him, made him hers.

He'd never wanted to be inside a woman so much. And it was even better once he was there.

"Ohohoh…I want…so much…I want…." She kept

struggling to speak, to tell him how she felt, what she wanted. Sweet.

"I know, baby." He wanted, too. He wanted all of her. It was primal, carnal. He wanted to take her here on the earth, like the creature of nature he was. Raw emotion plowed through him and he thrust deeper, then deeper still.

"More." She locked her ankles across his ass and repeated the command, pulling him deeper into her. "More."

"I don't want to hurt you."

"You won't," she said, steadying her gaze so he would know she meant it. "I want more."

So he allowed instinct to rule and thrust hard.

"Oh…that's…so…good. I'm coming…too soon."

He smiled at the despair in her voice. There would be more. He could promise her that. He quickened his pace to catch up with her climax, then exploded inside her, as relentless as a bullet. He caught a last glimpse of her face in the thrall of orgasm before he was lost.

Lost.

He rode the feeling, unable to do anything but enjoy the woman who gripped him with her arms, her ankles, her sex, not letting go, never letting go.

She was both soft and strong. Her skin was as soft as butter, but it was resilient, pliant and sturdy. She was like that, too, he knew, deep inside, where he connected with her in a way he didn't want to acknowledge.

They both quieted, breathing hard. He started to roll away, but she held him with her heels and looked up at him. "That was great," she said with a satisfied sigh.

He nodded, his heart still pounding in his ears. He needed a little distance, a break to collect himself. He caught sight of his camera a few inches away, the medium lens in place, and reached for it.

"What are you doing?" she asked when he pointed it at her, touching her hair.

"You look incredible. Lean on your elbow for me."

She turned on her side and gave him a seductive look, blocking her nipples with her arm. Very nice. "So, you are my artist, capturing the inner me on film?" She fluffed her hair and spoke in a teasing voice, shifting her leg to hide her pubic area, which was fine with him. He wanted that to be his alone to see. "That's a fantasy I have, you know," she said.

"A fantasy, huh?" He pulled her hair forward, the dark red waves gentle beside her cheek. Midday sun dappled her skin through the trees, turning her body into an impressionist painting. Leaf shadows arrowed from her breasts to her belly, adding texture.

"I've never been naked for a picture," she whispered.

"I've never been naked taking one, either. First time for everything." He ran his hand along the soft topography of her hip. "It'll be fine, Samantha. Trust me."

She relaxed under his touch. He felt that—deep—her trust of him and wanted always to be worthy of it.

She closed her eyes on a sigh and when she opened them again, they were blue fire. *I want you.*

He was shaking so badly he could hardly hold the camera to his eye, but he snapped the shot and it was perfect. He'd captured her in her double glory—soft and fierce, innocent and carnal, shaky and sure. She plain took his breath away.

At this moment, nothing mattered to him but her. Not the case, not being a cop, not his personal rules of conduct.

What the hell was happening to him?

SAMANTHA WATCHED Rick's eyes change color like a mood ring, going from hot to cool so fast she almost gasped. He was sorry they'd had sex. He would apologize now and stop them again. She couldn't let that happen. This was way too good to give up.

"Don't be sorry, Rick. Please." She rose on her elbows and pushed him to the blanket. "We're great together. Just let that be enough for now." She cupped his face, kissed his forehead, stared down at him, willing him to agree with her.

He was trying to smile, but she could tell it wasn't easy.

"I know you want sex to mean more," she said. "And it does." More than she'd expected it to, anyway. More than adventure or discovery or a fantasy fulfilled. It had been glorious and moving and tender and powerful. She hadn't quite grasped all the implications, but she knew she wanted more.

"Sex can mean plenty all on its own," she said. She grasped him and he went immediately hard.

"When you do that I stop thinking," he said, his eyes flaring hot.

"That's good. Don't think. Just feel." She straddled him, rose on her knees and guided him smoothly inside her. "Feel this," she said, leaning forward so he cupped her breasts. "Feel me. All…of…me." She dragged out the words, rocking as she spoke.

"Oh, yeah," he said, swept away. She loved that she was driving this restrained man crazy. He looked at her as if he'd never seen anyone more beautiful.

She'd never felt more like a woman. Her blood sang with the thrill and power of this moment. Talk about a fantasy fulfilled.

She and Rick were naked under the sky, surrounded

by nature. A bird called nearby, the creek gurgled past, and wind rustled the aspens and hissed through the pines that stood guard over them while they engaged in this most primal of all acts.

"This is another fantasy of mine," Samantha said, looking down at Rick, seating herself firmly on him, so that he reached her deep inside. "Having sex out here...like this."

"That's good." He gripped her hips to keep himself from going too deep.

"I have more," she breathed, fighting to hold a thought while sensations rushed through her in wave after wave.

"You want more, huh?" Rick said. "How's this?" He pressed his thumb to her clit, which electrified her so much that she cried out. *More fantasies* was what she meant, and she had to explain it, but it was almost impossible to speak with his thumb stroking her, sending aching waves of pleasure along her nerves, making her ride him helplessly faster and faster as her entire body strove for release.

"Yes, more," she panted out. "You finding me alone in my studio and tying my wrists..."

"Tying your...wrists?" He was clearly struggling to understand her words. He thrust up into her, meeting her downward stroke with wonderful force.

"Rick, help me...with my fantasies," she managed to say. "Make them real."

"Oh, yeah," he said, filling her, claiming her, reaching up into her, deep and demanding. She wasn't sure he had even grasped what she meant.

There was something in his face, a feeling, a need she met when they made love this way. She wished she could photograph him, catch this expression. And then she caught it—the double image she strove for in her photographs. There was Rick's desire, his drive to have her and to please her—that was obvious—but beneath that was…loneliness.

Rick was lonely. And, furthermore, so was she. She felt her soul rise up to say, "Me, too," the connection an arrow shooting through them both, pinning them together. And she wanted more than anything to make him happy, to be with him, to let him make her happy, too.

But that was too much. And way too soon. They were making love, enjoying their physical connection, nothing more. She closed her eyes and focused on what was real—her body rocking on his, in the open air, his thumb stroking her higher and higher, bringing that delicious rush of release ever closer.

Feel this. Feel him. This was what she wanted. To share this pleasure, this driving urge, this mind-blowing burst of ecstasy. Not to settle in, lock on to one man. She pushed away the impulse, but it rang in her like the finest crystal goblet tapped to capture silent attention.

Rick called out her name, thrust upward and released himself inside her, pushing her into climax, too. She cried out, her voice sharp in the quiet meadow, rolling on the breeze like the sensations washing through her, wave after wave, until finally she collapsed onto Rick's chest.

He held her and their hearts banged at each other through ribs and muscle and skin, both of them breathing hard.

Samantha relaxed into an easy peace on top of Rick, who stroked her back, soft and slow. She wanted a picture of this—something to hang on to forever as a memory—but she couldn't move a muscle.

"I bet we've got a frame or two left," Rick said, as if he'd read her mind. She felt him extend a hand, grab the camera and hold it above their bodies. She wiggled into his armpit and he angled the lens to catch them just to the collarbone.

She imagined the proof sheets of this day—sun-kissed desert vistas, rising red cliffs, the creek from all angles, the wildlife they'd captured, Rick's snap of her mud-streaked face and now the two of them together. Stalking the wild climax. Forever proof of their lovemaking in the woods.

She cuddled into him, comfortable and so happy. Then she noticed her leg itched. Then the itch moved. She leaned up to check and found ants crawling on her legs and his. "Ants!" she said and brushed them off her shins and Rick's thighs.

"I can fix that," he said, rising to swing her into his arms and stride toward the creek.

"What are you doing?"

He only grinned and kept walking.

"Don't you dare. It'll be too—" Before she could say *cold,* icy water brushed her bare bottom and Rick was up to his thighs in the creek. She squealed.

"It'll feel good in a second." He stepped into a deep spot and they both went under. The water went from frigid to brisk to mellow in the five seconds it took to reach the bottom and thrust up from the rocky creek bed.

Breaking the surface, Samantha threw herself onto her back to float, the sun deliciously warm on her water-chilled face.

For a few minutes, they floated and played, splash-

ing each other and holding on tight, until they wearied
and scrambled onto a flat boulder together to let the sun
soothe their chill-bumped skin.

It was lovely and lazy on the warm sandstone. After
a bit, Samantha rose on her elbow to look down at Rick,
who lay with his eyes closed looking gorgeous—a sun-
bronzed god sent to earth to pleasure women. Well, one
particular woman. Water gleamed on his skin and clear
diamonds of it were suspended in his chest hair.

Even with his eyes closed, she could see the lonely man
she'd caught in her mind's eye. Something in her wanted
to answer the emptiness in him. Had it come from losing
his brother? Had that made him feel lonely and lost?

She felt close to him. Maybe that wasn't good, considering how limited their relationship had to be, but she
wanted to understand him even better. "It must have
been so hard on you to lose your brother," she said.
"Were you close?"

Rick's eyes flew open. "Whoa, where did that
come from?"

She couldn't tell him what she'd seen in his face. "I
was just wondering about what you told me before. I
mean about your brother being killed. And how that
must have affected you. You said your parents were
wrecked, but how about you?"

"It affected me, sure. We weren't exactly close…Brian
wasn't what he seemed. Hell, it's complicated."

She waited. She could feel him struggling with his
own emotions. "Tell me, Rick. Please."

For a second, he disappeared from behind his eyes,
hiding out as he'd seemed to do that first day, and off and
on since, going from interested to watchful, easygoing
to intense. Friendly, but not fully present, and very wary.

But then he returned to her, as if dragged by an intimacy he couldn't resist, like an animal drawn from the forest by the warmth of a campfire on a cold night.

"Brian didn't get shot helping a client," he said. He pushed himself to a sit, grabbed a pebble and tossed it into the creek, watching the ripples swell outward. He didn't look at her, just continued speaking, his arm on one bent knee. "He went there to buy coke."

"Really?" she asked, sitting up to be sure he knew he had her full attention.

"Oh, yeah. His client was a low-level dealer and Brian already owed him for a grand's worth of product he'd 'borrowed' to sell to his yuppie friends, but snorted instead. He showed up wanting more, can you believe it?"

"Oh, dear."

"Yeah. My brother had cojones. But the dealer was already in deep with his supplier, who sent someone to whack them both. Nine millimeter. Mowed them both down in seconds."

"How awful."

"Yeah." He shifted his body to look at her now. "I knew one of the cops on the case and he kept the drug angle out of the report, so it looked like just a drive-by. Better for my parents. They think Brian was so brave helping that poor innocent client in that deadly neighborhood." His smile was crooked.

"You protected them," she said. He'd prevented them from hearing hard truths about their older—and favored—son. She understood that impulse. She was doing the same in a way with her own parents. If they knew about Bedroom Eyes, what pride they had in their only child would fade to black, she was certain. Better they didn't know.

"Did the client get your brother hooked on drugs?"

Rick gave a silent laugh. "No. Brian managed that all on his own. My brother liked things to go easy and feel good. Drugs were a shortcut to that. He liked shortcuts. That's why he chose criminal defense. Lots of rich scum happy to pay plenty to stay out of prison."

"That's a shame."

"Don't get me wrong. Brian wasn't a bad guy. He was always good to me. Loaned me money, found me a job once, sent me his friends' cars to work on. He just didn't mind working the system to get what he wanted." He paused. "He sort of got lost." He shot her a look full of anguish.

"It happens sometimes," she said.

"Yeah. But I didn't step in. I was too busy taking my own shortcuts. Not drugs, but anything else that felt good or wild or fun." He tossed another rock, this one more fiercely.

"You couldn't live your brother's life for him," she said gently. "If you'd tried, he'd probably have told you to go to hell."

"Did you know him?" He was trying to joke, but she could tell her reassurance hadn't gotten past the barrier in his eyes. He felt responsible for letting his brother's life end the way it had. *I think you earn love and guard it with everything in you.* That was Rick's belief and, in his mind, he'd let his brother down. Her heart ached for him. Here was the source of the pain and loneliness she'd seen. It was Rick's self-imposed exile because he didn't think he deserved love.

"And after he died, you changed your life?" He'd gone into the army, she recalled.

"I turned it around, yeah. Brian's chance to straighten

out, do the right thing, get married, have a family, all that was gone—" he snapped his fingers "—like that. So I had to make up for it, do what he couldn't do." His sense of mission burned in his eyes.

"If it's what you really want. For yourself, I mean."

"Sure. Everyone wants to find someone special and settle down. You do, too, right?" His gaze dug in with surprising urgency.

"Eventually, sure."

"When you finish making waves?"

"Exactly."

"Who says you can't do that with one particular person? You splash around, but you have company." He shrugged, as if it were a lighthearted idea, but she felt the weight of deep interest in his words.

She answered slowly. "I don't work that way, Rick. When I was with Barry, I gave up what I wanted, forgot who I was, just went along with him and how he saw me."

"Barry was a prick. The right guy wouldn't do that to you." His words were low and slow and there were a million emotions in his eyes.

Did Rick want to be that guy? Was that what he was hinting at? She was startled by how wonderful that felt, warm and right, like a sturdy pilot light flaring to life deep inside.

Too soon. And all wrong.

She had to stick with what she was sure of—the heat between them and all the fun they could have.

"For now, I'm exploring," she said and smiled over at him. They sat together on this sun-drenched rock, as naked as Adam and Eve in the first garden, and she didn't want to waste one beautiful minute of it. "And that's where you come in."

She pushed on his shoulders so he would lie back and she lay over him, pleased when she felt him go hard under her.

He resisted for a second, as if he wanted to say something more serious to her, but she kissed his mouth, blocking his words and felt lust wash through him. "Did you say *come?*" he murmured, his eyes gleaming with renewed heat.

"Oh, yeah." This was what she wanted. To keep making love with Rick, to explore her fantasies with this wonderful man. Any more than that would be foolish to imagine—greedy, really. This was more than enough.

What if there's more here? The idea shivered through her like a premonition or a dream, but she pushed it away and kissed the lips of her Adam, her highwayman, her cowboy, her artist, her Rick.

13

"WHAT HAPPENED TO YOU?" Rick's partner stared at him as if he were covered in spots or wore a sequined gown.

"Nothing. Went up to Oak Creek for some pictures." And had sex with Samantha. Lots of it.

"That explains the sunburn, but not the…" Trudeau scratched his own neck to indicate something on Rick's.

Rick touched the tender spot he'd tried to hide with his collar—a love bite Samantha'd marked him with during the last frenzied round before they'd headed for home.

Realization dawned in his partner's face. "Ah, you and Samantha did the deed. I'm impressed."

No. He was shocked, plain and simple, Rick could tell and guilt shot through him like a shotgun shell, big and destructive. He'd blown it, he knew already. The closer he and Samantha had gotten to home, the more the implications of what he'd done had trickled into his awareness and they'd kept him awake most of the night.

"Drop it," he said, low, shooting a look across the station, not wanting to be overheard.

"Okay, but I get the details later, pal."

"So the electronics gear checked out?" Rick spoke loud enough for everyone to hear. He studied the printout Trudeau had handed him.

"Bought and paid for. Looks like Mad Man Sylvestri's electronics depot is a straight-ahead business, though they could launder money through it easy enough."

"The construction crew is working up there this week. I'll keep an eye out, but I don't get what he's up to. I'm still sleeping in the studio, but there's been no late-night action."

Bad choice of words. He'd half expected Samantha to show last night at Bedroom Eyes—he'd moved to the satin-covered bed in studio one, tucked up against the castle backdrop. She had *fantasies* she wanted to act out, for God's sake. When she didn't appear, he was both relieved and disappointed.

Also a bad sign.

Even though the mattress was far better than that damn futon in Mona's shop, he'd slept little, working out whether he should tell Samantha what was going on, maybe ask for her help with the investigation, or head straight for the lieutenant's office and resign over his breach of conduct.

He felt ripped apart, and his brain wasn't working worth a damn. He had to figure this out, do the right thing somehow.

"The bookkeeper's twitchy," he continued, needing to fill Mark in, "but if there are double books, Samantha knows nothing about them."

"You sound pretty sure of that." Mark raised a brow. He bristled. "And…?"

"Relax. Sleeping with the woman doesn't make her innocent, West, that's all I'm saying."

"Don't you think I know that?" he snapped.

"Chill. You'll do your job."

"I will. Yeah." He realized he was leaning from foot to foot, head thrust forward like he expected Mark to throw the first punch. Hell, he half wanted him to.

Rick had granted himself a window of private time up there at the creek, but in the cold light of the case, he saw he'd been wrong. Way wrong.

"What about your tail on Sylvestri?" he asked, backing away, forcing the tension out of his voice. "Anything there?"

"Oddly enough, the guy's spending a lot of time at the yarn shop, though we did pick up a debate over the cut—of what we don't know—at that strip club, Moons. Lots of strangely worded cell calls. Something's about to break, I can feel it. Anything at the other shops?"

"From what I've seen, Mirror, Mirror is clear."

"All of it?" His partner honed in on him.

"Yeah, all of it," he said, but his belly churned with acid. Mark doubted his judgment. And he had good reason. Rick wanted everyone at the center to be clear of Sylvestri's crap. Bianca, too, who, he was reasonably certain, was clueless. Had his hope that the Mirror, Mirror crew was innocent compromised his investigative skills? Dulled his instincts?

He was sure as hell distracted by this thing he had for Samantha. He couldn't get her out of his mind. Now that he'd had sex with her, it was even worse. He felt as though he traveled in a cloud. Had he lost his edge, tripping over his own dick?

"Whatever's happening there, I'm on it, all right?" he said, rubbing his face, weary and worried.

"Get some sleep, man. You look wiped. The case will come together."

He *was* wiped. Torn up inside. Besides sorting out what to do, he'd kept going through their time at the creek and how great it had been.

For the first time, the idea of settling down with one

woman for the rest of his life felt real. He wanted it. Not just because it was time, not just for Brian, but because he wanted to be with her. Samantha. Just her.

She was smart and kind and full of life and she just made him feel good, as if he had a place in the world, as if he belonged. As if he were home. He could see waking up with her every day and coming back to her every night.

But that was impossible. Even if the case didn't stand between them, Samantha wanted to *explore,* for God's sake. Crazy. Knowing what was out there, he wished he could tell her just to forget it, stick with him. He'd be whatever she needed him to be. He'd said that from the day he'd stood at her counter with his beat-up portfolio.

But that was crazy, too.

He was who he was—a good cop who put the job first.

He looked around the squad room at the officers who trusted him with their lives and knew what he had to do.

He had to end this thing with Samantha.

He'd had a weekend off the clock. And now he was back on duty. He'd phrase it in a way she'd understand. Or maybe he'd just let it drop, be friendly, but back off. Maybe she'd want that, too. She hadn't come last night, after all. Maybe she'd realized they'd had a good time and that was enough. He hoped so. He couldn't stand putting any more hurt in those clear blue eyes. He said goodbye to Mark and headed off to do the right thing.

SAMANTHA WOKE ON Monday morning feeling great. Her sore muscles reminded her of all the fabulous sex they'd had in Sedona and her brain bubbled over with fantasies she would soon be exploring with her man.

The ride home in the golden dusk had been dreamy

and they'd kept grinning at each other, laughing for no reason, all the way to her place.

I just might surprise you tonight, she'd teased, kissing him through the driver's window before she skipped up to her place. He'd agreed to sleep on the fairy-tale bed, so why not?

But she'd been tired and had decided to save it for the next night so she could choose a costume and arrange everything first. She couldn't wait to talk to Rick about it.

But he wasn't in the studio as she'd expected when she breezed in early, excited to see him, but a little nervous, too. Must have gone home to shower or run an errand or something.

She checked the calendar, reviewed some orders, made certain Rick's marketing call list was ready for him, all the while watching for him like a girl expecting her prom date.

Finally she saw him, heading in from the parking lot and her entire body trembled with pleasure. Her man. He looked so handsome, extra-tan from their day in the high-desert sun, and so tall. She wanted to meet him halfway and hug the hell out of him, but decided that was a little too eager, even for her.

He entered the lobby, then pushed into Bedroom Eyes.

"Hi," she said shyly, her heart in her throat.

For the briefest of seconds, his eyes sparkled with pleasure and a smile bloomed, but abruptly, as if he'd called his features to attention, his reactions went flat and dead, and he said, "Hello," in the neutral, polite tone of a stranger.

Just like that, she realized, everything had changed.

"Are you okay?" she asked, completely disappointed.

"I'm fine. Just tired. Maybe we overdid it yesterday." He gave her a half smile, then moved behind the counter to rummage around on the shelves.

"Overdid it? You think we overdid it?" After the glory of yesterday, the disappointment was like a punch in the stomach. But she wasn't going to let on. No way. Maybe Rick had a fear of intimacy as Mark had said. Maybe he just needed room to breathe. That didn't make it any less irritating. "What are you looking for?" she snapped at him.

"The ledger," he said, lifting it onto the counter.

"What for?"

"To look things over. Check for mistakes."

"Lester doesn't make mistakes."

"How would you know?" He shot her a look. "You don't ever check." She didn't like the judgmental tone in his voice. This wasn't the first time he'd made a critical crack about her business practices. He was basically a suspicious guy. "I look things over. Darien trusts Lester with far more money than I'll ever have, so what's the big deal?"

He shook his head as if she were being foolish.

"And furthermore, I don't appreciate how you grilled the poor man when he was here, either."

"You're too trusting, Samantha."

"I have good instincts about people."

"You can be wrong." He looked almost angry.

"Oh, yeah? I hired you, didn't I?" she snapped.

"Yeah, you did," he said, looking so hurt, she almost apologized. "Look, I need to check with the workers upstairs. After that I want to touch base with Val and Blythe and Mona. You okay for a while on your own?"

"Of course I'm okay. I was okay before you got here and I'll be okay when you're gone." She was royally pissed now. How dare he make her sound helpless? Why did the man have to make everything so complicated?

"I know that, Samantha. I do." He didn't even have the decency to snap back at her. He sounded almost melancholy. What the hell was going on with him? Just when she thought she'd figured him out, he went all mysterious on her. Maybe she should just give up.

AT MIDNIGHT, SAMANTHA unlocked the front door to Mirror, Mirror and stepped into the lobby, the security lights bright enough that she didn't need the penlight on her key chain to see what she was doing. The velvet dress she'd borrowed from the costume room before leaving work swished against her knees, as soft on the inside as it was plush on the outside. She loved this dress.

She was giving them one more chance. Rick was sleeping in the studio, she knew, since she'd spotted his Jeep parked a block away. Why not in the lot, since his secret was out? One more Rick mystery. But tonight she was sleuthing out only one riddle: Would he come out and play with her?

Her heart pinched with hope.

Rick had spent the day roving the center, pretending to check on everything but her. When they had crossed paths, their eyes had never quite met. If it weren't for that darling hickey peeking above his collar, she'd have had no clue they even liked each other, let alone had made wild love at Oak Creek.

Tonight she would either fix what was between them or end it altogether. Oak Creek had been fabulous enough for any woman, of course, but if there was a chance to enjoy more fantasies with this incredible man, she owed it to herself to try.

Right before she'd left the studio, she'd arranged studio two for her ravishment fantasy, setting up the black filigreed arch, laying out the velvet sash and arranging clumps of red, black and gold candles here and there.

In the lobby, she glided to Bedroom Eyes, unlocked the door and eased in, her heart racing.

She stilled and listened. Nothing. Rick was probably asleep. She would wake him with a kiss and bring him into her fantasy in the neighboring studio. She scooped off her slip-ons and tiptoed barefoot down the hall, her heart thudding so loudly it seemed to reverberate against the walls.

At the door to studio one, she peeked in and saw him in the bed. Under the satin spread, his big body rose and fell with the slow breaths of sleep. She tiptoed closer.

At least he'd opted for a real bed instead of that rock-hard futon in Mona's shop. The guy was seriously into self-denial. Maybe they could try out a mild domination game. But only after she was certain Rick didn't consider more sex a betrayal of his higher purpose. Lord.

She thumbed on her penlight, shining it away from him so she could better see his face on the pillow, strong and square, his jaw a clean line below shadowed cheeks. He was naked to the waist. Oh, my.

For a second, she considered curling into his arms, cozy and content, to match his slow, deep breaths and drift to sleep tucked against his protective body, surrounded by his warm smell, heated by his skin. In the morning they would wake, make love, share coffee and the paper and whatever the day brought.

But that was way too domestic for Samantha. That was something Mona would cook up. Samantha had hotter adventures in mind. She let her eyes trace Rick's sleeping form and imagined him waking, reaching out to her with strong arms and skilled fingers.

The image made her desire for him rise swiftly, lifting her into deep water, where she'd never feel the bottom or ever want to. She wanted to wake him with a kiss—Sleeping Beauty in reverse—and begin the adventure, but first she had to light the candles in studio two and make sure everything was perfect.

RICK JERKED AWAKE. *What was that?* A noise. What? And where? Had another shipment come? He should have stayed on Mona's awful couch to better track any action out back, but he'd been so tired and his back hurt like hell.

He rolled out of bed, grabbed his gun and moved to the door. The noise wasn't coming from out back. It was down the hall. In studio two? He heard the swish of fabric, the click-click of a lighter. Was it Samantha?

Seemed unlikely. They'd hardly spoken all day and he could tell he'd hurt her feelings without saying a word. If she'd overcome her anger and come to him, she sure as hell wouldn't be rummaging around in another studio. She was a woman who went for what she wanted. If she wanted him, she'd go for him. And, dammit, the idea sounded good.

So who was in the studio? He held his breath, extended his gun in ready position, lunged into the open door and aimed at a bent figure.

Samantha, he realized immediately, and she was lighting candles. Huh? Already a dozen gold flames licked at the dark, wet pools of wax under each one.

He released the trigger, but before he could shove his gun into the back of the jersey shorts he wore for sleep, Samantha turned and looked up at him, hair flying away from her face. "Rick! What are you...? Was that a gun?"

She didn't look nearly scared enough.

"What the hell are you doing here?" he asked, though the sexy black dress hanging off one shoulder made it obvious, not to mention all the candles. "I could have shot you dead." His head pounded from leftover adrenaline.

"That's very sexy," she said in a sultry voice, swaying closer on bare feet. "It makes you seem so...dangerous." Her eyes gleamed and she licked her lips.

"What have you got in mind, Samantha?" he said. One of those fantasies she'd tried to explain up at the creek, no doubt. She was inches away now, her breasts swelling upward, her locket shining in the candlelight.

"I'll tell you," she breathed. "Today did not go well, I know. We argued. We avoided each other. The creek was intense and you needed some space. I get that. Now, it's time to just enjoy each other, don't you think?"

"Samantha, I—"

"Can you do that, Rick? Forget your rules and just be with me? Nights can be ours. Like this. We need this."

She searched his face, her eyes shining up at him in the candlelight, wicked and hopeful, sweet and demanding, and it was all he wanted in the world.

God help him, he was powerless to deny her.

He took her trembling body into his arms and kissed her, long and deep, holding tightly, sinking into her taste, the smell of her, the taut strength of her small body.

"Yes," she breathed into his mouth, then she dragged herself away, holding up one finger. "Stay right there."

He obeyed. He stood riveted to the floor, knowing he'd do anything she wanted—bark like a dog, dance naked on the roof, anything. With Samantha, the rules meant nothing anymore.

She grabbed a strip of cloth off a shelf—a sash of some kind—then braced herself against the intricately worked metal arch, black and shiny in the red-gold light of all those candles.

With her arms behind her, her breasts were half-bared in the black dress. A wave of nearly uncontrollable desire filled him. He wanted to take her, grab her up and thrust into her, make her moan. There were a bunch of buttons down the middle of that dress. How fast could he pry them open?

Still standing against the arch, Samantha lifted one arm over her head and extended the strip of cloth with the other. "Tie me up, Rick," she said, jutting her chin to make up for the tremor in her voice. "Then tease me. Nice and slow."

Slow? Was she kidding? He wanted to rip off her clothes and jam into her. Screw this fantasy nonsense.

But he saw how determined she was and he couldn't disappoint her. If she wanted to play games, he would play games. He put his gun on a shelf, safely out of the way, and went to accept the sash she held out to him.

"You want me to tie you up?" he asked, running it through his fingers.

In answer, she lifted the other arm against the arch and crossed her wrists. "Yes. Then make me beg for more."

She was pale against the dark metal—pale and vulnerable—waiting for him to restrain her. She trusted him, was giving herself over to him, even though she was a little scared. He knew that because he knew her well—better than she realized. Her bravado moved him. And made him vow to protect her from every imaginable harm.

He wanted to pull her away from that unforgiving metal, take her tender body into his arms, carry her to the bed and make love to her.

How do you see me, Rick? She'd asked him once. *In leather? Velvet? Silk? Something see-through?*

Right now, he pictured her in simple cotton panties in the middle of a pillow fight—feathers flying, giggling like a girl—and he wanted to nab her and pin her to the sheets with his body and his joy.

What the hell was wrong with him?

Her. Samantha. She was what was wrong with him. He loved the take-no-prisoners temptress and the tentative innocent beneath the bold moves.

The soft velvet of her dress cupped her curves, stroked her skin. She rocked her hips forward and back in a slow grind, a move that was clearly arousing her.

Lust pounded through him, as hard and heavy as a sledgehammer.

Just give the lady what she wants.

Easy enough to take hot, hard pleasure in her, ignore the fact that she made him want so much more.

He stepped closer, his body nearly brushing hers, and her pupils dilated with pleasure. The candles flickered around them, sending up threatening shadows, as if they'd discovered each other in a dangerous place and were only safe in each other's arms.

"Rick," she breathed, softening against the arch.

He ran his thumbs across the peaks of her breasts through the velvet. Her nipples were tight beads through the thick cloth. No bra. Just dress. Was it soft for her on the inside, where it touched her skin?

She gasped with pleasure.

He stopped. "You want to be helpless? Is that what

you want?" He deliberately spoke roughly, guessing she wanted that.

She nodded happily. "Yes. Absolutely. Make me helpless."

"Be warned. I won't stop until I've had my fill," he said, playing her game for her.

"You won't stop?" she said breathlessly.

"Not until I'm finished with you."

"How many times will I come?"

"As many times as I make you," he growled, wrapping the velvet strip around and around her wrists.

"Oh," she breathed, her eyes wide. "That will be wonderful."

"No, it won't. You'll beg me to stop." He yanked the tie tight for effect, fighting a smile. "Is that what you want? Say yes or no."

"Yes."

"Yes, *please,*" he added, then surprised her with a finger against her clit through the dress.

"Oh, yes, please, yes." The way she quivered turned him to steel. He'd just promised her multiple orgasms when all he wanted was to bury himself in her and ride the pleasure of mutual release.

This was what she wanted, though. She stood with her legs slightly apart, her hands tied above her head, swathed in black. She wanted him to be her master. That was a laugh. What man could ever master Samantha?

He ran a finger slowly between her breasts and down her belly through the soft dress.

"Oh, yes." She closed her eyes, anticipating more, rocking her hips forward, so he stopped. Her eyes flew open. "Don't stop."

"But I want to," he lied. "I want you to ache for me." He moved so his lips were millimeters from hers.

"I do, I ache for you." She leaned forward for a kiss. He allowed the barest contact and then pulled away.

She moaned. "Please…"

Ah, hell. He gave in and kissed her, sliding his tongue inside for a probing taste of her. Her tongue lapped at his, eager, desperate, so he dragged away his mouth and surprised her by popping open the top button of her dress, baring her breasts almost to the nipple.

Samantha's greedy gasp made her locket quiver in the middle of her chest. He ran his tongue around the medallion, then traced the line where the velvet touched her skin, finally shoving his tongue deep enough under the fabric to reach a nipple.

She writhed and wriggled, then pushed her hips against him.

Fighting his instincts, he shifted his lower body away, so she couldn't make contact and focused on wetting her breast, pressing his tongue across her nipple, over and over. He lifted his head to check her reaction.

"Oh, more. Please more," she moaned.

Instead, he thumbed the second button open. Now her breasts were completely exposed—white and fragile, framed by the dark cloth, served up to him in the red-gold light that seemed to threaten and promise at the same time, the golden medallion their only decoration. Her nipples were moist knots that he wanted to take into his mouth.

"Suck them, *pleeease.*" She held back her shoulders, offering up her nipples for his mouth, urgent, demanding.

"Don't rush me, lady," he said, aching to do just what she asked. He took a step away from her.

"Don't go," she said, tugging away from the arch.

"I will do what I please to you."

"Okay," she said, sagging against the metal that held her, despairing. He knew how she felt. He was as mindless with lust as she was limp with frustration, but her game demanded delay.

Still, there was no point in torturing themselves. He moved close enough to take a nipple into his mouth and suck it deep.

She gasped in surprised gratitude and rubbed against him.

He repeated the act on her other breast, loving the taste of her and the way she rocked so hard against him that the arch jerked. She was close to climax and, hell, she'd earned it, so he shoved his hand under her dress and stroked her clit through her thin panties, loving the soft, swollen secret of her.

She gasped, then wiggled on his finger, jerking once, twice. "Rick, oh, oh, I'm coming…."

He loved the desperate happiness in her voice as the waves passed through her for long seconds. Just as she finished, he slid a finger inside, hooking deep to nudge her G-spot so that she shrieked in abrupt delight, "Again. I'm coming again…I can't…" But she did, moaning and rocking on his finger, shaken by a second orgasm.

When she stopped moving, he stroked her softly, then slowly took away his hand.

"That was so incredible," she said.

"I'm not finished with you," he said. Not by a long shot. He was near the breaking point himself, his cock aching behind his zipper. She looked like raw sex to him, the top of her dress open, offering her swollen breasts to him, her nipples shiny with his saliva, her breaths coming ragged and wild.

The animal drive to take her would no longer be denied. He grabbed both sides of the dress and yanked it apart.

She gasped in happy shock.

Under the dress, she wore only a black see-through triangle of cloth over her sex. She was breathtakingly beautiful, standing there helpless, but still in charge, the dark tie against her pale skin, her fair body open to him, waiting for him, for what he would do next. He wanted to take her, make her his, but first he had to taste her again.

He dropped to his knees, and pressed his mouth to her mound. She was warm and quivering and the scent of her sex filled his head. Her sweet tang was heaven to him. The tissue-thin fabric was soaked with her juices and he licked her through the cloth, bracing her firm ass with his hands.

She pushed herself at him and seemed to be trying to jerk her hands free. To dig her fingers into his hair, he'd bet, but the tie held. She was at his mercy.

He vowed to make it worth all the trouble she'd gone to. He nuzzled her with his nose, then decided the panties had to go and yanked them down so he could stroke her with his tongue. He loved the soft, swollen tension of her sex, so hungry for more. He used slow, even strokes and when she sped her movements, so did he.

"Oh, you're doing it again…. Oh, I'm coming…."

Her release pulsed against him, like the wildest taste of life on his tongue. The heart of her in his mouth. And he was so grateful and so glad.

"Rick," she breathed. "I can't take any more."

He smiled and trailed kisses up her thigh and her stomach, rising to his feet. "Oh, yes, you can," he said and, in the spirit of her game, added, "And you will."

"I will?" she said, flushed, but still eager. Thankfully because he had no more self-control left. His cock felt bigger than his entire body, as if it held all the want and need he'd ever felt in his life. And the woman who stood naked before him was the only person who could quench it.

He paused to admire her, her arms tied high, wrists trapped, her hair tossed and tangled around her face. Her breasts trembled, and her thatch of pubic hair was stark against her pale skin. Her thighs gleamed. She slid her hips forward and back, craving him just as he craved her.

Now he would have her.

He shoved off his shorts and kicked them away.

Samantha's gaze traveled down his body, stopping at his cock. "You're going to take me now?" she breathed.

"Yes. I'm going to take you."

"Will you do it hard?"

Heaven help him, he might tear her in two. "Spread your legs," he ordered.

Instantly, she complied.

The sight of her with her hands tied, legs spread drove him to grab her by the ass, lift her and plunge deep into her moist heat, filling her to his hilt.

"Oh, yes," she said, wrapping her legs around him. "Harder. Please, harder." The flames in her eyes flickered like the candles beyond her body.

He pulled out and drove in again.

"Like that," she moaned. "Yes. Again. Do it."

He pumped in and out, again and again, feeling something in him give way, slip out of his control and go to her.

Her climax tightened around him and he exploded into her, burying his cock into her space, his face in her neck.

Climax number four for her, he vaguely realized.

A respectable score in any sex game. But he was tired of playing.

Still panting, he reached up to untie her hands and she slumped against him, her open dress hanging around her body. He kissed her mouth, so happy to hold her in his arms, to feel her fingers in his hair, hanging on for dear life.

"Come to bed," he said and started to lift her into his arms.

She stopped him, remaining on her feet. "I can't," she said, struggling for oxygen. "I have to go now."

"You can sleep with me," he said, reaching for her.

"But that would spoil it…the fantasy." She smiled. "Now I have to slip away in the night."

"Come on, Samantha. Forget the game. Let's go to bed." He would be happy to give her screaming climaxes all night long.

"It's what I want, Rick. And tomorrow night, I'll come back and ravish you, okay? You'll love it." She held her dress closed, reached down to button the two or three buttons that hadn't been ripped off. When she was finished, delicious gaps of pale flesh peeked out where buttons were missing.

He didn't have the heart to argue with her. Instead, he helped her blow out the candles so that the studio smelled like the end of a birthday party, smoky and a little sad.

What was wrong with him? He was going along with her like a damned puppy dog, instead of making things clear, telling her how he felt, what he wanted, or, hell, who he was.

He walked her to her car, kissed the lips he'd bruised, pulled the buttonless top of her dress over her breasts to hide them from late-night drivers, and watched her pull away.

He was in big trouble. He stood barefoot in the parking lot of a stakeout where, instead of watching for crime, he'd made love to a woman who'd barely stopped being a suspect.

He looked up at the full moon and wanted to howl.

14

"THAT FEELS SO GO-O-OD," Samantha said, "but what about the butter*sco-o-o-otch?*" She could hardly get the words out because Rick was licking the hot fudge slowly and carefully from her left breast and down the line he'd painted to her sex.

"Not sure there's any left after what you did to me," Rick said, chuckling against her flesh. "Mmm. Let's see if I can dig up a little for down below."

She heard the click of a spoon, then Rick shifted lower on her body and she felt warm liquid, followed by his tongue's stroke. She moaned in helpless pleasure.

"Mmm," he murmured against her sex. "I think I like you just plain, no toppings."

In seconds, she'd rocketed off to another delicious climax, completely forgetting about the whipped cream in the kitchen.

Rick slid up her body and cuddled her close.

"That was so great," she said. "And there's so many more foods we can try."

He groaned. "I'm stuffed," he said, kissing her behind the ear. "I should get going. Want me to scrub you down in the shower? Get off the last of it?" He chuckled against her, pushing his erection between the cheeks of her bottom. "Get you really, really clean?"

Tonight, she'd insisted they be at her place, though Rick had been reluctant to leave the studio—so strange how he clung to the place—because they'd need to shower after the sex-and-food adventure.

"I'm too tired," she said. "And I'm sore." Doing the stripper-seducing-a-businessman fantasy the night before had strained her inner thighs. Sliding down the beam she'd pretended was a chrome pole must have done it. Or maybe it was doing it against the wall that left her aching.

She sighed. It was all great, no matter how sore and tired she got. They were both exhausted, having hardly slept for the four fantasy nights they'd shared.

"I should get back to it." He pulled himself up to a sit.

"You sound like you're on duty. We don't need security at the center. Rest a while. You're tired." She patted the bed.

He struggled with something inside him—more rules, no doubt—but finally fell back on the bed. "I just can't leave you alone," he said, sounding sad about it.

"I don't want you to." She pulled him close behind her for a cuddle. She knew she shouldn't say that or feel this way. Far too cozy and comfortable for a fantasy lover.

Definitely against her own rules.

"You feel good in my arms," he said. "Maybe I'll just rest my eyes for a few."

She smiled and held his arms across her breasts. Before long, she felt him go heavy in sleep. And she just held on, happy to have him wrapped around her, happy to have him stay all night. Another rule out the window.

Samantha opened her eyes to morning light spilling through her sheers, the sweet aroma of an ice-cream parlor filling the air, and Rick's body spooned around hers.

She waited for panic or regret to take over, but it didn't. She liked that he'd spent the night. She liked that their bodies were glued together by sweat and sticky butterscotch. She felt close to him. She felt right.

She lifted her arm from where it stuck to the pillow-case and licked off the butterscotch streak.

Her movement disturbed Rick, who twitched, then gasped and jerked up, as if he had to run somewhere fast. He saw her and relaxed back to the mattress. "Hey, beautiful." His smile reached all the way to his green eyes. So appealing. Thrilling, really, that she'd gotten past Rick's cool barriers and reached him.

They'd reached each other, truth be told. He was a wonderful lover, as in tune with her body as the lub-lub of her own heart, but it was more than that. In his arms, Samantha felt understood, valued, almost adored.

It was wonderful.

She might be falling in love with him. It certainly wasn't her plan, but she felt too good to give herself a hard time about it. She basked in the smile he saved for just her and looked deeply into his eyes. There was only a faint mysterious shadow left in their green depths. She'd figure that out soon enough.

"What time is it?" she asked him, not moving to check the clock.

He lifted his wrist so they could both see his watch.

"Still early…good," she said. "I'm too tired to jump up."

"Me, too," he said, groaning. "What have you done to me?"

"It's exhausting living a double life, isn't it? Ordinary photographers by day, secret fantasy lovers by night." She laughed, but he didn't.

After a strained pause, he said, "Yeah, a double life is exhausting." Something bothered him about that, but she wasn't about to let him go moody on her.

"It's bad enough that my real life is secret from my parents."

"What do you mean? You aren't obligated to explain your sex life to your folks, you know."

"They don't know about Bedroom Eyes."

"Why not?"

"Because they'd be shocked. They'd think what I do is pornographic." She cringed just picturing their reaction. "They think I just take regular portraits."

"So explain it to them like you did to me."

"They'd never understand."

"If it makes you uncomfortable, take more regular portraits, Samantha."

"What are you saying?" She rose on her elbow. "You know why I do what I do."

"Why limit yourself? Plans change. People change." His eyes burned with emotion and she realized he was talking about more than photography. "Sometimes what people want changes."

He was talking about her, about them together.

The idea tugged at her, but it also scared her, made her feel pulled under and lost. Was she falling for the first guy she had great sex with? That seemed so small town.

"Not for me," she said firmly. "What I want hasn't changed." She had to stick to her goals. She couldn't let this new glory change everything, no matter how powerful it was.

She caught the hurt that flared in Rick's face before he covered it with his neutral mask. His eyes swirled cool, nature's shining green fading to a sad olive. And she felt an answering pain deep inside, as if she'd said no to something big and important.

She had to get past the moment, ease the tension. She noticed a streak of chocolate on his jawline and ran her tongue along it. "Mmm. There's whipped cream in the kitchen…."

He smiled, but didn't speak. Just rubbed at the spot she'd licked on his jaw. "I'd better get going." He pushed out of the bed, mostly to hide his hurt, she was sure. She knew him well enough now to interpret some of his mystery.

She put her feet to the floor to join him, to smooth the moment by making love in the shower, except then the phone rang. At seven-thirty? Who would be calling this early? She frowned and answered it.

RICK SOAPED UP, CURSING himself for letting emotions swamp his good sense. Samantha no more wanted to get involved with him than she wanted to camp out in a blind for three days for a shot of a kit-fox den. His thing, not hers.

He was falling in love with her. She made him feel complete, understood, a part of something. But he was making too much of what was, in essence, the games she wanted to play. It was seductive and confusing. He wasn't cut out for any of this nonsense.

He rinsed off, letting the water sluice over him, remembering how it was to wake up to her sleep-soft face. No makeup, no costumes, no games. Just her, bare and beautiful and open to his touch. Hell, his heart.

He didn't want her in a velvet dress he could rip away or with her nipples drenched in chocolate, or certainly not in any of the role plays they'd enacted or the ones she wanted to do. The cop-and-suspect gem she'd proposed had stopped his heart.

He had his own fantasies. The everyday moments people in love took for granted. Samantha in his favorite muscle shirt heating up something at the stove while he set the table. Or washing the Firebird together, spraying each other with the hose. Fighting over the covers in winter, lying naked on the sheets on muggy August nights.

Hell, his fantasies were just as silly as hers, maybe more so, because there wasn't a cold chance in hell they'd happen.

Not me, Rick. What I want hasn't changed.

He was lathering his hair when Samantha entered the shower and stepped under the water with him.

The need to wrap himself around her rushed through him like the hot water pouring down his body. Maybe she just needed time. Maybe she'd come around.

He started to reach for her, but she grabbed the soap and started scrubbing herself. "I've got to get to the studio. Bianca just called. She wants to help us with the wedding shots."

"Bianca wants to help?" Rick struggled out of the haze he fell into when Samantha was naked anywhere near him.

"Yes. Her yarn shipment's here, but Darien's handling that himself. He told her to go shopping, if you can believe it. Basically, *get lost.* He hurt her feelings. So of course I said she could assist."

She rinsed her body, her hands streaking across her breasts, down her thighs. She bent her leg and he could only stare, his mind struggling with the implications of her words.

"Darien's handling her yarn shipment?" Rick shook himself alert. This was important.

"Yeah. It's strange. She told me the other day that he actually ordered the yarn for her."

"He what?" He stilled, his attention tight on her words. He no longer felt the water or even saw her beautiful body.

"He fussed about the shelf dimensions, even, and now he insists on setting up the store. You'd think it was his knitting shop."

"Yeah, you would. Excuse me." He shifted her slightly so he could rinse the last of the soap off his body and stepped out of the shower, thinking hard. If Sylvestri wanted his wife out of the way, something more than fuzzy wool and knitting circles was going on at Bianca's Yarn Hut.

Had they all been asleep at the wheel? Or was he the only one with access to the clues he'd been blind to? He recalled Bianca's visit where she'd talked about Darien and the blankety-blank photography class, but he'd had to take Mary Jane Sizemore back for her shoot and had missed the rest of the discussion about the yarn shop.

"We can keep Bianca busy, can't we?" Samantha called to him through the door. "Darien's niece Elisha is helping with costumes, but Bianca can assist with setups, right?"

"Sure. Yeah." He had to get out to the yarn shop in Scottsdale. Let Mark know and take off. "Listen, since you've got help, Samantha, I need a couple of hours to handle some personal business. That okay with you?"

"Huh? I guess…" Through the frosted glass, he watched her go still. "Is something wrong?"

"I'll get back as soon as I can." He pushed out of the room to dress and take off, aware he'd bewildered her, but unable to fix it at the moment.

Maybe when he saw her again, they'd have grabbed whatever had arrived at the yarn shop and arrested Sylvestri and it would be all over. Samantha and her friends at Mirror, Mirror would be completely in the clear. He'd tell her what he'd been doing and they could take it from there.

Maybe all they needed was more time together.

For now, he had a job to do. He put in the call, then set off. The shop wasn't far, so he'd likely be first on the scene.

WHAT THE HELL WAS WRONG with Rick? Samantha wondered, driving to Mirror, Mirror. Was he so hurt that she'd turned him down that he had to run away? Rick had never been flaky. No. He'd acted as if it was important. What was he up to?

Another Rick West mystery. There was a message there. She didn't really know the man. He was a wonderful fantasy lover and that was all he could be. She shouldn't get comfortable. Probably didn't want to. Eventually, it would turn ordinary as it had with Barry maybe. Before long she'd forget who she was and what she wanted. Maybe they should stop.

No. No. No. Everything in her protested the idea.

Luckily, she had work to do, so she pushed away the quandary for now, grateful to find Bianca and Elisha waiting for her in the Mirror, Mirror parking lot.

Bianca was signing off on the floral delivery when Samantha walked up to the pair.

"Just in time," Bianca said and introduced her to Elisha.

The girl made her feel odd...uneasy, really. It wasn't the Goth look or the pierces or even the barbed-wire tattoo running up her forearm. It was something predatory in her eyes, a calculating glitter that made

Samantha glad the girl wouldn't be staffing the cash register this week.

Maybe that was unfair. Bianca trusted Elisha and she seemed eager enough to get started when Samantha led her to the dressing room. Pointing out the hats and wigs, Samantha noticed that the top row of cupboards sported new locks. Very odd. Darien and his storage, she guessed.

"Got it, Samantha," Elisha said, drawing her attention back. "Consider this room handled. Don't even think about it." She seemed almost too confident, but Samantha soon had her hands too full to ponder the combination of false confidence and a predatory gleam.

First, she had to listen to Bianca's ideas about the flowers and the grapes she'd bought. Lord. The woman had been reading too many art photography books.

Then the clients began arriving and all strangely overdressed. Summer clung to the October days and it was easily eighty degrees outside, yet the women wore blazers or light sweaters, the men leather jackets, suit coats or shiny athletic sweatshirts. Many were from Chicago, which might be chillier, so perhaps they'd driven straight from the airport, but still…

The women were tattooed and hard-eyed like Elisha and they wanted to pose as biker chicks or hookers in black leather and vinyl, grousing when Bianca brought a flower anywhere near them.

The girls bothered Samantha, but the men were downright scary. The wedding began to seem more like a World Wrestling Federation convention than loving nuptials. And there was none of the usual wedding-party giggling and chatting, either. Maybe these were the distant relatives and the close ones would show up later in the week with stars in their eyes.

She wished Rick were here. They made a good team and his steady solidity calmed her. But she didn't have time to think about Rick right now either.

"How about a flower to cover that?" Bianca waved a tiger lily over the skull tattoo between the breasts of a dangerous-looking blonde sitting, elbow on a side-angled knee, on the black leather ottoman. The woman had obviously worn the black-leather vest to display the tattoo, not hide it.

The blonde ignored Bianca and glared at Samantha. "Just take the picture, wouldja?"

"Got it," she said, snapping the release, grateful the wedding clients would be gone soon. This job would bring in a lot of money, but she almost dreaded the rest of the week, hating how these clients clashed with the warmly hopeful atmosphere of Bedroom Eyes.

The blonde clumped off in jackboots, chains clanking like the ghost of Jacob Marley.

"I'm getting the feeling these girls don't even like flowers," Bianca said thoughtfully. "And that last girl ate all my grapes."

Samantha tried not to roll her eyes. Only a couple more hours of this and the day would feel normal again. The last wedding client was due at two.

"Bianca, what the—bleep—are you doin' here?" Darien stood in the doorway to the studio, his face red, his tone furious. "I told you to go—bleepin'—shopping. Let's get the—bleep—out of here."

Samantha was startled by the change in the man she'd only seen as cheerful and friendly and solicitous.

"Darien, honey…" Bianca said, startled and embarrassed.

"Let's go," he said, grabbing her arm impatiently.

"I'm sorry, Samantha. I don't want to strand you." Bianca clearly didn't know what to make of Darien's behavior.

"It's fine. Just a couple more clients and Rick should be here in a moment."

"If you're sure, hon." But Darien was tugging her out. Samantha heard Bianca's faint words—something about her duty to a friend—then she was gone. Another strange event in a very strange day. And where was Rick, anyway? How long could his errand take?

AT BIANCA'S YARN HUT, Rick pushed his handcuffed prisoner into the nearest chair, which happened to be a doily-decorated rocker. Sitting there, the guy looked like he'd been strong-armed into visiting his granny.

Nearby, Mark ripped open a skein of silver-flecked yarn. Tightly wrapped packets of powder tumbled to the table and he added them to the pyramid of baggies he was building. Dangerous drugs in sweet lengths of yarn. Ingenious, really.

Rick had reached the scene in time to block the delivery van from leaving the back lot and now had the driver and two loaders in custody. A third officer watched the other two perps.

No Darien, though, dammit.

Thank God Rick had been at Samantha's place for Bianca's early morning call or they might have missed this entirely. A rationalization, he knew, but he'd take it for now. The heat was off Mirror, Mirror and all they had to do was snag Darien and Rick would be free of his undercover assignment.

"Where's Sylvestri?" he demanded of his captive.

"I just deliver the goods."

"You're not helping yourself here, pal. You think Darien Sylvestri would protect you? He'd save his own ass first and to hell with you."

The guy tightened his jaw, considered the idea, then sagged. "We made another delivery last night, okay?"

"Give me an address."

The guy named familiar cross streets and Rick had him describe the building. It was Mirror, Mirror Beauty Center, no question. Adrenaline rushed through him. This guy had dropped off a shipment when Rick was supposed to be staking out the place. Instead, he'd been licking chocolate off Samantha's body in her town house.

"Mark."

Trudeau turned from where he'd been piling up baggies of dope. "Yeah?"

"Something's happening at Mirror, Mirror. Call it in. I'm heading out there." He had to be sure Samantha and the other shop owners were okay. If his carelessness or inattention or, hell, lust, had put them in danger, he'd never be able to live with himself.

How DID A PERSON get the name *Billy Bones?* Samantha wondered, snapping the man's photo. He was huge, with a Neanderthal brow and slicked-back hair. His black leather vest, sweat-stained leather hat, chained-to-his-pants wallet and scuffed biker boots looked too natural to be a costume.

"And one more," she said, clicking the shot. She'd only taken two frames. The last thing she wanted was to capture this guy's inner light—probably an inky black blot.

"Yeah." He tipped his hat at her, then tromped toward

the door. He paused to bend down and sniff Bianca's abandoned flowers. Maybe he had a soft spot somewhere in his soul.

He was the last of the wedding clients, thank goodness. She'd done fine without Bianca, but she sure wished Rick had been here if for no other reason than to tell her she wasn't crazy for finding these people a little frightening.

Samantha removed the film from the camera, marked it, then headed up front to check the schedule for the next day, feeling a heavy sense of dread. If it weren't for Bianca, she'd cancel.

She bent to pick up a cowboy hat that had been left in the hall and carried it to the dressing room.

Except the door was shut, the knob twisted to the locked position. Odd. It hadn't clicked though, so she pushed the door open and what she saw shocked her cold.

Billy Bones stood in the middle of the room pulling his leather vest over a smaller plastic vest that seemed to consist of dozens of compartments bulging with white packets. Behind him, Elisha stood on a ladder reaching into one of the locked cupboards for what looked like more white packets.

"Hey!" Billy yelled, then headed for her, moving fast.

Samantha dropped the hat and backed up, but not quickly enough. Billy grabbed her, forced an arm behind her back and locked his forearm under her chin.

"I'm sorry," she choked out. "I'll be in my office. You just finish up in here. Whatever you're doing."

"Take it easy, Billy," Elisha said, jumping off the ladder. "Don't hurt her. Darien will be pissed."

"Just shut up and get the stuff. You can't lock the damn door?"

"I locked it. You didn't shut it. I can't do everything. Jamming this stuff into the vests is hard work. The pockets are sewed too tight and—"

"Shut your hole and do your job." Billy shifted one hand and Samantha tried to pull away, but he yanked her back and jabbed her with something hard. A gun? "Don't move."

Her legs went liquid and she had the desperate need to pee.

Meanwhile, Elisha had loaded her arms with baggies. "What do I do with all these? I was supposed to have four days to move them."

"Ya got four minutes. Wad 'em into clothes and take them out to the van."

While Elisha balled the baggies into a black cape, a red kimono and a pink robe, Samantha tried to figure out how to escape. Would they kill her? Or take her to Darien?

She couldn't believe Bianca knew this was going on…whatever it was. Drugs, probably. Had all her clients today walked out with plastic vests filled with narcotics? What a nightmare. If she could just…wake…up.

Elisha bundled up the clothes like a load of laundry, then rushed out of the dressing room. Billy yanked Samantha out into the hall after her, pushing her forward.

What was that self-defense move with the top of your skull and your elbow? He was holding her so tightly, though, pressing on her windpipe, that she couldn't maneuver at all.

"No one moves. Police."

The harsh voice made them all freeze. It was Rick, she saw with relief, standing in the Bedroom Eyes doorway aiming a gun at Elisha, who'd stopped dead in her tracks. "Hands on top of your heads. Do it. Now."

Elisha dropped the clothes, scattering drug packets everywhere, and put her hands on her head as instructed.

Billy tightened his hold on Samantha and moved the gun to her temple, turning her body to jelly. "I'll shoot her," he growled at Rick. "Drop the gun."

Samantha fought the urge to whimper.

"It's all his stuff," Elisha whined. "He forced me to help. I'm a prisoner. He has a gun. Like you can see."

"Pick up that shit," Billy yelled, "and get the hell out of here."

"No one leaves, no one acts crazy," Rick said in a deadly calm voice Samantha had never heard before. "Backup's on the way. Let's work this out before they get here. You, lie facedown, hands on the back of your head." He jerked his head at Elisha, who obeyed.

"Like this?" she called up, her voice muffled.

"You chicken-shit bitch," Billy muttered.

Rick inched forward, keeping his gaze on Billy. "Let's work this out now, what do you say, man?" He was talking slowly, coaxing, as if Billy Bones were a rabid dog.

"Drop the gun now!" Billy squeezed Samantha's throat so hard she had to cough.

"Kidnapping's federal. Let the lady go. We know about the knitting shop. All we want is Sylvestri. You can help yourself here."

As soon as Rick passed Elisha, lying on the floor, the girl slithered up and out the door. Rick didn't even look. His gaze was trained on Billy.

"You think I won't shoot her? Huh? Do you?" Billy shouted, squeezing Samantha so tightly she could only wheeze in air. "Drop the damn gun!"

Rick considered the guy for a second, then seemed to give in. "Okay. Weapon's down." He set his pistol on the end of the counter. "Take it easy."

"More like it." Billy yanked Samantha to her knees, crouching behind her.

Rick lunged forward, as if to grab her, but Billy pointed the gun at him. "She's picking up the stuff and then we're outta here. Tell the cops to stay clear." Unsteady on his haunches, the guy braced himself on the counter to his left, which wobbled.

It was loose, Samantha remembered, and she and Rick were at opposite ends of it. She looked up to catch Rick's eye, then tilted her head at the counter, telling him what she intended to do—shove the counter over Billy's body.

Rick gave a slight nod. "Someone could get hurt," he said, echoing his words that first day, when he'd offered to fix it, so she knew he understood her plan.

"Get all them bags," Billy said to her, glancing at her, then back at Rick.

She balled up some of the baggies into the robe, thinking hard. She had to distract Billy for a second and get inside the counter. Her pulse pounded and her body tingled with terror, but part of her slowed and steadied, completely calm. She wasn't about to let this creep carry her out of here. She leaned forward and deliberately shoved bags to Billy's right.

"Dammit." When he reached to get them, she moved inside the counter and put her weight against it. At first nothing happened, but then Rick must have shoved, too, because the thing gave way. She heard her computer monitor explode against the floor.

Billy grunted as the counter knocked him over, and

by the time she looked over the counter, Rick had grabbed the guy's gun and was dragging him to his feet.

"Are you all right?" Rick asked her, yanking Billy's hands behind his back.

"Y-y-yes," she managed to say, realizing her teeth were chattering uncontrollably. She was vaguely aware that her throat hurt and she was shaking so hard she felt as if she might tumble over.

"Sit before you fall," Rick said, kicking her computer chair closer to her. She collapsed into it, surveying her tipped-over counter, her wrecked monitor. The CPU had stayed in its slot and Billy's body had softened the fall, so maybe only the monitor was ruined.

What was she thinking? She'd nearly been kidnapped or killed or both and she was worrying about her equipment?

She looked at Rick, who was handcuffing Billy. Rick had handcuffs? *Police,* he'd said. She knew about the gun from the other night. She'd thought it was *cute* that he was acting like a security guard. But he wasn't a security guard. He was a cop.

A *cop.* Working on a case? Staking out Mirror, Mirror? It was too shocking to grasp all at once.

"You weren't in the army?" she said faintly, knowing how crazy that sounded, but she was rethinking everything she knew about Rick in these kaleidoscopic moments. She became aware of sirens in the distance, getting louder.

He shot a glance at her. "We've been watching Sylvestri for months. I'm sorry I wasn't here for this, but what you said about the knitting shop made me realize I had to get out there and—" He stopped abruptly, nodded at his captive, telling her he couldn't talk in front of the guy. "I'll explain everything when I can."

He yanked Billy over to the waiting area and shoved him to the couch. The huge man in leather and chains looked silly on the pink velvet sofa. "I want a lawyer," he said, completing the transformation from big, bad biker to fat, pathetic loser. She should have kneed him in the nuts and saved Rick the trouble of rescuing her.

"You get a lawyer and you can forget any breaks," Rick snapped. "Work with us now. Last chance."

The sirens, now screaming, stopped abruptly, and she watched through the glass as police officers lunged out of two cars and into the Mirror, Mirror lobby.

Seconds later, an officer took over watching Billy, while Rick led the others farther into the studio to talk, leaving her sitting there, miserable and confused. And angry, it turned out.

The mystery of why Rick had wanted to work at Bedroom Eyes had been solved in a few terror-filled moments. He was investigating Darien Sylvestri. And Bianca?

And her?

Had he been investigating her, too?

She jumped to her feet, wanting to demand the answer, and started for the hall, then realized she couldn't interrupt him now. The answer was obvious, anyway, as she recalled all the questions, him poring over her books, grilling Lester, even asking her if she took more graphic photos.

She turned back, planning to sit and wait, but her eye fell on her computer. The green light was still on. She squatted to check it and noticed a tiny piece of metal dangling from the shelf above—looked like a hook of some kind. It turned out to hold the end of the shelf closed. Inside the hollow slot, she found a ledger just like the one she used. Opening it, she immediately recognized Lester's tiny, precise handwriting and lots of big, big numbers.

Oh, dear.

"What have you got?" Rick spoke from above her.

"You were right to suspect Lester," she said, handing up the book. "There's a false shelf and this was in it."

"You didn't know about this?" he demanded, flipping through the pages, giving her a stern look. He was a different person entirely—cold and terse. Not friendly, not teasing, not warm at all. A complete stranger.

"Of course not," she said, anger spiraling through her. He had suspected her, all right. That was clear.

"I have to ask," he said, softening his tone. "Finding this is important to the case. It explains why Darien said Bedroom Eyes was *prime*."

"He said what?" She felt sick at the thought that her generous landlord had used her in some terrible crime.

Rick's eyes raked over her, his mouth tight, as if he had so much to say. "Look, I have to go. They caught Sylvestri at the Deer Valley Airport." He glanced at the officers near Billy and turned so his back was to them. "I told them you knew nothing, but you'll have to answer questions."

"Of course. I'll answer any question anybody has," she snapped. "I did nothing wrong."

"I know that, Samantha," he said, grabbing her hand. She thought he wanted to offer comfort, but he only placed a business card in it. "Talk to this lawyer. Larry Tucker. He's a friend of Brian's. Decent guy and very smart."

"I need an attorney? I'm in trouble?" She went as cold as ice.

"You hold the lease here and we don't know how

Sylvestri will characterize your involvement. This is just in case."

"How do you characterize my involvement, Rick? Do you think I'm part of this?"

"Not from the moment I met you, Sammi. Call the guy."

She stared blindly at the card.

"They'll bring in Mona, Val and Blythe. He can help them, too."

"My friends are in trouble?"

"Like I said, just in case. I'm sorry you had to be part of this. I'd hoped it was all at the yarn shop, but it wasn't." He swallowed. "And there's one more thing."

"What?" She couldn't take any more bad news. She hadn't even thought about her friends being involved.

"It would be best not to mention our…about us…."

"You mean that we're sleeping together?" Bitterness made her voice crack. "I bet there are rules about sleeping with suspects, right?"

"It was wrong. I should never have let it happen."

"No kidding." But she was stung by his words. She'd had the best time of her life and he wished it hadn't happened? Meanwhile, he'd been lying to her about himself, about everything. Hell, he'd put her in danger. And she'd fallen for it. Like a small-town fool.

"Just don't say anything about us," he said again. "We don't want to give them a reason to doubt my word about you."

"What about *my* word about me? Isn't my word good enough?" On top of everything, now she'd be treated like a criminal.

It had been happening all around her and Rick had said nothing—pretended to be her assistant, helping her with clients and the other shops, all the while suspecting them all of being crooks.

"Why didn't you warn me?" she said. "After all the time we've spent together? All we meant to each other?"

"I wanted to, believe me, but I couldn't." His eyes dug deep, a fierce green, as radiant as fire. "I'll explain it all when I can. Just don't think the worst until we talk. Promise me that."

"I won't promise you a damn thing, Rick," she said.

She thought he'd been her partner, that he loved her work, too, hell, that he was falling in love with her. Instead, he'd been spying on her every move, looking to arrest her, her friends, Bianca, Lester. Because of him, police swarmed her beloved center with cameras and crime-scene tape and she might need an attorney to stay out of jail.

"That's fair." His shoulders dropped and the intensity in his eyes faded to a cool neutral. "I'll fix what I can. I promise you that." Then he took off.

She wanted to call him back, turn back the clock to this morning when they'd woken up sticky with sundae sauce, ready to make love. In the hours after that, her whole life had been turned upside down. The scary tattooed people had paraded out her door wearing plastic vests padded with drugs. She'd had a gun pointed at her head. She'd risked her life catching a drug dealer.

Bedroom Eyes would never be the same. It even smelled weird—of sweat and metal and chemicals and fear. She wanted to crawl into a hole somewhere and cry for hours.

Worse, she wanted Rick to hold her, explain it all away, make everything right. That, she knew, was impossible.

It would never be right again.

15

GET BACK TO SAMANTHA and fix it. The thought was a drumbeat in Rick's head all the way to the station, during the interview with Sylvestri—even while he cooked up a way to get the man to confess—he wanted to get to her, straighten it out, somehow erase the betrayed look in her eyes.

He'd managed a couple of calls to her home and her cell, but got no answer.

It might be too late. Love was fragile, he knew to his soul. You had to protect it with everything in you. He hadn't done that. In a way, it had been impossible, because from the beginning he hadn't been able to be honest with her. Their whole time together had been built on a lie.

He had to make sure she got out of this okay, no matter what. He knew she'd called the attorney because the cop who interviewed her had said Tucker was there.

Despite his worry, Rick had managed some decent police work. Sylvestri had screamed immediately for his attorney, but it had been Rick's idea to send in Bianca and she'd shamed the man into confessing.

Darien *had* intended on retiring. This was to be his last job. He might be a lying sack of shit, but he loved his wife, though Rick was in no mood to be touched by a tender moment.

He was too busy dealing with what an ass he'd been. Yeah, he'd gotten the word on the yarn-shop delivery and drawn the right conclusion, gotten back to Bedroom Eyes before anyone had gotten hurt, but that didn't change all he'd done wrong.

Getting involved with Samantha had cost him his edge, risked the case and hurt her—hell, had almost gotten her killed.

Why didn't you tell me? Because he couldn't. The memory of her face when she'd asked him if he'd suspected her burned through him like acid.

His questions about the ledger she'd found had sounded like accusations, he knew, when he'd just been verifying the chain of evidence, keeping her in the clear. He ached to talk to her.

Except what could he say that could possibly make this right? For her or the job?

His squad mates wanted to take him out for beer at Jade's after the shift. That felt wrong. He should be cut from the case, kicked off the force maybe, not be tossing back brews, accepting high fives.

In the john, he splashed water on his face to clear his head, then glanced into his guilty eyes. The eyes Samantha said looked like Oak Creek moss. Damn. He wanted to punch through the glass and smash his reflection to bits.

Back in the squad room, Mark looked up at him. "What's the deal? You look like you lost your dog. You solved the case, bro."

He shrugged away his partner's back slap, leveled his gaze and ground out the truth, "I wasn't at the stakeout last night."

"You weren't? Then how did you...?" Trudeau stared at him.

"Samantha got the call at her place. Early this morning. I was there."

He watched Mark put the pieces together, react, then work his game face back into shape. "You did your job. The case got solved."

Rick held his silence.

"Hell," Mark said, leaning in, speaking low, "if you hadn't slept with her, we'd still be doing surveillance."

He shook his head. "It was wrong. For the job. And for Samantha. I took advantage."

"Sawyer's smart. She knows you were doing your job."

"By sleeping with her?" He looked around to be sure he hadn't been overheard.

Mark took in his expression, read between the lines. "Talk to the woman. Straighten it out with her."

"What the hell am I going to say? I'm sorry? An apology can't fix what I've done." He realized he'd clenched both fists and was trembling with frustration.

"Take a couple hours off the clock. Go see her. Meet us at Jade's after."

"Yeah." He ran his fingers through his hair. "I'll do that. I'll go talk to her." He had to make sure she was all right, offer his help where she needed it. He might not be able to make it right, but he could make it better.

SAMANTHA LOOKED through the peephole at Rick. She'd only been home from her police interview for a couple of hours and she was still pretty shaky. Her impulse was to run to him and let him comfort her.

But the man on her porch was now a stranger to her. Always had been, really. She'd played a dangerous game, turning him into her fantasy lover, then losing herself to the dream of what she'd thought they shared.

She took a calming breath and opened the door to a man she didn't know at all.

"Are you okay?" he asked.

"I survived," she said simply, backing up to let him in.

He stepped inside, and raised and lowered his arms, as though he wanted to hug her, but didn't dare.

He was right not to try. She turned on her heel and led him into the living room, where she sat in the chair, leaving him the couch, far enough away that she wouldn't be able to catch every flicker of emotion in his eyes. She'd misinterpreted those eyes and those emotions all along.

Rick sat on the closest corner and leaned toward her, elbows on his knees, eating up all the space she'd intended to keep between them. "I'm sorry, Samantha." He looked so anguished that her heart ached for him. That was ridiculous. She was the one who'd been suspected, lied to, tricked, put in danger.

A wave of outrage rose in her and she was glad. "Sorry that you thought I was doing pornography and dealing drugs and laundering money and God knows what else?"

"I was doing my job, Samantha."

"Your job? You mean as my assistant? Doing whatever I needed?" Those words had meant so much to her at the time.

"You have every right to be angry," he said. "Did the questioning go okay?"

"I somehow escaped getting charged with any crime, if that's what you mean." She paused and softened her tone. "You were right about the attorney. He's good. He got me through it. And the girls, too."

"If I could have been there to help, I would have been."

"But you had another job to do, didn't you?" Her

words were bitter, but she couldn't help it. "Mirror, Mirror is ruined, you know. They took my computer, all my photo files, and Mona and Blythe's appointment books. They can seize the building, but I guess you know that. Racketeering laws or something."

"I'll see if there's any flexibility, Samantha. I'll help however I can."

"Forget it. I'll handle my own problems from now on." She paused, guilt and regret swamping her. "I just feel sick that I dragged my friends into this mess." They'd been brave and supportive despite the disaster she'd brought down on their heads.

"You didn't know Darien was scum," he said, clearly trying to ease her guilt. "How could you?"

"I should have known that lease was too good to be true." She'd made mistakes, too. Rick had told her she was too trusting. She'd trusted Darien and she'd trusted Rick. "If there's a trial, I'll testify. It's the least I can do."

"There won't be a trial. I got Bianca to talk to Darien and he folded."

"He did?"

"Yeah. He didn't want her to be ashamed of him. If it's any consolation, Darien seems to really love his wife. You should have seen them. He apologized for letting her down. The man was almost in tears." He spoke haltingly, the ghost of a smile on his face. "It was like you said your pictures do—remind a couple of why they love each other."

She just stared at him. "Stop pretending you believe in what I do, Rick. All that 'I see what you mean, that makes sense,' bullshit you dished out when I told you why I do boudoir work was so I'd tell you I was dealing smut, right?"

"No. It wasn't like that—"

"Just stop." She held up her hand, angry and hurt and confused. She didn't want to redefine Rick. She'd fallen in love with how he was.

"I'm sorry I couldn't tell you what was going on. You have to understand—"

"Oh, I understand. You couldn't tell me because I might be part of it. Get your free bag of drugs with every portrait!" She felt tears slide down her cheeks. Angrily, she wiped them away. No more crying. She was done with that.

"I was wrong to do what I did. Up at the creek and—"

She couldn't stand hearing him talk about their time together like *that* was the mistake, instead of the real one—Rick's lies and pretense. Along with her small-town naiveté.

"Stop taking credit for everything, Rick," she said with a sigh. "I was the one who pushed the issue. You made up a girlfriend and when I ignored that, you gave me that crap about wanting to settle down with one special person. I should have listened."

"It wasn't crap." Determination flashed in his eyes. "I do want that." *I want you.*

Looking into his eyes made her lose her footing, slip into water that was too deep for her again. She couldn't be trusted to know the truth about Rick anymore.

"You tried to say no. That's my point." She sighed again, shaky and disgusted with herself as much as him. She'd ignored his signals and stupidly fallen in love with a fantasy. She was a fool. "Was it all a lie? Everything you told me about yourself? Who you are? Who you were? What you've done?"

"I went into the academy, not the army, after Brian

died," he said softly. "Everything else was true." He settled his gaze on her face, holding her tight. "Look, I know I've blown your trust, Samantha, but I'll do whatever I can to fix this. I'll find out if there's any way you can keep the center. If not, I'll help you find a new location. If you need money, I can take out a loan—"

"Stop it." She raised a hand. "I don't want your money, Rick. Whatever you can do to help me help my friends would be good. I have to make it up to them somehow. But I'll deal with my own mistakes." Including falling in love with an undercover cop investigating her.

"I want to fix this for you."

"Forget it, Rick. We both got carried away. There is one thing you can do. Stop thinking of what happened between us as all bad. It was a fantasy, a dream, and we both enjoyed it. At least I did."

"I did, too, Samantha. More than I can say." She saw what that admission cost him in the tension in his jaw, the agony in his eyes.

"But it's over and we're back to real life," she continued. "I've got a studio to rebuild and you've got police work to do." She tried to sound matter-of-fact, but the words hurt so much she knew it showed.

"Is that what you want? To forget what happened?"

Something in his eyes made her heart throb, but she ignored it. "What else can we do? I don't even know you, Rick."

"Yeah," he said and the green fire in his eyes went out like a blown fuse. "I don't know myself anymore. I was always a good cop, everything by the book. Until now. I was wrong and I'll pay the price for that."

His grim tone startled her. "What price? Are you in trouble? Because of...because we slept together?"

"I should be. I have to tell my lieutenant, leave it in his hands."

"What will happen? Will they fire you?"

"Hard to say. But I can't live like this. I let the job down. And myself. And you."

"Don't give up your career because I talked you into something you didn't want to do in the first place."

"I'll be okay with whatever happens," he said and his face softened with so much tenderness tears sprang again to her eyes. He cupped her cheek. "I screwed up big, I know. You probably have a hard time believing anything I say, but I only want the best for you, Sammi."

She let the tears spill over her lids and race down her face.

"You don't want advice, I know," he continued, "but don't fight so damned hard to change. Mona's right about that. You know who you are and what you want."

He stared deep, searing her, so that even after he looked away, stood to go, the burned-in spots remained, like the afterimage from a camera's flash.

Was he right? Did she know what she wanted? And had she just let him walk out her door? She was too confused to figure it out. Her whole world had tumbled around her ears, and lay smashed and broken at her feet, unrecognizable.

One idea rose in her mind. Rick was going to confess their relationship to his lieutenant, who might fire him.

That was unacceptable. No way could Rick lose his job because of her. He was as devoted to police work as he'd seemed to be to her. That hadn't been fake, she knew for certain.

She grabbed the phone book and flipped to the blue-edged government pages, blinking her eyes clear so she could find the police listings. She'd call every station in town to find Rick's boss and she'd talk and talk and talk until she straightened this all out. They'd both lost a lot over what had happened. She wasn't about to let him lose his career.

I DON'T EVEN KNOW YOU, RICK. All the way to the station, Samantha's words rang in his head, pulsed through his bloodstream, beat a tattoo in his chest.

He had to talk to the lieutenant, come clean and take his lumps. It was the only way he could live with himself. He owed it to Samantha, to the job, to himself. He prayed Darien's confession made the case strong enough that his bad behavior wouldn't damage it.

In the squad room, he found people standing around Mark's desk. "Check out the jugs on this one," Rocky Marston said, holding out a paper Rick recognized as a photo proof.

All of Samantha's work was evidence in the case now. It would be weeks, maybe months, before her negatives and computer files would be returned to her.

Over the past weeks, he'd blocked out the inevitability of this outcome, pretended it would all work out. Samantha had been right. They'd been living a fantasy, a dream, and now he was facing the brutal reality of the mess he'd made of it all.

"Hey, it's the man of the hour," Rocky said, noticing him. "You took some of these, you lucky prick?" He waved the proof he held in Rick's direction.

"I want naked women," Mark said, "These are all scenery and coyotes."

"I love coyotes. Let me see," Jessie said. She yanked the sheet from Mark and studied it.

With a jolt, Rick realized that was the Sedona shoot they were talking about. "Can I have those?" He reached, but Jessie said, "Whoa! This is you, West, and, here, with a woman... Isn't that Sawyer?" She looked up at him, startled.

"Where?" Marston moved to look over her shoulder.

"It didn't affect the case," Mark said, trying to help, but making Rick sound as guilty as hell. The room fell silent as his fellow officers put two and two together. Soon the whole precinct would know he'd slept with a suspect.

"I'm going to talk to the lieutenant," Rick said firmly. "Right now."

"It's nobody's business." Mark gathered the proofs from his silent squad mates, shoved them into the envelope and reached for the one Jessie held. She handed it to him, keeping her eyes on Rick.

"I'm accountable for what I did." Rick swallowed over his dry throat, determined to face the people he'd let down. This was the whirlwind he'd reaped by failing to be the cop he'd always believed himself to be.

"If you tell Lieutenant Stone, he'll have to act," Mark said. "He'll take your badge. What's the point of that?"

"I violated regulation," he said grimly. "I'll take the consequences."

"Let it go, Rick," Jessie said. "It doesn't change anything. We're behind you." Looking right at him, she took back the Sedona proof sheet, held it up and deliberately tore it in half. Mark and Rocky each took a half and ripped it in two, handing the torn pieces to the officers on either side, who did likewise, then solemnly carried the scraps to the wastepaper basket.

"I'll take care of the negatives, too," Mark said.

They nodded all around him, moving closer, surrounding him with their stubborn support.

"I can't let you destroy evidence for me," Rick said.

"Don't do this," Mark said, grabbing his shoulder.

"I have to." He turned for the lieutenant's office, feeling their eyes on him, their silent attention at his back, as he moved forward to take whatever came.

Lieutenant Stone waved Rick into the office and Rick stood at attention while he finished up a phone call. "What's on your mind, Detective?" he said, putting the phone back in place.

"I need to explain my behavior on the Sylvestri case, sir." He felt rooted in place, determined to do the right thing, but sick with guilt all the same. "I broke regulation, sir. I got involved with—"

The lieutenant held up a hand. "I believe you want your rep in the room if you're going to talk about broken regs."

"That's not necessary, sir."

"You may have a point. I just hung up from a woman who gave me an interesting hypothetical."

"A what?" He stared at the lieutenant. What the hell was he talking about?

"She asked me what might happen to a cop who got involved with a witness. Hypothetically. He was off duty, of course, but she wondered if this cop might be in trouble."

Samantha had called the station. Trying to help, which was nice of her, but it didn't change anything. "Sir, listen, I—"

"I'm not finished, Detective. She also explained that this hypothetical cop is a good man, a credit to the force, and he went above and beyond the call of duty—hell, she went on and on about all he did that was right and good and honorable."

"Sir?" He started to interrupt, but the steely glare Lieutenant Stone shot him made him stop.

"Do you want to know what I told her?"

He opened his mouth, started to speak, and settled for "Yes, sir."

"I told her the cop should keep his mouth shut and just do his job."

Rick swallowed hard. "I don't know what to say, sir."

"Don't say anything. Just be the good cop you are. There's a squad of men and women out there who trust you with their lives. Take a look." The lieutenant yanked the blinds up and Rick saw that everyone stood there, waiting for the outcome of this meeting, eyes steady, expressions grim.

He felt the sting of emotion. Despite everything, they trusted him. The lieutenant did, too, it seemed.

Rick looked at the man, his chest so tight it hurt. "Thank you, sir. I won't let you down. Or them."

"I don't think you have it in you, West. We need more cops like you, not fewer. For God's sake, use good judgment from now on. Especially with the hypotheticals."

"I intend to, sir."

"And that lady had a pretty high damned opinion of that cop. I couldn't shut her up about his morals, his principles, his integrity. That hypothetical cop must have done something right."

"I hope he did, sir. I do."

Rick left the office, emotions swirling through him. The trust of his squad and Lieutenant Stone touched him deeply. Samantha's heartfelt defense, too. Everything he'd always believed about his obligation to others and what he could expect in return was tumbling around inside him.

Despite what he'd done, they still believed in him, trusted him, had faith in him. He thought about what Samantha had said about a woman who loved him not needing him to be perfect. *If she loves you, she'll forgive your flaws and mistakes.*

Was there a chance she loved him?

But his mistakes had been huge. Could she forgive him anyway?

"IT WAS A MISTAKE to sleep with him," Samantha said to her friends, nibbling on a chocolate boob, trying to relax into the shoulder rub Mona was giving her.

"I don't see how," Blythe said licking a blue cock pop. "You wanted it so much. You had to go for it. And this tastes more like grape than blueberry, Val, *FYI.*"

Samantha had invited Mona, Blythe and Valerie to her town house to commiserate about the disaster, but all three were more interested in talking her into making up with Rick than bemoaning the fact she'd set them up in business in the middle of a drug deal.

Mona, happily in love with Chuck, planned to be a mobile therapist for a while. Blythe would lease space at her old salon and Valerie would go back to mail order until Samantha found a new location for Mirror, Mirror or, if Rick could pull strings, reopened the center.

"You're not supposed to know what you're doing in love," Mona said. "That's the magic of it. Remember? You told me that yourself. Oooh, save me that strawberry vagina." Val had snagged a box of sex candy on her way out of the shop and they were all enjoying the loot.

"This wasn't love. It was a fantasy," Samantha said, dragging her locket back and forth on her chain. "The man doesn't even approve of my work. He even told me I should take regular portraits."

"What's wrong with diversifying?" Val shrugged.

"That's not the point. I'm not giving up who I am for a man."

"Was he asking you to?" Mona said.

No. Rick would never do that. He'd been trying to help her with her own uncertainty about her parents. Besides that, he'd happily played sex games with her for days, even when she could tell he'd rather just make simple love—no chocolate, no costumes, no playacting. "He wants a wife and I want a life," she said weakly.

Mona stopped rubbing. The other women just stared at her, telling her with their eyes she was full of it.

"You're going to snap that necklace right off its chain," Valerie said, grabbing the locket she was tugging on. "Let me see." She opened the locket and sighed. "I loved that outfit on you."

Mona stopped rubbing her shoulders and leaned in with Blythe to look. "You look so hot."

"It was my first bedroom photo."

"To impress Barry, right?" Mona said. "You look a little shaky."

"I *was* shaky." But not anymore. She thought about the photo Rick had taken of her. The one on her bedside table.

"Hang on a minute," she said. "I want to show you guys something." She brought it back and handed it to Valerie, who still held her locket. "What do you think?"

"Great bikini. Do I sell that?"

"No. It's one of my costumes, Val. And that's not what I mean."

"I like your hair this length," Blythe said, tapping the glass.

"Yeah, but what else do you see?" she said. "Don't I look more confident? Like I know who I am and what I want?"

"Absolutely," Mona said. "You look in charge."

"And like you just ate a big piece of the best chocolate cake in the world and you can't wait for seconds," Val said, "now that I look more closely."

"Or like you just got laid," Blythe added.

The girls burst out laughing.

When Samantha didn't reply, Mona said, "We're just kidding, hon."

Samantha was lost in the photo. Rick had caught the double image she tried to capture in all her portraits. She could see it here—her confidence, her sexiness, her readiness, her triumph. All of her right in this little square of exposed paper. She did know what she wanted.

"Did Rick take the shot?" Mona asked gently.

She nodded. She thought she needed the photo to remind her not to settle, because she feared she'd lose herself in someone else's view of her. But she wouldn't do that. Not anymore. And Rick would never ask her to.

"He's good," Mona said.

"Yes, he is." And not just as a photographer. Or a fantasy lover. He was good in all the everyday ways. She'd told him she didn't know him, but she did. And it was about time she forgot fantasy and went for the real thing. With the man she loved.

TWO HOURS AFTER HIS MEETING with the lieutenant, Rick sat in a booth at Jade's Grill and let Rocky pour him a beer. He wasn't quite used to the idea that he still had his job and the loyalty of his squad mates, but he was doing his best to get into the moment.

"So, now that it's over, what was it like to have naked ladies prancing around you every day?" Marston asked, sitting across from him, next to Jessie.

"It wasn't like that," Rick said. "What Samantha does is professional and respectful. She captures the real person."

"Oh, I bet," Marston said, rolling his eyes.

"Tell you the truth, Rocky, you should take your girlfriend in for a picture. Seems to me you take her for granted."

"What?"

"Oh, yeah, you do," Jessie said. "Standing her up for dinners, expecting her to do your laundry. You're lucky she doesn't leave your fat sorry ass."

"Hey," Marston said, but the truth had hit home, Rick could tell. He did take the girl for granted.

"And Gloria would like a photo, too, Mark," Rick added. "Because of how you'll react to it. You'll see her new again. Samantha opens people's eyes. I've seen it over and over."

"I don't know about my girlfriend, but I'd pay to have Jessie get a shot like that," Rocky said. "We'd pick out your outfit, wouldn't we, guys?"

"Sit and spin, Marston," Jessie said, but she leaned closer to Rick. "So, how does it work exactly? My boyfriend kind of wants a picture for his wallet."

"For his wallet, huh? Oooh." Marston again. Jessie slugged him this time. Hard.

Rick explained a sitting to Jessie. As he talked, he remembered how each shot Samantha took held heart and hope and, hell, magic. And, even more, he realized he'd loved helping her take them. People shots weren't so bad. Lately, it didn't hurt so much to look into their hearts, their hopes, their shy dreams.

In fact, he felt honored to be part of it.

Because of Samantha and what she'd taught him.

He looked up and saw that Marston, Mark and three other guys were drinking in every word, not even touching their beers. Bedroom Eyes was just down the road. The photos on the wall would still be up. Maybe he could snag some new clients for Samantha...and talk to her, too, about what he'd been thinking.

"Come on. The studio's a block away. You can see for yourselves."

He dialed Samantha's number. He'd surprise her with new clients for down the line. And he'd surprise her with his heart. And pray to God she meant what she'd said about love being sturdy.

He knew his love was strong, for sure. As he waited for her to answer, he felt as if someone had wrapped a fist around his heart and wouldn't free a beat until he got her back, convinced her to spend her life with him. He wasn't so sure about the rules anymore. Except for one: When you find a person to love, don't let her go without a fight.

Samantha pulled up to Bedroom Eyes, her heart in her throat, her breath coming shallow and quick. Rick wanted her to meet him here to talk. He'd sounded mysterious, but also warm, and he'd made her hopes soar.

She didn't know what to think. Really, she was *afraid* to think. She just jumped into her car and drove to the studio, pulling up in front behind Rick's Jeep and another SUV.

Through the window, she could see Rick pointing at one of her pictures and talking to four people—she recognized Mark among them—looking for all the world as if he were leading a gallery tour. How bizarre.

The lobby entrance was unlocked, the crime-scene tape pulled away, and she hurried to the Bedroom Eyes entrance, pausing outside the door at the shock of seeing through the glass door the tipped-over counter, remembering all that had happened here since that morning.

She shoved open the door and everyone turned to her.

"Samantha," Rick said, his eyes brimming with emotion—love, maybe, and hope. "I want you to meet some of my squad mates. I was trying to tell them about your work and figured that seeing was believing."

"How nice," she said, her heart spilling over with love for him.

"You do wonderful work," a woman said. "I'm Jessie."

Samantha shook the hand she extended. "Thank you very much."

"And how much does something like that cost?" the man next to Mark asked.

"That's Rocky Marston," Rick said to Samantha, "and he makes every nickel squeak." Rick turned to Rocky. "Less than you lost on the Suns game and it'll change you both for the better."

His words made her smile. Where had she ever gotten the idea that Rick disapproved of her work? It was her parents she was worried about and maybe they wouldn't be as judgmental as she'd feared. It was high time she found out. Even if they were horrified, it wouldn't change what she did or how she felt about her work. She was through seeing herself through others' eyes.

"Take that woman," Rick said, nodding at one of the

photos. "She came in here looking like hammered shit—cold and scared hammered shit. Samantha warmed her up, brought her out of herself, captured that extra something about her that—"

"We get the idea," Mark said, holding up his hands, rolling his eyes with affection. "Book us for photos, Samantha. Once you get going again. And while you're at it, got any time shares? Rick seems to think you walk on water."

"You can use my cameras until your equipment's released and we can rent studio space," Rick said to her, already doing what he could to help her, just as he'd promised he would.

"I'd be honored to take your pictures," she said to the group. "Anything for Rick's friends."

"Great then. Terrific," Rick said.

"Yes, great," she said. They just stared at each other. She drank him in, looked into his green eyes, which, if they were windows to his soul, were flung wide to let in all the light there was. For the first time, Rick was completely present, fully himself, and she realized she loved him even more in the bright day of reality.

She'd hidden, too, in her fantasies.

She became aware that the silence had gone on too long. Finally, Jessie cleared her throat. "So, uh, we'll be taking off, right, guys? Nice to meet you, Samantha. Take care of this guy." She patted Rick's arm.

"I hope to," she said, looking up at him.

The door closed behind the cops and Samantha and Rick were alone in Bedroom Eyes again. "That was nice of you, Rick."

"It's the least I can do after all that happened because of me."

Love has to be earned. He still believed that. It would be up to her to show him love could be freely given. Without fear. With faith.

"How did it go with your lieutenant?" she asked, figuring he must still have a job, considering that he'd brought folks from his station here.

"He gave me another chance. They all…believe in me." He shrugged, seeming mystified.

"Of course they do. They should. You deserve it."

"Thanks for calling him. It means a lot. Your doing that."

"I had to. I believe in you, too, Rick."

"How can you? You were right. You don't even know me."

"Oh, yes I do," she said, her voice low with the intensity of her feelings. "I know everything that counts. I know that you're loyal and honest, that you have honor and principles and—"

"I love you," he blurted. "That's the main deal. All this time I thought I should settle down, have a family. Because of Brian, I guess. And for me. But I didn't really want that. Not until I met you. I guess…" He paused, swallowed, then pushed himself to speak. "I was waiting for you."

"Oh, Rick," she said, rising up on tiptoes to meet his lips.

He pulled her into his arms and held her tightly, and she felt safe and protected and so loved. This was real. This was better than all the fantasies in the world.

She broke off the kiss and looked into his open green eyes. "I love you, too, Rick."

"So love is pretty sturdy after all." He looked so happy, as relieved as a child, that she kissed him again.

"I can't believe I fell in love with the first man I had great sex with."

"Sometimes you just get lucky." He winked at her, the smart-assed, wicked Rick back again.

"Sometimes you do." She looked around at the wreck of her studio and felt like the luckiest woman in the world.

"So, we're starting over, right? Allow me to introduce myself. Samantha Sawyer, I'm Rick West. I'm a cop. A good one. I work hard, by the book, love my work, but I won't let it interfere with our life together."

"Nice to meet you, Rick West. It's kind of scary to me, you know, you being a cop. Thinking of you getting shot at or hurt. That'll take some getting used to."

"I don't take unnecessary risks, Sammi, and with you in my life I'll be even more careful."

She considered that closely. It wouldn't be easy, but every life held risk. She would adjust. She smiled up at him, knowing they had all the time in the world to work things out.

"I guess this means you're quitting as my assistant."

"Sorry." He grimaced.

"I won't need help for a while anyway." She sighed. Maybe when she did, Bianca could work for her. She was taking that class, she'd need a distraction from the mess with Darien, and Samantha enjoyed working with her.

"I can help on the weekends," Rick offered.

"Oh, no. On the weekends, we'll be far too busy to be in the studio." She pushed her body tight against his, tucked her fingers into his hair and looked up into his eyes, delighted by the emerald heat she saw there. There wasn't a shadow in his eyes, no hint that he'd disappear from her or the love growing between them. He was hers. For good.

"Busy, huh?" He nuzzled her neck and spoke into her ear, "I suppose this means more of your sex games? I haven't got all the butterscotch off me yet."

"Just a few more…" she teased, shivering with desire.

"One request? Can we skip the cop-and-suspect one?"

"Too close to home?" She laughed. "No problem. Actually, I'm excited about just plain us, fantasies not required. I think we're pretty damn sexy all on our own."

"Whatever you need me to be, Samantha, I'll be," he said in that low, steady way she loved.

"I'm counting on it. We'll take it slow, okay? Not get carried away."

"Whatever you need."

She loved when he said that. "What I need right now is you, Rick. The rest I can build again."

They stood together, in the messy wreck of all she'd built, but she'd never felt happier in her life. Her work would go on. Her studio was in her heart, in the way she saw the world through her lens. She'd bring her dream to life again.

She was enough just as she was. She didn't need a photo of her sexy side on her bureau or around her neck to remind her. She could be a small-town girl, shy and repressed, or a sultry temptress, wild and wanton, or anything in between. She was all that and more, under the skin and in her soul. And she'd found a man who loved her for it.

And, more importantly, so did she.

Blaze.

Sue Johanson's Hot Tip

Forbidden Fantasy #1

Having a new man in your bed every night (but, of course, he's really the same guy).

Do I Know You...?

Having "multiple lovers" in a committed relationship requires only a little imagination and the passion of a true actor. Whether you're playing the "saucy wench" to his "strapping young knight" or the "warden's wife" to his "escaped prisoner," role-playing can turn your mundane sex life into an Oscar-worthy turn-on. Start the seduction with a trip to the local costume store and I guarantee you'll have more fun than a kid on Halloween night. Remember, there's no harm in pretending every now and then—even if you're secretly imagining that it's really Brad Pitt in bed with you!

Sue Johanson is a registered nurse, sex educator, author and host of The Oxygen Network's Talk Sex with Sue Johanson.

Photo courtesy of Oxygen Media, Inc.

If you enjoyed what you just read,
then we've got an offer you can't resist!

Take 2 bestselling
love stories FREE!
Plus get a FREE surprise gift!

Torn between two lovers?

That's Zoe McNamara's latest dilemma. She hasn't had
any men in her life lately...and now she's got two! So
what is she going to do about the electrifying chemistry
she has with sexy Jed Calhoun—and with mysterious
Ethan Blair? And when is she going to realize they're
one and the same...?

TWO HOT!
by *Cara Summers*

Book #259, on sale June 2006

Do *you* have a
forbidden fantasy?

**Look inside every *Forbidden Fantasy* book
for Hot Tips from Sue Johanson!**

*Sue Johanson is a registered nurse, sex educator, author and host of
The Oxygen Network's* Talk Sex with Sue Johanson.